SLOW BURN

What Reviewers Say About Missouri Vaun's Work

The Mandolin Lunch

"Two timid school teachers find love in this cozy lesbian contemporary from Vaun. The result is touching…"—*Publishers Weekly*

The Sea Within

"This is an amazing book. *The Sea Within* by Missouri Vaun is an exciting dystopian adventure and romance that will have you reading on the edge of your seat."—*Rainbow Reflections*

Chasing Sunset

"A road trip romance with good characters that had some nice chemistry."—Kat Adams, Bookseller (QBD Books, Australia)

"*Chasing Sunset* is a fun and enjoyable ride off into the sunset. Colorful characters, laughs and a sweet romance blend together to make a tasty read."—*Aspen Tree Book Reviews*

"This is a lovely summer romance. It has all the elements that you want in this type of novel: beautiful characters, great chemistry, lovely settings, and best of all, a nostalgic road trip across the country." —*Rainbow Reflections*

"I really liked this one! I found both Finn and Iris to be well fleshed out characters. Both women are trying to figure out their next steps, and that makes them both insecure about where their relationship is going. They have some major communication issues, but I found that, too, realistic. This was a low key read but very enjoyable. Recommended!"—Rebekah Miller, Librarian (University of Pittsburgh)

"The love story was tender and emotional and the sex was steamy and told so much about how intense their relationship was. I really enjoyed this story. Missouri Vaun has become one of my favourite authors and I'm never disappointed."—*Kitty Kat's Book Review Blog*

Spencer's Cove

"Just when I thought I knew where this story was going and who everyone was, Missouri Vaun took me on a ride that totally exceeded my expectations. ...It was a magical tale and I absolutely adored it. Highly recommended."—*Kitty Kat's Book Reviews*

"The book is great fun. The chemistry between Abby and Foster is practically tangible. ...Anyone who has seen and enjoyed the series *Charmed*, is going to be completely charmed by this rollicking romance."—*reviewer@large*

"Missouri Vaun has this way of taking me into the world she has created and does not let me out until I've finished the book." —*Les Rêveur*

"I was 100% all in after the first couple of pages and I wanted to call in sick, so I could stay home from work to immerse myself in this story. I've always enjoyed Missouri Vaun's books and I'm impressed with how she moves between genres with such ease. As paranormal stories go, this one left me thinking, 'Hmm, I wish I was part of that world,' and I've never read a book featuring vampires or weres that left me with that feeling. To sum it up, witches rock and Vaun made me a believer."—*Lesbian Review*

Take My Hand

"The chemistry between River and Clay is off the charts and their sex scenes were just plain hot!"—*Les Rêveur*

"The small town charms of *Take My Hand* evoke the heady perfume of pine needles and undergrowth, birdsong, and summer cocktails with friends."—*Omnivore Bibliosaur*

"I have a weakness for butch/femme couples so the Clay/River pairing worked for me, even if their names made me laugh. I like the way Missouri Vaun writes and felt like I got to know the folks in Pine Cone in just a few short scenes. The southern charm is front and center in *Take My Hand* and as River Hemsworth discovers, the locals are warm and welcoming."—*Late Night Lesbian Reviews*

Love at Cooper's Creek

"Blown away...how have I not read a book by Missouri Vaun before. What a beautiful love story which, honestly, I wasn't ready to finish. Kate and Shaw's chemistry was instantaneous and as the reader I could feel it radiating off the page."—*Les Rêveur*

"*Love at Cooper's Creek* is a gentle, warm hug of a book."—*Lesbian Review*

"As always another well written book from Missouri Vaun—sweet romance with very little angst, well developed and likeable lead characters and a little family drama to spice things up."—Melina Bickard, Librarian, Waterloo Library (UK)

Crossing the Wide Forever

"*Crossing the Wide Forever* is a near-heroic love story set in an epic time, told with almost lyrical prose. Words on the page will carry the reader, along with the main characters, back into history and into adventure. It's a tale that's easy to read, with enchanting main characters, despicable villains, and supportive friendships, producing a fascinating account of passion and adventure."—*Lambda Literary Review*

Birthright

"The author develops a world that has a medieval feeling, complete with monasteries and vassal farmers, while also being a place and time where a lesbian relationship is just as legitimate and open as a heterosexual one. This kept pleasantly surprising me throughout my reading of the book. The adventure part of the story was fun, including traveling across kingdoms, on "wind-ships" across deserts, and plenty of sword fighting. ...This book is worth reading for its fantasy world alone. In our world, where those in the LGBTQ communities still often face derision, prejudice, and danger for living and loving openly, being immersed in a world where the Queen can openly love another woman is a refreshing break from reality."—Amanda Chapman, Librarian, Davisville Free Library (RI)

"*Birthright* by Missouri Vaun is one of the smoothest reads I've had my hands on in a long time."—*Lesbian Review*

The Time Before Now

"[*The Time Before Now*] is just so good. Vaun's character work in this novel is flawless. She told a compelling story about a person so real you could just about reach out and touch her."—*Lesbian Review*

The Ground Beneath

"One of my favourite things about Missouri Vaun's writing is her ability to write the attraction between two women. Somehow she manages to get that twinkle in the stomach just right and she makes me feel as if I am falling in love with my wife all over again."
—*Lesbian Review*

All Things Rise

"The futuristic world that author Missouri Vaun has brought to life is as interesting as it is plausible. The sci-fi aspect, though, is not hard-core which makes for easy reading and understanding of the technology prevalent in the cloud cities. ...[T]he focus was really on the dynamics of the characters especially Cole, Ava and Audrey—whether they were interacting on the ground or above the clouds. From the first page to the last, the writing was just perfect."—*AoBibliosphere*

"This is a lovely little Sci-Fi romance, well worth a read for anyone looking for something different. I will be keeping an eye out for future works by Missouri Vaun."—*Lesbian Review*

"Simply put, this book is easy to love. Everything about it makes for a wonderful read and re-read. I was able to go on a journey with these characters, an emotional, internal journey where I was able to take a look at the fact that while society and technology can change vastly until almost nothing remains the same, there are some fundamentals that never change, like hope, the raw emotion of human nature, and the far reaching search for the person who is able to soothe the fire in our souls with the love in theirs."—*Roses and Whimsy*

Writing as Paige Braddock

Jane's World and the Case of the Mail Order Bride

"This is such a quirky, sweet novel with a cast of memorable characters. It has laugh out loud moments and will leave you feeling charmed."—*Lesbian Review*

Visit us at www.boldstrokesbooks.com

By the Author

All Things Rise

The Time Before Now

The Ground Beneath

Whiskey Sunrise

Valley of Fire

Death By Cocktail Straw

One More Reason To Leave Orlando

Smothered and Covered

Privacy Glass

Birthright

Crossing The Wide Forever

Love At Cooper's Creek

Take My Hand

Proxima Five

Spencer's Cove

Chasing Sunset

The Sea Within

The Mandolin Lunch

Slow Burn

Writing as Paige Braddock:

Jane's World The Case of the Mail Order Bride

SLOW BURN

by

Missouri Vaun

2022

SLOW BURN

ISBN 13: 978-1-63679-098-5

THIS TRADE PAPERBACK ORIGINAL IS PUBLISHED BY
BOLD STROKES BOOKS, INC.
P.O. BOX 249
VALLEY FALLS, NY 12185

FIRST EDITION: AUGUST 2022

CREDITS
EDITOR: CINDY CRESAP
PRODUCTION DESIGN: SUSAN RAMUNDO
COVER DESIGN BY JEANINE HENNING
COVER PHOTO BY MICHAEL RYAN

Acknowledgments

My Father was a firefighter for the U.S. Forest Service. In his prime, he and his crew got dropped into places out west like Colorado and Montana to fight wildfires. He'd be gone for three weeks at a time and would come back to southern Mississippi bearded and thin from the experience.

I grew up hearing stories about close calls and how one time, they got caught and had to seek shelter in some huge rocks. He said the fire blew up and that it sounded like a freight train bearing down on them. His best friend wanted to make a run for it and my dad wouldn't let him. To this day, his friend credits my father with saving his life. The fire burned over them so hot that day that it singed the tops of Dad's ears and melted the name tag off his hardhat.

This is real hero stuff and it continues every year.

I would like to thank the firefighters who work every fire season. As someone who lives in an area that is regularly required to evacuate for wildfires, I'm personally indebted to all of you for your hard work and bravery.

I first thought of writing this story after a particularly scary event in which my wife and I got stranded on Interstate 80 trying to evacuate to Sacramento, CA. While we were driving east on I-80, two fires converged and jumped the freeway, closing all lanes in both directions with flames within sight, climbing down the hillside. I'll never forget that experience. The mere smell of smoke brings the memory back in an instant.

Hopefully, I was able to capture some of these real-life experiences, past and present, in this story.

I'd like to thank my beta readers, Jenny, Vanessa, Alena and my wife, Evelyn. Special thanks to Michael Ryan for the beautiful cover photo. A special "thank you" to the support team at Bold Strokes Books. Cindy, Sandy, Rad, Ruth…you're the best.

And to my readers…thank you for sharing the journey. Stay safe out there.

Dedication

For Evelyn

Chapter One

The faint glow of the horizon line was like a fulcrum as the weight of night tipped toward day. Grayson Reeves sat on a canvas folding chair near the opening of her crew tent and pulled on her boots. She lingered there, with elbows propped on her knees, and watched as the blueish glow turned to purple and then pink. The Sierra foothills were gorgeous at sunrise. Around her, firefighters began to stir with the routines of morning. The air was crisp and painfully dry in her nose and throat. But the juniper-scented breeze that caressed her face almost made up for it. She stood up, placed her hands on her hips, and arched her back as she took a deep breath and then exhaled.

Gray's back was stiff and her right shoulder sore from digging in the dry earth for long hours the previous day. She rotated her aching shoulder as she strode toward the mess tent for food and coffee. The faint smell of smoke quickened her steps. Adrenaline began to pump through her system like sips of caffeine. Fire season had that effect.

The low hum of conversation greeted her as she entered the mess tent.

"Morning." Gray was low-key, not chatty first thing in the morning. She brushed past her friend Shane as he cleared his breakfast plate. She served herself some coffee. Crew members from various teams huddled at long folding tables shoveling food into their mouths. Firefighting burned serious calories so it wasn't a good idea to eat light.

"Morning to you too." Shane downed the last of his coffee and tossed the cup into a plastic bin along with his empty breakfast plate.

"You're a little too happy this morning." Gray already knew why. "I guess Alissa hasn't dumped you yet."

"Dude, she's so into me." Shane punched her shoulder, causing her to slosh coffee on her fingers.

"Ouch, that's hot." She switched the cup to her other hand and wiped her wet fingers on her pants.

"You are such a baby. How did you ever become a firefighter?" Shane assumed a thinking pose, with his hand under his chin. "Oh, yeah…right… Me."

"You wish."

"Did you sleep in today or what? You almost missed breakfast." He grinned.

"Ha-ha, very funny." Gray couldn't remember the last time she'd actually slept in. A firefighter's day usually started around five a.m. She sampled the brew. Not too bad for camp coffee.

At five feet and eleven inches, Gray would have been considered tall in most circumstances, but she was dwarfed by Shane's six-foot, four-inch hulking frame. He looked like one of the Avengers, like Captain America with a square jaw and disarming smile. Mr. Perfect in every way. Which would've been completely annoying if he wasn't so damn likeable.

Gray and Shane had been friends since her first day on the job. He'd taken Gray under his wing and showed her the ropes. Wildland firefighting was mostly a guy's world, but Shane made her feel supported and encouraged. Not that the men in the crew weren't supportive. As far as that went, they had a great group of guys. Dave, especially, made sure that Gray didn't feel like an outsider. But still, women fighting fires faced different challenges. Shane helped Gray succeed and that meant a lot to her, the newbie. He had five seasons under his belt by the time she joined the Helitack 407 crew.

Helitack was basically a blend of the words, "helicopter" and "attack." It was a term coined in the fifties to describe crews transported by helicopter to wildfires. A helicopter could provide rapid, highly maneuverable transportation, which allowed the helitack crews to quickly assess a wildfire and come up with a plan of attack. Gray loved the exhilaration of being on the front line of attack.

Year one as a wildland firefighter had been tough though.

Gray thought she was in shape until she tried to pass the rigorous fitness trials required to become a firefighter. Looking back now, she could see how far she'd come. Two years in the field and she was stronger than she'd ever been. Year three she'd joined the helitack crew. This was a great job. Where else could you spend all day outdoors, get in shape, and feel like what you were doing mattered—preserving wild spaces and people's homes, sometimes even saving lives. Not that she was trying to be some sort of hero or anything, it was just that a regular job indoors for long hours never appealed to her.

A chance encounter with a wildland firefighter along the Pacific Crest Trail when she was twenty-six and searching had set her on this path and she'd been on it ever since. It wasn't a *get rich* sort of profession, but money wasn't everything. And maybe someday she'd grow tired of living in a tent and actually put down roots somewhere. But for now, this was exactly where she wanted to be.

By the time the Forest Service made the "mutual aid" call requesting help, Gray had finished her eggs and gulped the last of her coffee. She hustled out of the mess tent to grab her gear. A minute later, the helicopter rotors were a blur above her head, thumping like a giant heartbeat that she could feel against her chest as the crew of the 407 loaded into the Super Huey. As the copter left the ground, a churning plume of gray smoke was visible in the distance.

"Looks like we're gonna have a busy day." Dave studied the terrain—steep hillsides covered with loose rock and scruffy brush. Dave was part of the crew, of which Gray was the only woman. He was seated next to Shane, across from Gray.

The 407 was a crew of seven, plus their helitack commander, Vince Walsh; and the pilot, Greg Webber. By the time the helicopter's skids touched down the air tankers had already made two water drops. Thick smoke darkened the sun as the team of firefighters disembarked.

"Okay, huddle up." Vince had to shout to be heard over the rotors as the chopper lifted off.

The fire had burned nearly ten acres and was spreading upslope, pushed by a light wind along the canyon. Vince had already confirmed that air tankers had made retardant drops on the right flank along the upper section of the fire, but they weren't able to get lower on the slope because of the steep canyon walls.

Gray and her crewmates were standing on a loose gravel bed near the south fork of the Stanis River, about a half mile away from the fire. After receiving the briefing and tactical plan from Vince, Dave led the crew as they walked single file from their landing zone to an old logging road near a campground. Two backcountry campers scuttled past them headed in the opposite direction. They looked scruffy and shaken, their backpacks lumpy and half-zipped as if they'd packed in a rush. The campground had been evacuated and these backpackers looked like the last two to get the word to leave. Cell service was spotty in this area, which made evacuations difficult.

Gray followed Shane as they turned toward the right flank of the fire.

The 407 was the first ground crew on site. Sweat trickled down Gray's back beneath her well-worn flame resistant Nomex shirt. The temperature was climbing and the wind was hot. Ground vegetation was brown and brittle from months of drought.

Gray shifted her pack on her shoulders to allow some air circulation as she followed Shane and Dave. Gray's gear consisted of a GPS unit, two-way radio, first aid kit, six quarts of water, MREs, Gatorade, and a scraping tool. She didn't have a twenty-five-pound chainsaw braced on her shoulder today so she was feeling almost too light as they trekked uphill. The rest of the guys followed, single file behind her.

"It's fucking hot already." Shane glanced back. He was a few feet ahead of her. Every boot fall kicked up a powdery puff of fine dust.

"Yeah, it's called fire season, you may have heard of it." She loved to heap on the sarcasm whenever he complained. "Who's the baby now?"

Shane laughed.

Fire season used to be shorter, now it extended from August all the way through the end of October, or until seasonal rains began to fall. Gray could see now that the fire was above and below the road. The right flank of the fire beneath their position was backing very slowly into the wind. Vince's tactical plan to anchor the fire from the road down to the river seemed good.

Vince had pointed out two safety zones—the riverbank and the gravel road. Firefighters were always looking for planned escape routes. The basic plan was to circle the fire, cut it off, and force it to move in a different direction. Gray dropped her pack at the edge of the road. From here they'd rely on hand tools and chainsaws to cut fire lines.

The seven-member crew fell in behind Vince as he headed down slope.

"I really love this job." Shane grinned at her. "You know, except for the smoke and fire."

She couldn't help laughing, even though she'd heard the joke before. Laughter eased the tension and made the work lighter.

Gray swung the scraping tool with steady, even strokes. They'd been on site for only three hours, but it already seemed like a long day and her arms were feeling it, especially her stiff shoulder. The rising temp didn't ease the fatigue.

Flying embers were igniting spot fires, so Dave went back to the road to get a water pumper. That's when the wind shifted.

Gray looked up. The wind was picking up. A little tingling sensation had settled in the short hairs at the back of her neck. She tried to spot the crew chief, Vince, through the thickening smoke. Vince had been fighting fires for ten years. He never took chances. If he wasn't worried, then she wasn't worried.

The wind was blowing for real now. Like some angry gray ghost chasing them from below. If they got into trouble, the pre-planned escape route was to retrace their path to the safe ground of the gravel road, which meant a steep ascent and then they'd follow the road back down to the dry creek bed.

The wind suddenly increased.

Despite the heat of it, a chill ran down her spine. Gray glanced down the ravine. If flames started to climb behind them, the steep terrain was so dry the entire slope would be blazing in minutes. She rotated again to look for Vince.

Gray heard the roar first, then she saw it. A wall of flames racing up the slope toward their position. It was blowing up! It roared like a jet engine about to take off.

Dave must have seen it too because in that same instant he shouted down at them from the road.

"Get out of there—now!" Dave yelled.

Gray and Shane started running up the slope behind the rest of the crew.

"Move!" Vince shouted back at them. "Move faster!"

Gray and Shane had been in the lowest position, closest to the bottom of the steep, narrow canyon. Shane was beside her and then he began to pull ahead. The ground was uneven and so brittle that it crumbled as Gray climbed toward the road. She slipped and tried to stop herself with her hands, dropping the scraping tool. Gray slid for several feet before she could catch herself. She'd lost ground and the super-heated, roaring flame was almost on top of her—like a blowtorch breathing down her neck.

Suddenly, Shane's hand was around her arm near her shoulder. He tugged her roughly up and then shoved her from behind. She scrambled up the steep incline, practically on all fours. Gray broke through the dry brush at the road's edge just as Vince shouted the command to deploy. Her heart thumped in her chest. Gray took a deep breath, but that only brought on a coughing fit. The air was so dry and smoke-filled that it burned her throat.

"Deploy shelters!" Vince shouted again somewhere nearby and then someone else echoed the command.

"Deploy shelters now!" It was Dave that shouted the second time. He was a veteran firefighter. There was urgency in his voice which did nothing to ease Gray's fear. If Dave was rattled, then it was definitely time to panic. Nothing *ever* spooked Vince or Dave and now they were both shouting at the crew to hunker down.

Were they going to make it? Was this it?

The fire was coming like a freight train. The narrow canyon had turned into a wind tunnel, increasing the intensity and speed of the fire. There was no time left and no chance of escape. Each firefighter carried an aluminized one-person fire shelter, like a single-person tent, that they hoped never to use. Deploying the shelter in a strong wind was no easy feat either.

"We're deploying here!" Vince was making sure everyone knew the plan. "Remember your training," he shouted at Gray, who was struggling to manage the cover in the windstorm.

On her right, Shane worked to free his shelter. He'd crested the climb to the road barely a minute behind Gray. He'd lagged because he'd helped her.

"Shane, hurry!" Shouting sent her into a coughing fit.

They'd done this training exercise a million times and the familiar routine calmed Gray a bit, offering the illusion of control. She'd unzipped the carrying case, pulled out the shelter, and shook it open. It whipped out like a sail in the wind and she'd had to wrestle it back. She climbed into it like a sleeping bag open on one side, pulled it over her head and lay face down. She kept her face as close to the ground as possible. The goal was to stay as near to the ground as possible where the air would be the cleanest and coolest. Her knees and elbows became anchors to hold the shelter down against the wind.

Blistering hot air radiated on all sides, from below and above, stealing moisture and oxygen away as it swept past. Fires this hot created their own weather systems, which generated their own wind, and this one was intensifying. No sun reached the ground through the thick black-brown haze as she'd dropped to her knees on the rocks of the gravel logging road.

Seconds after Gray had taken cover, the first wave of heat and noise swept over her. Embers and debris rained down on the thin shelter. From inside, she tried to knock hot chunks off while constantly shifting her weight to keep the edges of the shelter pinned down. Nearby, trees burst into flame with a loud whoosh. She tried to peek out to check Shane's status, but smoke and hot air poured in.

Bad idea.

Luckily, they were close enough together that they could call out to one another. Someone shouted something, but she couldn't make it out. Then she heard Shane trying to calm someone down, it sounded like Jake, the newest member of the team. Jake clearly wanted to make a run for it. But he'd never outrun a fire like this. Running was a death sentence. Super-heated air would fill his lungs the second he left the shelter.

"Jake, you're gonna make it," Shane shouted.

"I can't take it!" The pitch of his voice sounded off, desperate.

"Yes, you can!" It was comforting to hear Shane's reassurances even if they weren't meant for her.

Gray's impulse was to run too. But if they could stay down they might actually survive; making a run for it was suicide.

Gray tried to settle her mind but failed. All she could think of was how little she'd done with her nearly thirty years on the planet and how no one would miss her if she bought it in this rugged ravine in the Sierra foothills. Suddenly, out of nowhere, she was angry. Maybe that was just a coping mechanism. Why had this happened? Why was she here? She'd been running so long she'd almost managed to forget why.

Her knuckles ached from clenching the shelter's edge. Panic took hold and her heart beat so fast it was making her dizzy, she was afraid she was going to pass out.

Keep it together. Keep it together!

Gray heard a roar like some enraged demon from the depths, like something from a horror movie. Flames passed through their deployment and along the steep rocky terrain. Trees popped loudly. Things were quiet for an instant; the heat ebbed momentarily.

Then the second wave of fire hit them.

Chapter Two

The phone was ringing—again. What could be such an emergency? Faith Owen shuffled magazines and discarded potato chip bags searching for the demon device. She'd heard it ring from the bedroom at least five times. Then the ringing started again, incessantly. She was forced to drag herself out of bed and search for the damn thing. When had she even turned the ringer on anyway. *So annoying!*

"There you are." She snatched the phone up mid-ring and silenced it.

Faith checked the screen before answering it. Only her best friend, Kayla, would be brave enough to be *this* annoying. If she didn't pick up she knew Kayla would just keep calling until she answered.

"You know, some of us like to sleep in." Faith flopped onto the sofa. A crunching sound caused her to shift sideways. She'd just killed a half-eaten bag of Oreos. Faith tossed the bag onto the already piled high coffee table.

"Sleeping in? It's almost one o'clock." Kayla was far too awake.

"Is it?" Faith squinted at the shaft of sunlight slicing across the room from the almost-drawn drapes. This clue did seem to support the news that it was midday.

"What are you wearing right now?" Kayla's question was matter-of-fact.

"I don't think we have that sort of relationship." Faith couldn't help the sarcasm.

"In your dreams. I'll bet you're still in your pajamas surrounded by empty potato chip bags."

Faith catalogued her immediate surroundings. Kayla's statement was a bit too accurate. Was her condo bugged? She'd seen movies, she knew the laptop camera could be hacked. Faith leaned forward and checked that her laptop was closed and off.

The truth was she'd slept in a T-shirt and sweatpants; she hadn't even made it into her pajamas before snacking herself into a food coma while bingeing Netflix rom-coms. She'd shouted at the screen every time something stupid happened or one of the love interests missed a major cue regarding their relationship. Romantic comedies were evil. They made you believe love could last. They made you believe you could trust people.

"And your point is?" Faith tried not to sound miserable, but she was.

"Listen, sweetie, you have to move forward." The combination of Kayla's sweet Southern accent and the concern in her words was going to make Faith start crying. Again. "You have to leave the house. You need to eat something green…and put on real clothes."

"I know." Faith sniffed.

The breakup with Sam had really thrown her. Partly because she hadn't seen it coming, partly because she'd thought she and Sam had something real. What did real even mean anymore? She obviously had no idea.

"I want you to come to Sky Valley." Kayla took a breath. "Listen, my grandparents' house is empty right now. We don't have to rent it for the season. You could stay there and work at the café with me, and do your art thing."

"I don't know—"

"Faith, honey, you need a change of scenery. Somewhere far enough away that you don't have to be afraid to leave your house and bump into Samantha Stevens at the grocery store."

"That's not why I don't leave the house." Faith knew that didn't sound convincing. She was a terrible liar.

"If you don't drive here this instant I'm going to come get you myself."

Faith knew Kayla well enough to know she meant it.

"Okay, okay, maybe you're right." She exhaled loudly. "I'll just come for the weekend."

"Come for a month, maybe two. The leaves are already beginning to turn. It's beautiful here. It's the busy season…we need you…and you need to be needed." A bell chimed in the background. "I just got to the café so I need to run. Tell me you're packing right now and leaving. If you start driving soon you can be at our house for dinner, okay?"

"Maybe you're right." Faith wiped at her cheek with the sleeve of her T-shirt. "Thank you."

"Hey, who loves you most?" Kayla was playful.

"You." Faith couldn't help smiling.

"That's right, me." She heard the muffled thud of a car door closing. "Drive safe and call me from the road."

"Okay."

"I love you."

"I love you too." Faith clicked off. She took a deep breath and sank into the soft cushions. *This place is a wreck.*

Kayla was right. She needed a change of scenery in the worst way and Sky Valley, North Carolina, was one of her favorite places in the world. If she left now, she could be there in four and a half hours. The drive from Raleigh was mostly highway and it was Saturday midday, so traffic shouldn't be too bad. Folks who were headed to the quaint ski village in the mountains of western North Carolina were probably already there for the weekend.

Faith shuffled to the bedroom and faced the mirror next to the open closet. She'd been wearing the same sweatpants for three days and they sagged unattractively in the seat. Her hair had the uneven, disheveled look of sleep, and matted curls brushed the shoulders of her faded T-shirt. *What is that?* She leaned closer to the mirror. There was a remnant of a potato chip in her hair. *Beautiful.*

Wallowing had hit an all-time low. A tear gathered at the edge of her lashes, and she wiped it away with her fingers and took a deep, shaky breath.

She gave herself a stern look in the mirror.

Okay, Faith, this is the first step to getting over her. Four weeks was more than enough wallowing. *Seriously. Have some self-respect.*

Faith tugged a duffel bag from the top shelf of her closet and tossed it onto the bed. Then she selected a few shirts, jeans, a couple of dresses and began to pile them on the foot of the unmade bed.

The weather would be cool in the mountains, maybe she also needed a few sweaters. She rotated to look at the growing pile of things on the bed. Her subconscious was clearly packing for a month, definitely more than a weekend.

Otis slinked by, leaning against her legs as he passed. She reached down to rub his head between his ears. He yawned and stretched. Luckily, she'd chosen a cat instead of a dog at the shelter two years ago. Cats were great pets for wallowing. Otis would sleep all day with her if that's what she wanted to do. He never seemed to care whether she left the house or not.

"Well, boy, how do you feel about taking a little trip?"

He purred and rubbed his head against the side of her leg.

"I'll take that as a yes." She felt lucky she'd gotten him when she and Sam split up. Having someone to take care of had probably saved her, even if that someone was a twenty-pound cat.

Faith left the pile of clothes and headed to the second bedroom which doubled as her studio. If she was going to stay for a month, then she'd need to take supplies along. Not that she'd been able to do much work lately, but maybe she would finally break through this creative block. She was always happier when she could paint. Maybe it was like some sort of color therapy.

Faith opened a large plastic toolbox and loaded up tubes of paint and brushes. She laughed as she fought the urge to pack only dark colors. *The color palette for breakups.* Then she selected sheets of stiff illustration board and sketchpads and slid them into her portfolio case. Maybe she'd bring a few small blank canvases, just in case. There was no need to take too much, but just enough, in case inspiration found her again. And if she decided to stay longer she could always drive into Asheville and pick up more canvases.

Wow, that thought was almost optimistic. It seemed the act of simply packing to leave had improved her outlook a little.

The breakup with Sam had hurt, but more than that, it had badly shaken her confidence. Faith was unbalanced by Sam's sudden and abrupt rejection. It seemed to come out of nowhere and the fact that she hadn't had one clue about it made it seem as if Sam had been gaslighting her for months. Sam had deflected any moments of doubt or questions as if Faith was just paranoid, or worse, needy. She'd never considered herself to be a needy person.

If she hadn't caught Sam with Elaine, she might never have found out the truth.

Faith took a deep breath and exhaled slowly.

One step at a time. Take a shower, get dressed, and finish packing.

She turned on the shower and instead of waiting for the hot water, she stepped into the cool stream. It took her breath away for a moment, but the shock of the cool spray felt good.

Kayla waved from the porch as Faith stepped out of the car. Kayla walked out to meet her, pulling Faith into her arms. It felt good to be held by someone. Faith squeezed her eyes closed and held onto Kayla for longer than necessary.

"How are you, sweetie?" Kayla released her and stroked her face like a doting big sister.

"I'm fine." Faith sniffed. "Okay, not fine, but I'm happy to be here."

Kayla peeked into the car.

"You brought Otis."

"Well, I thought…what if this turns into more than a few days." Faith shrugged. "I didn't want to leave him at home. He's sort of become my furry security blanket."

Kayla's husband, Dan, joined them just as Faith opened the Volvo's hatchback. Dan was as handsome as ever, in that outdoorsy sort of way. He had short brown hair, a firm jawline, and a neatly trimmed beard. He was wearing his usual attire, jeans with paint splatters all over and a long-sleeved Henley T-shirt, unbuttoned just enough to show chest hair. Which she was sure most of the ladies loved, but was completely wasted on her.

"It's great to see you." He smiled and hugged her. "I just cranked up the furnace, so the place will be nice and warm when you come back after dinner."

Faith always joked with Dan that if the carpentry thing didn't work out, he could always launch his second career as an L.L. Bean model. He looked great in khakis and button-downs.

Dan grabbed the suitcase out of the back while Faith rounded the car to lift Otis's pet carrier out of the passenger seat. He meowed loudly.

"We'll get him settled inside and unload your stuff, then you're coming to our house for dinner. Dan is grilling chicken. I even convinced him to add a few skewers of vegetables."

"I hear they're healthy."

Faith smiled at their banter.

"I'm really glad you brought art supplies." Kayla reached for the portfolio.

Faith followed Kayla and Dan into the house she'd been in a million times when Kayla's grandparents still lived there, and a few times since then. The cozy, century-old frame house felt almost like a homecoming. Kayla and Dan had made a few updates to the kitchen, reworked the electrical and plumbing, and done some repairs to the hardwood floors, but mostly the house was how Faith remembered it. The living area was downstairs with three bedrooms upstairs. There was a bathroom on each floor, the upstairs bath added sometime in the eighties.

Otis wasn't released from the kennel until Faith returned with his litter box. She settled him into the downstairs bathroom. It seemed best to acclimate him in a small space while she had dinner. When she got back she'd let him roam and explore.

"Okay, boy, just relax. I'll be back soon." Faith filled a small saucer with water and put it next to a bowl of dry food.

He crouched near the food and began to eat. She felt lucky that he was such a mellow cat. Nothing seemed to ruffle his calm demeanor. Maybe she should aspire to be more like her cat. She pulled the door closed.

The drive to Kayla's place would only take ten minutes. They lived close by. Dan climbed in the back and let Faith sit up front while Kayla drove.

"I'm really glad you're here." Kayla reached over and clasped Faith's hand.

"Me too." She squeezed Kayla's hand.

What Faith needed now was time with friends. She was grateful to have Kayla and Dan in her life. As she'd gotten older, she realized true friends were rare and should be cherished.

Chapter Three

*T*hey'd cut a fire break, but the line had been breached by fast-moving flames, urged on by the shifting wind.

Gray needed to get higher. Only a few more feet to the gravel roadway. She glanced over her shoulder to check for Shane, but Shane wasn't there. She rotated to backtrack, but a tendril of arching flame pressed Gray to the ground, cutting off any retreat. She turned again toward the road.

She was on the road now, under the shelter. The brittle rock beneath her palms felt hot as if at any moment it would melt into lava. Gray struggled to breathe, she tried to beat back her fear. With trembling fingers, she loosened the protective blanket and lifted to survey the destructive inferno. The wildfire sounded like a hurricane now, the oppressiveness of it bearing down on her like a freight train. Chunks of charred debris fell all around, glowing lumps of hot embers bounced off the dry, rocky surfaces.

Shane was dead and so was she.

This was it.

Panic took hold, her heart thumped against her ribs. She was trapped. The end of everything was heat and choking smoke. She was utterly alone.

There was no one to call.

No one was coming to save her.

Gray jerked awake, gulping air. She sat up, braced on outstretched arms. The thin bedspread dropped to her waist. Gray blinked rapidly taking in her darkened surroundings. The dingy hotel room where the air smelled of stale drapes and old carpet, but not smoke.

Gray was alive.

Against all odds she'd survived. Shane had not.

I am here. This is now. Gray swung her legs over the edge of the bed, silently repeating the phrases to herself. She waited for her heartbeat to slow before she attempted to stand up. The counselor at the hospital had shared this method with her. In times of fear or stress, Gray repeated the mantra to remind herself that she was still here and not still on some scorched hillside.

She picked up the bottled water from the bedside table and parted the heavy drapes with her free hand as she took long sips. The headlights on I-40 zipped past in the distance. There was some comfort in the low hum of the freeway. Life carried on, despite whatever tragedy might happen in the world, life carried on. People kept moving forward. The world didn't stop.

The highway sound, comforting as it was while she was awake, had most definitely invaded her sleep and triggered the dream. It didn't take much to trigger the memory. Even the normally pleasing scent of wood smoke sent her right back to the rocky ravine, fighting for her life.

If she hadn't stumbled.

If Shane hadn't come back for her.

The events of that day played in her head every time she shut her eyes. Was it her fault Shane hadn't made it? Gray couldn't help thinking that was the case.

Her crew still waited for the final California Department of Forestry report on exactly what happened, and why. The preliminary CDF report of the burnover suggested Shane had died from super-heated air, a bad seal on his shelter. But Gray couldn't help thinking the time he'd lost when he'd come back for her had cost him his life.

Had it been worth it to save that little patch of ground?

In moments of anger, no.

But then Gray thought of the bigger picture. The fight hadn't been for a single blackened hillside, but for the land itself. The foothills of the California Sierras were full of game, timber, and a wilderness that drew hikers and campers enough to keep rural communities alive. So, she revised her answer. *Yes, it was worth it.* That charred hillside was just a small part of a much bigger ecosystem that affected lots of people.

Gray checked her phone. It was three thirty. Maybe she should just start driving. She was in Tennessee, not too far west of Nashville. If she left now she'd be in western North Carolina by breakfast. She might as well get going. There was no way sleep would return.

The motel she'd chosen was of the vintage variety. A single-story building with bright blue doors that all faced the parking lot. The last time she'd stayed in a place like this was with her grandma. They'd flown to Mississippi for her cousin's wedding. She'd shared a room with her grandma who'd gotten out of bed every hour all night long to check that her suitcase was still locked. Gray regretted now that she'd been short-tempered, but she was much younger and didn't understand that her grandma was simply afraid.

Until recently, Gray hadn't really understood irrational fear.

The times she was thinking of now, more than a decade ago, were about a different kind of fear. Back then, Gray was more on edge. Being in the closet added a level of stress to every situation. She could see that now and wondered why she'd been so afraid to be out. The truth was she'd probably been more scared of her own feelings than the reactions of others. She'd kissed the wrong girl in high school and feared ridicule that never really came. She got lucky, but still, high school was a lonely place for someone in hiding. She'd come out to her grandma, blurted it out over dinner one night. *Grandma, I'm gay.* Her grandmother had been a little confused about exactly what that meant. Hailing from a different generation, it was hard to explain, since she wasn't exactly sure herself, having had only the briefest of experiences.

Shortly after that, her grandmother's memory began to fail her, so those sorts of conversations became less important. Her grandma loved Gray and accepted her, even though she didn't truly understand her. Her grandma had always offered Gray a safe haven because her parents were a different story.

Gray's mother had a distinct picture in her head of who her daughter should be, of how she should conduct herself. When Gray refused to conform, well, things didn't go so well. That had been part of the allure of California. Distance. It was as far as she could get from North Carolina and the space allowed her to be completely herself—whoever that turned out to be. Or at least in the beginning that's what she'd told herself.

As she stowed her bags in the Jeep she noticed that the lights in the office were on. The parking lot had scattered puddles from an overnight rain. The air smelled of damp asphalt, a complete contrast to the bone-dry conditions in California. She literally hadn't seen grass until she reached Colorado. Living in the west had sharpened her senses to notice and appreciate weather, especially rain.

A bell chimed as she stepped through the lobby door. A sleepy looking middle-aged man shuffled out of the back room.

"Good morning." He reached for the room key she'd just set on the counter. "Gettin' an early start?"

"Yeah, couldn't sleep so I thought I might as well hit the road." Gray noticed the coffee pot across the room. She tipped her head in that direction. "Mind if I take a cup for the road?"

"Help yourself. I can fetch some cream if you need it."

"Naw, I just drink it black." She took a sip and headed for the exit. She paused in the open door. "Have a good day."

He waved and returned to whatever he'd been watching on TV in the back room. The bell chimed again as the lobby door whooshed closed behind her. Gray took a few more sips as she stood in front of the door enjoying the damp, pre-dawn air. Somewhere in the distance a dog barked as she crossed the parking lot.

As she merged her Jeep Wrangler onto the interstate, she puzzled over her decision to drive home. Funny how someone could still call a place home that hadn't offered shelter—emotionally or physically—in years. Glimpsing death had gotten her thinking about years long past. About things left unsettled, about things that she knew still held sway over her even as an adult. Baggage, that's what people called it, and she reckoned that's exactly what it was. Well, Gray needed a place to stow hers for a while. Just long enough to figure a few things out.

Yes, the solace of home was what she needed. Luckily, home was in a place far from fire season. A place where the hillsides were covered with broad-leafed hardwoods instead of dry grass and brittle live oaks. Yeah, the mountains of western North Carolina were just what she needed. At least, that's what she hoped.

Chapter Four

F aith squinted into the pre-dawn darkness from the kitchen window. What was that large black shape at the edge of the tree line? She leaned across the sink for the light switch. With the interior light off, she'd be able to see better.

Is that a bear?

Black bears had become much more invasive in the area, like oversized racoons foraging through unprotected trash receptacles, and when they could find an open door, even kitchen pantries.

She studied the large shape for any sign of movement but saw none. The faintest glow from sunrise warmed the grass between the house and the stand of hardwoods. Now that she had a better look it was obviously just a jagged tree stump. The wind had been fierce the previous night and the old oak at the edge of the yard had been broken at the spot where the trunk split in a vee. She could now see limbs scattered at the edge of the lawn, the bulk of the trunk having fallen sideways at the edge of the yard. Faith had worried the ancient tree wouldn't last another winter. Now the old hardwood would have a second life as firewood. That is, once she talked Dan into coming over to cut it up for her. She had tried to be the outdoorsy type, but she had her limits. And a chainsaw was definitely beyond her skills.

There hadn't been a bear. That was the good news. And the tree hadn't fallen on the house, also good news. But, wait…something was burning.

The toast!

The interior of the toaster oven glowed orange. She quickly flipped the glass door open and turned the dial to "off." Faith used a fork to skewer the blackened ember—formerly a slice of whole grain bread—from the little toasting rack. The charred square smoked all the way to the sink where she tossed it, doused it with water, and then fanned the air with a dishtowel to disperse the smoky haze.

Faith put another slice of toast in the oven. This time she'd pay attention.

She covered a yawn with her hand. She hadn't slept well. She hadn't been sleeping well for days. Leaving Raleigh for Sky Valley had definitely been the right decision. But sometimes late at night she just couldn't shut her brain off. She'd replay endless loops of conversations with Sam, regretting things she'd left unsaid. Oh yeah, she could think of every comeback in the world now that it was too late. Her tired brain was full of a million clever things she wished she'd thought to say in the moment. Typical.

You need a change. The words of her best friend, Kayla, echoed inside her head. Kayla had been right. As she buttered the toast and took a bite, she considered Kayla's words.

Thankfully, Kayla had convinced her to come to Sky Valley. What was supposed to be a week had turned into a month. Sky Valley was busy in autumn when all the leaves turned, but it was even busier when it started to snow. Ski lodges filled up with tourists and Kayla needed Faith's help at the café more than ever, especially during the Christmas holiday. And as Kayla had so succinctly put it, Faith needed to be needed. Work at the café was a great distraction for now. Faith had a steady group of clients she did freelance artwork for, but during the holidays all of that usually slowed down.

After finishing her toast, Faith carried her tea out to the edge of the yard where the old tree had broken apart. The ancient tree was at the edge of a thick grove. In the presence of the silent hardwoods, time slowed.

Tree time was an enjoyable pace.

In long ago summers when she used to visit with Kayla's family, Faith would carry her sketchbook to a small clearing in the grove and then wait and watch. Dappled light would shift through the leaves changing shadows, causing her to notice small details whenever the sunlight shifted. An abundance of water in early spring made moss at the base of the trees come alive with intense chartreuse green. It was almost impossible to capture the intensity of that green on paper.

But she'd been unable to do much painting since Sam left, and there was no time to linger this morning. It was her turn to take the breakfast shift at the café so she needed to get dressed and get to work. Since Kayla was letting her stay in the house rent free, the least she could do was go in early a few times a week so that Kayla could sleep in. Her painting work and the firewood could wait until later.

"Hi, boy." Faith paused on the porch to stroke Otis. "Do you want some breakfast?"

Yes, she was talking to a cat. Something she found herself doing even more lately. Faith wondered if that was a good or bad sign? Maybe neither.

She held the screen door for Otis and let it softly bang closed before she followed him to the kitchen. He seemed pleased with the selection of cat food she'd scooped onto a saucer for him.

The wall clock told her she'd taken a little too much time with her morning routine. She needed to dress and get going. Faith reached for a blouse with three-quarter sleeves and pulled it on over a tank-style T-shirt, leaving it unbuttoned. The jeans she'd chosen were a little snug. She fell back onto the bed and inhaled to button them, certain it was the dryer's fault and not the late-night stress eating she'd been doing lately.

Faith lingered in front of the bathroom mirror after brushing her teeth trying to decide if her slept-on damp hair was too unruly to wear down. She swept her fingers through it to tame the curls a bit and put a hair tie around her wrist for later. If it was too hot in the afternoon she'd just wear it up.

A warm lip color, not quite red but a bit bolder than pink, seemed like the right choice.

Otis waited at the door, grooming himself by the time Faith had her bag and keys in hand.

"Have a good day, little man." He slinked out onto the wide front porch and lay down. Ah, to have the life of a cat. Without a worry in the world and no place to be and in no hurry to get there if he did. *Tree time* and *cat time* had a lot in common and she envied both.

Faith backed her car away from the white, wood-framed farmhouse and turned onto the main road from the gravel driveway. The paved road to town angled sharply downhill and then right into a hairpin turn. This was not a drive to attempt if you were too sleepy or too tipsy or if the road was icy. Every other weekend, some teenager on a crotch rocket missed this curve and ended up in the trees. The rescue squad had fished so many motorcycles out of the woods over the years Kayla said she'd lost count.

This wasn't Faith's first layover in Sky Valley. She'd spent holidays here and summers with Kayla's family. Sky Valley was like a second home.

Faith waved at George Patterson as she passed. He was standing in the yard with a cup of coffee watching his tiny black and white dog tiptoe through the dew-laden grass. Only the retired got up this early. She supposed it was so he could make the most of every day, although he never seemed in a hurry, regardless of what he was doing. His wife, Elba, probably called his slow speed *George time.*

That thought made her laugh.

Sky Valley was where the Smokies met the Blue Ridge Mountains. The only way in or out was to take one of three curvy scenic roads that cut through the surrounding mountain passes into the valley, named for the sky because of its higher elevation. Winter snows sometimes forced road closures from here and along the Blue Ridge Parkway located not far away. But it wasn't that cold yet. The trees still had a bit of their autumn colors on display.

Sky Valley had been a popular family resort town in the mountains of North Carolina for many years. It was laid-back and still sort of old-fashioned, with vintage ski lodges, motels, and plenty of craft shops for tourists who liked to browse. In fact, Kayla's Sky Valley Café had been in her family since the forties and was a classy throwback to roadside diners of that day.

Kayla and Dan had taken over the café and lodge several years earlier and they were still working on updates. It helped immensely that Kayla's husband, Dan, was a part-time contractor because when they took over the place, especially the lodge, there were a million minor things that needed attention. The entire place was now beginning to glow with tender loving care.

Faith had first fallen in love with Sky Valley while visiting with Kayla during a semester break. It was by sheer luck that she'd met Kayla while in college and they'd become fast friends. When Kayla had decided to take over the business from her parents, Faith was almost jealous. At least with Kayla here full-time she got to visit whenever she wanted. She loved it here. The smell of the damp hardwoods in summer. The light filtering through the early morning fog. The pace of life. She loved all of it. Except Sky Valley's official sport, skiing. She was a terrible skier. Hot chocolate in the lodge was her sport of choice, at which she excelled.

Western North Carolina contained the highest mountains in the Eastern United States. There were more than a hundred peaks rising to over five thousand feet in elevation. It wasn't the Rockies, but the winter snows were beautiful and the autumn leaves so vibrant that visitors came from all over just to soak in the color. Faith felt lucky to be here. If she was going to hide out anywhere and nurse her wounded spirit, this was the place to do it. Having not been born here, Faith never took the beauty of the mountains for granted.

As she rounded the curve, something emerged from the greenery and into the road. It was a bobcat! Faith braked and watched as the smallish wildcat darted across the road and disappeared into the woods on the other side.

Chapter Five

A pile of trash greeted Faith as she parked behind the café. "Tyler Caldwell." She muttered his name as she walked past the carnage. Food debris and garbage was strewn all over near the dumpster at the back of the café. If she'd heard Kayla tell Tyler once she'd heard Kayla tell him five hundred times to make sure all the trash at the end of the evening was in the dumpster with the latch locked. Something, some creature, had surely had a feast given the mess they'd left all over the employee parking lot. She stepped carefully over a pile of shredded paper towels and entered the restaurant through the back door. The kitchen was warm and busy. Ed glanced over as he shuffled sausage patties around on the grill. She waved hello as she reached for the wall phone and dialed.

"Tyler?" His voice was raspy with sleep on the other end. "Yes, I know it's early. You need to get down here and clean up a huge mess." She waited for his confirmation and then hung up.

"How's it going?" Faith checked in with Ed before she pushed through the double swinging door to the restaurant's interior.

"Busy." He shrugged as he whisked eggs in a bowl. "Steady."

She could never get more than one word at a time from him, but he was a damn solid cook. He never got flustered, no matter how slammed they got at peak times. He'd been a cook during his tenure in the Navy and absolutely nothing riled him. Not even Sunday brunch, which was the café's busiest time. As she scanned the tables, it was clearly still early, the after-church crowd wouldn't arrive until much later. That was good. That would give her a little while to ease into the day.

Mr. Niebhoff was at the register with a ticket in his hand. He was usually the first customer on the weekends; he apparently never slept in. He was in his nineties and still driving, which made Faith nervous. She smiled at him as she made her way to cash him out. Nancy Jo joined her at the front counter. Nancy Jo waited tables alongside Faith.

Nancy Jo had grown up in Sky Valley and knew everyone in town. No one called her Nancy, or simply Jo, her first name was *Nancy Jo* as if it was all one word. She was the quintessential Southern belle, with long, blond feathered hair. And the enviable skill of friendly flirtation that bordered on a superpower. Faith had no doubt that Nancy Jo could get any man in the tri-county area to do any chore she needed done with a sway of her hips and a flip of her golden hair. It truly was a sight to behold. Every seat at the counter in the café was taken each morning from the minute they opened. Nancy Jo doled out coffee and feminine charm in equal servings to her rapt admirers.

Nancy Jo had offered to coach Faith, to share her gift. Maybe twenty years from now, if Faith ever decided to date again, she'd take Nancy Jo up on the offer. But for now, these were skills she was sure she had no use for. She might never date again.

Nancy Jo set the coffee carafe down and turned toward Faith.

"I can ring him up." She waved Nancy Jo off.

"That'll be six seventy-five." Faith waited for Mr. Niebhoff to tease a few bills from his wallet.

"You can keep the change." He smiled and tipped his head.

"Thank you. See you next week, Mr. N." Everyone had shortened his name to one letter. Few could pronounce Niebhoff and even fewer could spell it.

He strained to manage his cane and push the door open at the same time. Faith quickly stepped around the register to hold the door for him.

"Drive safe." She smiled as Mr. N. wobbled through the exit.

Faith dropped the extra change in the tip jar and was just about to help Nancy Jo deliver second rounds of coffee when she noticed a rather intimidating Jeep pull into the parking lot. It was matte green, similar to a military color. The driver didn't park in one of the angled spots right next to the front of the café but instead glided into one of the parallel slots a few car lengths away, which gave Faith time to watch the driver, a woman, round the Jeep and saunter with long strides toward the door. The Jeep was a four-door model with huge off-road tires. It looked as if it belonged on safari, not in quaint Sky Valley, North Carolina. And she didn't recognize the driver. That wasn't unusual since Sky Valley got lots of tourists, but this woman didn't strike her as a tourist. That was the second thing she thought. Her first thought was that this woman was very good-looking. She shook her head to dislodge the thought.

Not interested. Remember? Never dating again.

The tall woman was dressed in a brown jacket with fleece lining all around the collar which was partially turned up around her neck. Her stride seemed comfortable. She was confident, in well-worn jeans and boots. An unruly tuft of wavy dark hair softly shadowed thoughtful brown eyes as she entered the café and walked right up to where Faith was standing at the register.

"Hi." The stranger's voice was in the alto range and resonated with calm confidence.

"Hi." Faith's cheeks warmed. Did she know this woman? No. If they'd met before she'd certainly remember. But still, there was an unnerving sense of familiarity. _NOT interested_, she reminded herself.

"Um, can I just take any empty table?" The woman motioned toward the dining room.

"Oh, yes…anywhere is fine." Faith realized she'd been standing like a statue, openly staring at the stranger for several seconds, so embarrassing. "I'll bring a menu over."

Faith exhaled and reached for one of the glossy trifold menus before following the woman to an open booth near the windows.

"Can I get you a coffee to start with…or water?" Faith was annoyed by the tremble in her words. _Pull it together._

"Sure, coffee." The woman regarded Faith with an expression of wariness, as if the world was not to be trusted.

"Cream and sugar?"

"No thanks, just black."

The dark-haired stranger smiled only briefly, at which point the temperature of the air heated and woke a feeling of warmth inside her that until this moment had been stuffed down. The sudden shift might have alarmed Faith, probably should have alarmed her, but any wariness was overruled by curiosity.

Faith's hand shook as she poured coffee at the front counter. She took a couple of deep breaths to settle herself before delivering the heavy, white diner-style mug and the little tin cup of cream to the table. Only then did she remember the stranger drank her coffee black.

"Are you ready to order?" Faith slid the tin cup of cream across the table away from the mug of coffee and tried for nonchalance. Her own voice sounded far away. She'd have sworn they were the only two people in the restaurant. In the background, a dish clanked loudly to remind her they weren't.

"Um, can I get scrambled eggs and toast." Short dark hair framed the striking symmetry of the stranger's face. She had a straight nose, and an easy manner; everything about her suggested fairness and a firm handshake.

A firm handshake meant strong hands. Where did that come from? Why was she noticing a total stranger's hands? *Not interested! Never dating again, remember?*

"Would you like cheese on the eggs?" Faith tried to focus on the simple question rather than the distracting monologue inside her head.

The woman taking her order was so pretty that Gray had forgotten what she'd asked for. Hell, she'd forgotten where she was for a moment. The woman's nametag read Faith, and Gray was fairly sure this woman could restore hers. Faith had wild reddish auburn hair. The color was striking against her pale skin. Her wavy, long hair was so beautiful that it may have been where her power center resided, you know, if she was a superhero. Gray might have said Faith's hair was one of her most alluring features, until Gray allowed herself to notice Faith's eyes. Green, clear and brilliant in their ability to make you feel utterly exposed. She had a delicate aquiline nose and her face had an ageless quality, but Gray would have guessed she was in her early thirties.

"Sorry, what was the question?" She'd drifted completely.

"Cheese?" Faith repeated the question. "Would you like cheese on your eggs?"

"No, thanks…um, on second thought, why not." She handed Faith the laminated menu and their eyes locked for a few seconds. Warmth snaked through her entire system.

"Grayson Reeves! Aren't you a sight for sore eyes." Faith visibly flinched at the sound of Nancy Jo's voice just behind her. Nancy Jo had come from nowhere.

Gray suddenly remembered life in a small town—small world.

"Hi, Nancy Jo. It's been a long time." Gray smiled.

"Well, don't just sit there. Git up and give me a hug." Nancy Jo pressed the fullness of her curvaceous body against Gray the minute she stood. She knew Nancy Jo didn't really mean it the way it felt, but it still felt good. Nancy Jo's embrace reminded her she was alive and that not everyone in a small, Southern town was a church-going judgmental busybody. As a matter of fact, Nancy Jo probably had enough skeletons in her closet to rival Gray's.

"You two know each other?" Faith had lingered, which pleased Gray.

"This is the famous, or infamous, Grayson Reeves." Nancy Jo made introductions with a grand gesture with one arm while her other arm still draped across Gray's shoulder. "She's a local legend."

"Hardly." She extended her hand to Faith. "Just call me Gray."

"Hi, my name is Faith." Faith clenched the folded menu with a death grip, but after an awkward few seconds accepted her offered hand.

As she held Faith's hand, the warmth that had snaked through her system a few moments earlier from mere eye contact returned and with it a tingling sensation traveled up the tiny hairs of her arm. This woman was breathtaking.

"Where have you been?" Nancy Jo spoke, breaking the spell, and pulling Gray back to the real world.

"I've been out west." She shoved her hands in her pockets. "I thought I'd come home for a little while." She smiled at Faith who still hadn't taken her eyes off Gray.

"Um, I'll put this in." Faith seemed to suddenly realize she'd taken Gray's order but hadn't actually delivered it to the kitchen.

"I need to get back to my customers too." Nancy Jo patted Gray's shoulder as she took her seat. "It's good to see you, Gray."

"It's nice to see you too. And nice to meet you, Faith."

Faith nodded and smiled as she walked away.

Faith felt like she might pass out. *Just breathe.* She slid the ticket in the spinning order rack and then kept walking through the kitchen and out the back door.

"Are you all right?" She heard Ed call after her.

"I'm fine." Faith called back as the door swung shut.

She placed her hands on her hips and took deep breaths as she paced in small circles in the back parking lot.

Tyler was making a racket over near the dumpster as he attempted to clean up the mess.

That was just what her insides felt like. A tangled mess.

Who the hell was Grayson Reeves and why had Faith's reaction to her been so damn strong? Her safe hideaway had just been invaded by a very charming enemy element.

Not interested.

She'd just keep repeating that to herself until she believed it.

Chapter Six

Gray had hoped to get another chance to talk to Faith during breakfast, but Nancy Jo delivered the food and a coffee refill and then collected her check. Oh well, she'd have to stop in for another meal sometime. And it was a small town after all, they were bound to run into each other eventually. That was one of the ways a small-town environment could actually work in your favor.

Gray drove slowly along Main Street after leaving the restaurant. She steered with one hand draped across the steering wheel as if she were casing the scene, as if she were expecting to be recognized like some fugitive on a wanted poster. But having been gone for so long, she didn't see any familiar faces and even parts of Main Street were different.

The old five-and-dime was a yoga studio. That was a surprise. The hardware store remained, as did the historic courthouse. She followed the roundabout taking in the display of pumpkins and other autumn flair on the lawn near the wide front steps. The short streets surrounding the square were populated with a coffee shop and several gift shops, a bookstore, a chocolate shop, a music shop, and a pizza place.

Two miles from the main square, she turned right onto a paved winding road that climbed the hillside. Frame houses from the turn of the century dotted the rural side road. Some were in better shape than others. The yards showed years of neglect. Waylaid autos rusted in a few places, some nearly reclaimed by the encroaching vines and weeds. Her parents' old house was just below the ridgeline, sheltered from wind and weather at the base of a smattering of large granite boulders. Like the remnants of some giant's game of marbles. As a kid, she loved to climb and play on those rocks. She and her cousin Mark had constructed complex imaginary worlds amongst those rocks. They'd practiced swordplay with sticks and built forts.

The dirt driveway up to the rustic dwelling was rutted and uneven. She had to use both hands on the wheel as the Jeep lurched and bounced over the rough roadway to the house. The road definitely needed to be graded and treated with some fresh gravel. The house looked pretty good from the outside. The timbers were dark from age and weather, but they had the solid look of a structure that could withstand a hurricane if called upon to do so. Luckily, they didn't get many hurricanes in the mountains, just the residual tropical storms.

The heavy front door was stuck, probably swelled from the damp mountain air. Gray had to press her shoulder against it and put her weight into it to convince it to open. The hinges squeaked loudly.

Inside, the air wasn't great. It was damp and musty from lack of use. The clingy strand of an unseen cobweb attached itself to her face and hair. She tried to brush it away, but bits of it kept clinging to her fingers. She brushed them against her jeans. The rafters of exposed beams were gray with more cobwebs. Spiders were not her favorite and these would have to go.

Gray checked the huge stone fireplace. The flue finally opened after putting up a bit of a fight. Debris, mostly dried leaves and acorns, tumbled down creating a dust cloud and she coughed.

Next was the kitchen. She turned the handle at the sink, but nothing happened, not even a groan from the aging pipes. Well, she could work around everything else, but she couldn't stay here without water. The pump house was visible from the kitchen window. She'd have to take a look.

There was a small room off the kitchen. It had been added on where the back door used to be. The house had originally been built in 1902 but was expanded over the years like some project made from Lincoln Logs. The floor plan no longer made sense, and some of the walls were discolored in spots from original construction that had been altered. Walls pushed back or removed altogether leaving spaces of wood previously protected from the sun so that they were lighter in color. Crank-style windows had been added in the 30s. They were single-paned and offered no insulation, but they looked cool. They'd gather moisture in the wintertime when the fire was lit and warm bodies huddled inside.

Something crunched under Gray's foot as she approached the window of the ancient back door of the house. Broken glass was scattered about. She surveyed the room; nothing seemed to be disturbed or missing.

She wondered what sort of person had broken the window. The lock was old, fragile, and could probably have been forced open by a strong wind without having to break a window.

Whoever it was, they had to be hard up to stay in the house without heat or water. If that was in fact what they'd done. You'd definitely need a fire now. The thick walls held in the dampness and the chill. The whole place smelled like old wool clothing that had been left in the rain for too long and then stored in a closet.

The more believable story was that some kid had thrown a rock for fun. Vandalism was its own special brand of acting out. She still remembered what it had been like to be a teen who didn't fit in and how that was frustrating as hell.

Gray scuffed the glass aside with her boot and opened the door. She glanced back as she walked toward the pump house. There was moss in the shingles on the roof, but otherwise the house looked solid and showed little other wear from neglect. Each wall was constructed of five rough-hewn old-growth timbers. They were dark as pitch, with lighter bonding material in between. This cabin would likely survive anything—earthquakes, blizzards, maybe even a forest fire. In a fire, the roof would be lost, but probably the aging timbers would partly survive. Unless there was too much pitch in them. The thought reminded her of old-growth trees after a big fire. All that was left of them were the blackened trunks jutting from the ashes, refusing to give in, like a forest of the standing dead.

Experience with fires had changed her. She measured almost everything against its ability to withstand a big burn.

She shook off the mental image as she pulled vines away from the pumphouse door. Yep, the pump was frozen and she didn't know how to bring it back to life. There were lots of things she could do.

She was good with carpentry and woodworking, but she'd never had a knack for small engine repair. But she knew someone who did.

She fished her phone out of her pocket and dialed the number. A hawk circled overhead as she waited for her cousin Mark to pick up on the other end.

"Hello." He sounded busy.

"Hey, Mark, it's Gray."

There was silence on the other end.

"Mark? Are you still there?"

"Yeah, I'm here." There was a shuffling sound on the other end. "I thought maybe this was a prank caller." Then she heard the sound of a vehicle door slam. "How'd I rate a call from California?"

She couldn't decide if he was glad to hear from her or not. Mark was hard to read even when he was standing right in front of you, even harder over the phone. Admittedly, they didn't really chat that much over the phone. Had it been two years since they'd spoken? She couldn't remember.

"I'm not in California. I'm home...I'm at the house."

"When did you get in?"

"Just this morning." She cleared her throat. "I, um...I was thinking I might stay for a while."

He was quiet for moment.

"Well, I'll bet the house is cold as a well digger's butt."

"Yeah." She was relieved that he was warming up, sounding more like his old self.

"Is the water and power on over there?"

"The power and gas are on, so I can cook or whatever. But the well pump is frozen up." Luckily, she'd thought to get the power and gas sorted out before she made the drive.

"I can come take a look if you want." She heard a screen door bang. "I just need to check in with Christy and then I could head over."

"That'd be great." She was relieved. The first phone call to family was always the hardest.

"See you in a few." He clicked off.

Gray shook her head, amused at herself. She'd traveled all over the country alone, climbed hazardous trails along the continental divide, fought forest fires, faced all kinds of dangers, and still, talking with her family could reduce her to an insecure teenager in a matter of seconds. Mark wasn't one of the problems anyway, so why did talking to him bring everything back so fast? Probably because he'd been witness to all of it. So, talking to Mark, being with Mark just brought all of the awkward, awful teen stuff back.

It was good that she'd come back. Gray was an adult. She needed to quit letting her past affect her. And the only way to make that happen was to return home and deal with it.

A wave of regret washed over her as she stood in the backyard and looked at the house. She'd waited a long time to make things right with her mother. Mostly things had been okay with them in the end anyway. They'd at least come to some sort of understanding, if not agreement.

The house had started as a small one-bedroom cabin, probably a vacation home for some wealthy family in Asheville. Her mom had purchased it even before she'd married. Her parents had been divorced for several years when her mom passed away, so Gray now owned the house. In hindsight maybe it wasn't so much her mom as her dad who'd put pressure on her to conform. He'd remarried right after the divorce and moved to Florida. He never really cared for the mountains the way her mother did, the way she did. He'd been in Florida for years now. They didn't really keep in touch aside from the obligatory Christmas and birthday phone call. And even sometimes the birthday calls didn't happen. And she didn't even care, did she?

Gray slowly walked the perimeter of the overgrown yard to the tree line. The house sat on twenty acres. A narrow plot that extended from the road into the forest at a steep grade so that the only good building site was where the house sat. The rest of the land was, as her mother used to say, just forested space for your soul. Room for walking and thinking and spending time with the trees. Gray thought back to those times when she was younger, to those moments of communion with the trees. The silence of the wilderness always confronted her with the question of who she thought she was. As she stepped into the shadow of the trees she wondered if she'd ever really answered that question. She'd done the searching part for sure, but to what end?

Maybe answers hovered in the shadowed spaces among the old hardwoods.

❖

Mark had the well pump running in short order. He straightened from his hunched position over the pump as it hummed to life. He had aged well. Mark's physique still held from his high school football days. And although his hair had receded a bit in the front, there was still plenty of it. The only wrinkles on his face were the white creases of laugh lines near his eyes, his face otherwise tanned from labor outdoors. He'd mostly worked construction in the decade since graduation and the work seemed to have kept him fit and happy.

It was easy to see why Mark had never left Sky Valley. It suited him. He never chafed under the oppressive small-town-ness of it all. He easily fit in, plus, he'd married his high school sweetheart. Gray hadn't been that lucky. In fact, upon graduation, she'd felt that she needed to get as far away as she could to find space to breathe, to find room to be herself, hell, to figure out who she even was. Because she sure didn't know when she left. Yeah, she'd been back a few times, but never for very long. The pressure from family to conform, to fall in line, would begin to seep into her psyche the minute she arrived.

Or was that even real? Was it all in her head? Now that her parents were no longer around, she wondered.

"How long are you going to be here?" He wiped his hands on a handkerchief and then stowed it into his back pocket. He bent to pick up the wood handle of the toolbox he'd carried out to the pump house from his vintage Ford truck.

"Not sure yet." But the truth was that she was not eager to leave. She needed to stay for a while somewhere with plenty of rain and a low risk of fire. And right now, that meant being far away from California.

It was nice to be somewhere safe and protected. Funny how the place she couldn't get away from fast enough ended up being the first place she ran to for some sense of security. The mountains of western North Carolina embraced you, the coziness of the blue ridges made you feel sheltered.

"Well, Christy wants you to come over for dinner while you're here."

"That'd be nice." Gray followed him toward his truck. "How old is Hailey now?" She hadn't kept up with birthdays for her young cousin the way a doting relative should.

"She's twelve, going on sixteen."

Gray sensed a bigger story behind that statement.

"Well, it'll be great to see them both and catch up."

Mark stowed the toolbox in the back of the truck. He opened the driver's side door, pausing for a moment with his arm resting on the open window. He held her gaze for a moment, not in a challenging way, but in the way someone can when they really know who you are. Gray felt an unexpected lump rise in her throat. She averted her eyes and swallowed. When she turned back Mark was still there.

"It's good you're back." His expression softened. "Are you okay?"

"Yeah." But she wasn't sure she was.

Gray stepped around the open door and gave Mark a hug. He hugged her back and then released her quickly as if he felt suddenly awkward, the way men do sometimes when they've shown emotion they didn't really intend to show. He climbed in the driver's seat and spoke to her through the open truck window.

"I'll text you about dinner."

Gray nodded and waved as he backed the truck away from where she stood.

Chapter Seven

The crowd in the café thinned by the afternoon. Kayla had arrived just before the after-church lunch rush and was now busy bussing tables. This was the first breather they'd had to actually catch up.

"What did I miss this morning? Anything exciting?" Kayla paused near the front counter where Faith was standing.

"Nothing." Faith wiped the counter with a clean rag. Her mind kept wandering and she couldn't remember if she'd done the task or not. The countertop already had a bright sheen indicating that she probably had already done this at least once.

"Nothing except our friend here drooling over a returning local ghost." Nancy Jo sashayed past. She winked at Faith as she retrieved a piece of apple pie for a customer.

"Who?" Kayla perked up at Nancy Jo's teasing.

"Ms. Grayson Marie Reeves, in the flesh." Nancy Jo nodded for emphasis as she squeezed past Faith again on her way to deliver the oversized slice of pie.

At the mention of Gray's name, Kayla really did look as if she'd seen a ghost. She froze, holding a glass in midair. She had an expression that was hard to decipher. Was that anxiety or annoyance, or just plain surprise?

"You know her?" Faith tried to sound as if she didn't really care about the answer, but on the inside, she was all pins and needles.

"She knows her, as in, the *Biblical* sense." Nancy Jo paused at Kayla's elbow to reveal this juicy bit of news. She was enjoying this way too much. Nancy Jo hustled through the double swinging doors into the kitchen before Kayla could regroup and throw something at her. All Kayla could muster was a scowl.

Faith turned to Kayla, waiting for an explanation. Did *in the Biblical sense* mean what she thought it meant?

"Don't look so surprised." Kayla circled behind the counter and stowed the plastic bin of dishes. She stood next to Faith and continued, her voice not much more than a whisper, as if she were sharing some conspiratorial plot twist. "I told you about that time at summer camp."

"You did, but I thought her name was Marie." And then Faith realized what she'd said.

"It was, at the time. Grayson Marie Reeves. She even had long hair back then. People didn't start calling her Gray until her junior year in high school. At her own request, I might add. She cut her hair short too. It was a whole thing."

"You—and Gray?" Her voice cracked. Faith was truly and sincerely in shock.

"It was one time when we were teenagers. I was curious. Don't make a federal case out of it." Kayla frowned, then shrugged. "And you—" Kayla pointed at Faith for emphasis. "*You* should avoid her. Grayson Reeves is a player, which is the last thing you need."

Faith bristled a little at Kayla's bossy tone, but deep down, despite what her hormones were telling her, she knew Kayla was right. The absolute last thing she needed was a crush on some butch playgirl who would inevitably do exactly what Sam had just done. Hadn't Faith learned anything? Thank goodness she was finding out the truth about Gray now, before her imagination, and her hormones, ran amuck.

So, Gray was a player.

Obviously. I mean, just look at her. Faith found herself picturing Gray's brooding good looks, the way that little clump of unruly dark hair fell teasingly over one eye.

OMG, get a grip!

Faith picked up the plastic bin full of dirty dishes that Kayla had just stowed behind the counter. "I've got these."

She was thankful for a good friend who cared enough about her to intervene with the truth. She'd dodged a bullet. A sexy bullet, but lethal just the same.

Faith finished her shift, having started her day early. Driving home, she just happened to glance down a rutted dirt drive and catch a glimpse of Gray's Jeep. She'd thought that house was empty. She never saw anyone about the place.

So, that's where she'd gone. And now Faith would be driving by twice a day as long as she worked at the café. Or until Faith returned to Raleigh, which she had been in no real hurry to do. It had been great to be away. To not have to continually watch for her ex, for fear she'd bump into Sam when she was least prepared to do so. Kayla had definitely been right. A change of scenery had vastly improved her perspective. She might even break out her paints and get some work done when she got to the house.

Big things could happen. She was feeling better all the way around. So, she'd met a cute woman today, so what. That didn't mean she had to do anything about it, it just meant she wasn't dead inside. She'd begun to wonder.

Faith's phone chimed in her purse as she turned into the driveway at her place. She checked the screen as she got out. She stopped dead in her tracks and stared at her phone.

It was a text from Sam.

Just thinking of you. Hope you're okay.

What the literal hell? That was such typical Sam behavior. Sam didn't care about how Faith was feeling. Sam just wanted to reach out so that she could make *herself* feel better. If she really thought that then why did she have such a strong impulse to reply. Faith pinched the bridge of her nose, took a deep breath, and then exhaled slowly. For a minute, she considered blocking Sam's number, but she just couldn't quite go that far—yet.

Although, as she climbed the porch steps she lectured herself. Blocking Sam's number was probably exactly what she should do for the sake of self-preservation. Or possibly change her number, or maybe just never return to Raleigh. There had to be moving services she could engage to pack up and ship all her belongings so that she never had to actually return there in person.

Faith sat down on the top step beside Otis. She propped her chin in her hand and sighed.

"You are so lucky to be a cat."

Chapter Eight

As Faith lay in bed nursing a cup of herbal tea, thoughts of the day crowded inside her head. She tried her best not to think of Gray, but that was nearly impossible, and besides, what was wrong with a little distraction. It wasn't as if she was ever going to act on it. And thinking of anything or anyone was better than thinking of Sam.

Gray was no more than a mile away. Just down the road. What was she doing right now? What was she thinking? Faith could have sworn they had a moment at the café, but maybe that was only on her side of the equation.

Otis jumped up and curled up on the unoccupied side of the bed. He licked his paw, and when she reached over to stroke his thick fur, he began to purr. If she was lucky, he would share his sleep vibe with her and, combined with the chamomile tea, she might actually get some rest. But not just yet. She needed more of a distraction for her brain.

There was a sketchbook and a random assortment of soft-lead pencils on the bedside table. Sometimes doing a late-night sketch helped her relax. Sketching put her into sort of a Zen state. Drawing was definitely a form of meditation for Faith. She set the tea aside and started working on a loose outline of Otis. The gray stripes across his back faded to soft white fur on his stomach. The lines of his closed eyes were also ringed with white fur, as were all four of his paws—as if he was wearing a white mitten on each foot.

Faith had probably sketched Otis a hundred times and with every drawing, she noticed some small detail she'd never seen before. This time it was how one of his whiskers was askew from the rest, pointing almost forward. That was the thing about art, it was all about the seeing, and learning to see. You could draw or paint the same thing multiple times, but depending on lighting and angle it could be like seeing it for the first time all over again. Before Faith began to work on a painting she always did a series of sketches of the subject matter from various angles and with different lighting before settling on the final composition. Sometimes she never got past the sketching phase. Some things were best as pencil studies; some things were best left unfinished.

Her phone buzzed nearby and her stomach lurched. It was probably another text from Sam because she hadn't answered the first one. *Ignore it.* But she couldn't.

She flipped the phone faceup, expecting the worst, but instead it was a text from Dan.

Sorry for the late text. Just a heads up that my friend Mark is going to take care of the tree tomorrow.

The fallen tree was a bit of a mess. Faith assumed Dan would eventually get to it. He must be busier than she thought at the lodge if he was going to pay someone else to take care of it. Dan was a real *do-it-yourself* sort of guy. The sort of guy who could literally fix anything.

No problem. I'll be here. It was her day off and she'd planned to lounge, read, or maybe do some drawing—maybe even go for a hike.

Relieved that the text had *not* been from Sam, Faith set the phone and sketchbook aside and reached to switch off the bedside lamp. She closed her eyes and tried to get her brain to wind down. A yawn came over her, and she stretched and rolled onto her side.

"Good night, little man."

Faith let her hand rest on Otis's fluffy back one more time before she tucked her arm under the covers.

❖

Gray jolted from sleep. She pressed her palms to her eyes in a useless attempt to hide the images from view. But the images were all in her head. Ever since the fire, she'd had trouble falling asleep and continually woke up exhausted.

I am here. This is now.

The anxiety attacks mostly came during sustained silences, which evoked the quiet of the thin shelter after the fire had passed. Nighttime was the worst. She tried to stay up as late as possible. She even did sit-ups and push-ups beside the bed in a futile attempt to exhaust herself into sleepiness. Nothing made a difference. Most nights she sprang from sleep in a panic.

I am here. This is now.

Working as a firefighter required a person to operate under various threats—getting hit by a falling tree, or being killed in a helicopter crash. She'd known all of that, been cavalier about it in fact. But now her greatest fear was being burned to death and she couldn't shake it. Fire shelters weren't made to withstand the conductive heat from direct flames. Prolonged heat exposure while in a shelter meant you were likely dead. She couldn't help wondering what Shane's last moments had been like. Those thoughts haunted her.

Gray had never suffered from nightmares or constant fears, until now. She was spooked and wondered if she'd gone soft. She wondered if she'd ever be the same person she'd been before. Now, every memory was clearly defined by a hard line between before and after that fire.

She got out of bed and put on a sweatshirt over her T-shirt, then tugged a blanket from the bottom of the bed. The hardwood floor was chilly, but she didn't put on shoes. The house was cold, but for some reason she didn't tug on sweatpants either. She shuffled out to the living room in her boxer shorts. The first hints of sunrise bathed the living room in soft pink light. Gray stepped out onto the front porch and sat in the porch swing at the far side, facing the mountain. A warm glow lit the ridge with red-orange brilliance. Even with nowhere to be, Gray was unable to sleep in. Habit and bad dreams woke her just at sunrise so that she was seated in the porch swing just in time to see the blue ridges bathed in light.

She tugged the quilted throw a bit tighter around her shoulders against the early chill. The sun had painted the hills and hardwoods with an orange glow, but the air had not warmed to match. Food and coffee seemed like a good idea. Gray wasn't sure how long she'd been sitting on the porch, but her bare feet were getting numb. The first thing she did once inside the cabin was pull on socks.

It had taken a couple of days to get the place in working order. The pump was running, the gas had luckily never gotten turned off because Mark was supposed to check on the place and keep the heat on in the winter months so the pipes didn't freeze. There was a wall heater in the short hallway that separated the master bedroom from the kitchen and living room that kept freezing temps at bay. But in order to bring the house to a comfortable temperature in the winter you basically had to keep a fire going all the time in the massive stone fireplace.

Mark had kept the place from falling apart or freezing up, but he definitely wasn't a housekeeper. The spiders had nearly taken over, especially in between the hard-to-reach rafters of the large main living space. She'd had to get an extension ladder to knock them all down.

Gray rested her palm on the aged butcher block countertop while she waited for the French press to do its thing. A doe and her fawn appeared in her view from the kitchen window. The doe bent to feed on the lush, dewy early morning grass of the backyard. A light mist just beyond the deer hovered close to the ground making it look as if the trees were disconnected from the earth. That bit of fog would burn off within the hour.

Then something entered her view from the left. A tendril of churning gray turned the sky an eerie, dark color. Smoke. She took a deep breath. It was only chimney smoke from a wood fire at the Pattersons' place. Gray wondered if she'd ever be able to smell smoke without simultaneously getting a jolt of adrenaline in her system.

She poured coffee from the insulated silver French press into an old diner-style mug. Seeing the mug reminded her of meeting Faith at the café.

Under normal circumstances she'd have figured out some excuse to bump into Faith again, or maybe even been bold enough to track down Nancy Jo to get Faith's number. But Gray was feeling anything but normal; she was rattled and off her game in almost every way. She almost felt like a lost little kid. And in fact, she'd run home as if that was exactly what she was.

Feeling small inevitably made Gray think of her mother. They'd had their differences, in fact, they couldn't have been more opposite, but there had been mutual respect in the end. An acceptance of each other's differences. And love, yes, that unconditional love that might only exist between a mother and child. Gray had taken it for granted without realizing how singular it was.

Sure, Gray loved her father—didn't she?

But it wasn't the same. She and her father had never reached that place of understanding, not in the way she had with her mother. When her mother passed away her father was already long gone, he'd needed someone after their divorce. He'd needed a new life almost immediately. He'd found both and moved to Florida with his new wife.

Her father hadn't even wanted to take anything from his old life with him. Maybe everything reminded him of her mother, who knows. Anger and grief were different for everyone. She didn't understand her own and certainly didn't understand his. It wasn't as if he was going to actually sit down and talk with Gray about his feelings. From his perspective, only snowflakes and left-wing hipsters had feelings.

At any rate, all the *stuff* in the house was for Gray to sort out. She'd kept most of it. Well, not her mother's clothes, but the furniture, the books, and some of the small sentimental things. Standing in the center of the living room as she sipped coffee, she marveled at how nothing about the room had really changed since her mother lived here. Was that a good thing?

It was strange to be in the house alone, as an adult, without her mother. But at the same time the familiarity of it was comforting. Especially now. This was the only home she could run to.

Gray tried to remember what sort of life she'd imagined for herself as an adult. She was pretty sure this wasn't it. Well, maybe the adventure parts, but not this part.

Her phone buzzed on the coffee table. She rounded the couch to retrieve it. The text was from Mark.

Hey, are you busy today? Want to help me out?

Sure. She figured she owed him that for the pump repair at least. *I'll swing by and pick you up in an hour. Wear work clothes.* What was he talking about? All her clothes were work clothes. *Sounds good.* She wondered what she'd just gotten herself into. It didn't really matter. She had nothing better to do than stare at the walls and think way too much.

Chapter Nine

Faith checked the driveway again for Dan's friend. He'd mentioned the previous night that a friend of his was coming to cut up the tree and haul it away, but no one had turned up yet. She'd gotten up early and dressed so as not to get caught by a stranger in her pj's. Not that that would offer much of a tantalizing view, unless someone was into flannel lounge pants and a vintage T-shirt. She realized now she could have slept in a bit longer. Typical that Dan hadn't said exactly what time this mystery woodsman, Mark, would arrive and she'd neglected to ask. So, now she was just waiting around. As far as men went, Dan was terrific, but communication was not one of his strengths.

She dried the last of her breakfast dishes and hung the towel over the dish rack. There was enough coffee in the pot for one more cup so she added cream and sat at the kitchen table. She absently thumbed through an old issue of *People* magazine that she'd found in the living room. Kayla and Dan usually rented the house on Vrbo, so there was a random collection of magazines and books around for general vacation consumption. This particular issue was more than a year old so it was a bit of a time capsule. Nothing particularly interesting captured her attention. Pages of beautiful people doing beautiful things—mostly. Happy celebrity couples holding hands as they ventured out for weekend lattes.

Whatever. Just give it six months, then we'll talk.

Faith tried to remember what the vision for her life had been before reality ruined it. She was pretty sure it involved some picturesque house, white picket fence and all, in an equally picturesque town. Of course, in her fantasy-small-town-future-life, she had a spouse and children. That part hadn't quite worked out so well. She'd thought she was well on her way to creating the perfect life, but that had all been fiction. She'd thought that things would work out with Sam, but she'd been wrong—so wrong.

As things had ended up, her primary relationship turned out to be with her cat. Well, at least he was loyal and trustworthy, you know, in a cat sort of way.

The sound of wheels crunching gravel caught her attention. A white pickup truck with oversized tires and mud splattered halfway up the doors came to a stop near her car. The driver, Mark, she assumed, got out and started toward the front of the house. Faith walked out onto the porch to meet him. There was someone else with the driver, but she couldn't really see who it was until she was outside. Soulful dark eyes greeted hers. Grayson Reeves was inexplicably standing on her front steps. Gray removed the faded red baseball cap and swept her fingers through her hair.

"I'm sorry." Faith blinked and looked at Mark. He had said something, but Faith had been too distracted to hear it.

"Um, I was just saying that I'm Dan's friend, Mark." He had a friendly way about him. He was one step higher than Gray, who hung back as if she were feeling shy. "Dan said you lost a big tree on the property and we came by to split it up for you."

"Right." Faith nodded. "I'll show you where it is."

"Oh, and this is Gray." Mark introduced them.

"Yes, we've met." Faith smiled at Gray.

"Hi, Faith." The sun was rising behind the house, and as Gray looked up at Faith from the lower step, she squinted into the sun.

"Hi."

Gray took a few steps back to allow Faith to lead them to the fallen tree. Faith was at least three feet away from Gray, and still, her skin tingled from the electrified air between them. Mark was thankfully oblivious. Faith hugged herself. She pulled the cardigan more tightly as she walked them around the house to the side yard where the hulking tree lay in huge sections, sinking into the soft grass.

Mark nodded as if he'd assessed the situation and agreed with it but didn't say anything for a minute or so.

"Do you mind moving your car so I can back my truck in here?" He motioned with his hand to an open spot on the lawn near the trunk of the fallen giant.

"Sure, no problem. Let me just get my keys."

Gray hadn't said anything more than hello and wouldn't even look at Faith, but instead was intently focused on the tree debris. That struck Faith as odd. When they'd said hi just a few moments earlier there'd definitely been warmth between them. Now, nothing. Gray was doing a great imitation of an uninterested stranger. Well, Kayla had warned her about Gray, so, what did she expect. Hot one minute, cold the next. A player, that's what Kayla had said and the description was obviously accurate.

Faith wondered how Mark and Gray knew each other. There was a bit of a family resemblance. Were they related? Were they siblings? Their rapport seemed too cordial for siblings, at least based on her own family experiences. Her brothers teased her mercilessly, even now as adults.

Faith watched the work from a safe distance inside the house. She was fairly sure Gray couldn't see her peeking out from the guest room window, but just to be safe, she kept hidden behind the drapes. It wasn't like she was stalking or anything, she was simply observing. She was simply observing Gray use a chainsaw, while wearing some protective chaps over her jeans that were damn sexy.

It was hard to believe this was actually happening for real, in the real world, rather than in a cheesy scene from an indie lesbian film set in Portland. Faith couldn't have conjured a dreamier setup if she'd tried. *It's a good thing I'm not interested*, with an emphasis on NOT. *This is ridiculous.* After hovering just out of view for twenty minutes, Faith decided to do a load of laundry. Something about watching other people work and not actually working made her feel lazy. But putting in one load of clothes didn't take very long. Maybe she should deliver a pitcher of water outside and offer them a drink. Yes, that was the neighborly thing to do. And the gesture of kindness had nothing to do with wanting to get a closer look at Ms. Grayson Reeves, butch heartthrob in a Carhartt jacket.

Gray watched Faith cross the yard carrying a tray with a pitcher and two glasses. She let the chainsaw idle and enjoyed the view.

When they'd first arrived, Faith made her so nervous she could hardly look at her. Faith had this intense way of studying you, like she was committing personal details to memory or sizing you up or looking for the truth you didn't want to reveal. It was unnerving, especially given Gray's somewhat fragile state.

Sometimes she felt she was barely keeping things together, and if pressed, the facade would crumble. Faith was close now, so Gray killed the chainsaw and set it on the ground. Mark hadn't seen Faith yet as his back was toward the house. Gray touched his shoulder. She signaled with a tilt of her head toward Faith as she removed her safety goggles. Mark shook his head and kept working.

His chainsaw was loud so Gray motioned toward the front porch. Faith smiled and nodded. Only when they were at the steps, some distance from the noise, did Faith speak.

"I thought you might be thirsty." Faith poured ice water into a glass and offered it to Gray.

"I am, thanks." Why was her throat so dry?

They hadn't been working for much more than an hour and she was already taking a break. It wasn't like she was getting paid by the hour or anything, actually she was getting paid in firewood, which was no small thing. Heading into winter without a substantial wood pile would be a bad thing. Especially if she decided to hang around Sky Valley for a while.

"Should I pour a glass for Mark?"

"I think you can just leave it here. It doesn't seem like he's ready to take a break yet."

Gray took several big gulps, partly to avoid having to speak. Small talk was a challenge at the moment. She smiled at Faith just to seem friendly and because Faith was studying her again. She decided to attempt conversation, even if just to distract Faith.

"So, you're friends with Kayla?" That had to be the reason Faith was staying at Kayla's grandparents' house.

"Yes, we've been friends since college. We met at Chapel Hill." Faith tucked an errant strand of wavy hair behind her ear.

"Ah, you're a Tarheel."

"Well, I do have far too many T-shirts that are Carolina blue."

"If God isn't a Tarheel, then why is the sky Carolina blue?" Gray smiled again and scuffed at the ground with her boot.

"It seems conclusive to me." Faith quirked the corner of her kissable lips up in a playful smile.

Faith was hyperaware of Gray's body language. She maintained a cushion of air between them of no less than four feet. Gray kept one hand in her pocket as the other held the almost empty glass, as if she needed something to do with her hands at all times.

And they were talking about safe topics like, where'd you go to college? Now that Gray knew the connection she might realize that Faith would know all about the thing with Kayla. Which by the way, she was going to need a lot more detail about from Kayla very soon.

The noise receded and Faith almost jumped when Mark walked up to claim a glass of water. She'd been so focused on Gray that he'd surprised her. By comparison, Gray visibly relaxed the moment he joined them.

"Thanks for this." Mark air toasted with his glass.

"Thank you for dealing with the tree." It wasn't as if the tree blocked the driveway, but it did sort of make a mess of the yard.

"We'll stack some wood for you to use and then take the rest." Mark took a long swig of his water. "That's the deal I made with Dan—labor for firewood."

The barter system kept things running in a small town, there was no doubt about that.

"Let me know if there's anything I can do to help," Faith offered.

"We've got this." Mark set his empty glass on the tray that rested on a small round table near the porch railing, then tugged on his work gloves. He grinned at Gray as if they had just shared some inside joke.

"Well, I better get back to it," he said to no one in particular.

Faith watched Mark walk away and was pleased that Gray didn't immediately follow.

"So, chaps?" Heat rose to her cheeks. She couldn't help but notice how Gray was dressed, but she hadn't meant to say it out loud.

"Oh, yeah." Gray looked down at the protective leggings. The chaps had definitely seen some action. There were dark smudges and wear in places, so that the material had lost its color. "They are kinda cumbersome, but they'll save your leg if you get kickback from the saw."

Faith was relieved that Gray played off the flirtatious question as no big deal.

"What do you mean by kickback?" Faith wasn't remotely interested in chainsaw techniques, but she'd pretend to be if it kept Gray talking.

"That just means the teeth of the saw can sometimes get hung up on something and if the saw's momentum changes abruptly it'll sometimes literally kick back."

Gray was so sincere and serious, as if she thought chainsaws were the most interesting thing on the planet. It was adorable.

"If someone doesn't know what they're doing or they don't wear protective gear, well, you can get hurt pretty bad." Gray glanced toward the tree. "I should go help Mark."

"Sure." Faith nodded. "Let me know if there's anything you need." Gray had taken a few steps and then glanced back at Faith. "I mean, you know, anything you or Mark need. The two of you…both of you." She needed to stop talking like three minutes ago.

Gray smiled and nodded.

Faith shook her head and went into the house.

Chapter Ten

After working all day trimming, splitting, and hauling wood, a home-cooked meal with Mark and Christy was a welcomed invitation. Gray hadn't seen Christy or their daughter, Hailey, in several years. Actually, the last time she'd seen Hailey was four years ago when she'd come home to settle the deed. Hailey had been eight. It was hard to believe she was twelve now, a scary pre-teen.

"Hey, there! Come in." Christy greeted Gray at the door with a hug.

Christy was as pretty as always, maybe with a few more laugh lines around her blue eyes, but the sparkle was still there and the smile and the hug were real. Christy had always been able to light up a room. She was sweet through and through, the perfect girl next door, everyone's high school sweetheart. Christy dusted her hands on a well-loved apron with some sort of Smoky Mountain bluegrass festival logo on it. It was barely readable, likely having been washed too many times. Her straight blond hair was pulled up into a high ponytail, and her cheeks were red from the warmth of the kitchen. Gray followed her through the living room to the kitchen and immediately had to lose her jacket. She set the six-pack of hard ciders she'd brought on the island counter and then hung her jacket on the back of a nearby chair.

"Is there anything I can do?" Gray knew she wasn't much use in the kitchen, but it was polite to ask.

"No, no...just open two of those ciders and hand me one." Christy stirred something on the stove, used a small spoon to sample it, and then tossed it in the sink. "This chili is almost done."

She handed Christy a cider and they clinked the glass bottles lightly.

"Mark said you guys like cider. I hope this one is okay." It sort of tasted like apple juice for grown-ups to Gray.

"It's perfect, thanks." Christy held the cider with one hand and stirred the chili again. "This is on the mild side. Hailey doesn't like it spicy."

It was hard to picture having a kid. Gray didn't have many friends with children. A few of the guys she worked with in California had kids, but they weren't around very much. Mostly when her crew was together they were out in the field or tired to the bone. At least that was the drill during fire season. In the off season, for those who were single and without families to support, the income from the seasonal work could pay for skiing or surfing or travel in the off months. With overtime and hazard pay the money was pretty good. Good enough to coast for a couple of months when she wanted to. This was one of those times. What the plan was after that, Gray wasn't sure yet.

A towheaded kid barreled in through the back door and rounded the island, almost bumping into Gray. Was this Hailey? It had to be, but this kid was much more of a tomboy than the little girl in pigtails Gray remembered.

"Hailey! Don't run in the house." Christy frowned as she set bowls on the counter near the stove. "Say hello to your cousin Gray."

"My cousin?" Hailey rested her elbows on the counter and studied Gray.

"Yes, Mark and Gray are first cousins, so that makes you second cousins. Mark, honey, will you set these out while I get Hailey some water?"

Mark had joined them in the kitchen. He took bowls from Christy and placed them on the table. "Go wash up for dinner, Hailey."

She frowned but did as she was told.

"We got the last of the wood unloaded." Mark kissed Christy lightly on the cheek.

"I could have helped you with that." Gray hated to leave a job half finished.

"No, it's good for Hailey to have chores." Mark used the bottle opener after helping himself to a cider. "She's earning money to pay for that window she broke."

"You mean—?" Gray hadn't given the broken glass much thought since she swept it up and temporarily patched the hole with duct tape.

"Long story." Mark took a swig of his drink as a signal to change the subject when Hailey returned.

"What's a long story?" asked Hailey.

"The Bible." Christy placed a cast iron skillet of cornbread on a trivet in the center of the table. Then she sliced it into pieces like a pie, leaving the knife in the pan so everyone could serve themselves.

"I'll say grace." Mark held hands with Christy and Hailey after they were seated.

Gray clasped hands with Hailey and Christy as well, seated across from Mark.

"Thank you, Lord, for this food. We are grateful for this fine meal and for the hands that prepared it. Bless this food to the nourishment of our bodies and our bodies to your service. Amen."

"Amen." Christy softly echoed Mark.

Gray's mind wandered as they ate. It was always strange to be in someone's house who was the same age as she was, but with so much more responsibility. Christy and Mark had made a family together, maybe it hadn't been planned out exactly, but they seemed happy.

Christy had unexpectedly gotten pregnant at seventeen. And then it was like *happy graduation, you're going to be a mother*. She'd been a cheerleader, Mark played football, they'd been everyone's favorite couple in high school. Gray wondered what it felt like to be the hometown heroes who never left home.

It must be nice to belong and for it to always have been that way. She had no idea what that would feel like.

"I like your Jeep."

"Hailey, don't talk with your mouth full." Christy shook her head.

"You like Jeeps?" Gray was happy to talk about something they both seemed to have an interest in. Until then, Hailey hadn't said a word. "I can take you for a ride sometime if you like."

Hailey nodded but didn't say more.

Dinner was brief but flavorful. To be honest, Gray liked chili on the mild side too. Hailey blazed through her serving and asked to be excused. Gray got seconds of the cider for the three of them and they lingered at the kitchen table. Pounding footsteps signaled that Hailey had run upstairs to her room.

"I wish someone had warned me how tough twelve-year-olds are." Mark sank back in his chair. One hand held his cider which rested at the edge of the table.

"Mark." Christy's expression told Gray that the unspoken directive was, *hush*.

Gray leaned forward with her elbows on the table. She wondered if they thought she'd understand because Hailey seemed gay, or at least gay-curious. Hailey had all the earmarks of a baby dyke in the making. But Gray didn't know anything about kids and wasn't sure she should offer any advice from the sidelines. It had taken her years to figure out her own path for coming to terms with who she was. Hailey would likely have to chart her own course.

"Why not talk about it? Gray's family...maybe she understands more than we do." Mark's words softened.

Did they suspect Hailey was gay too or transitioning and they wanted her to weigh in as the big gay cousin from the Left Coast?

"She's been acting out and it's getting worse." Mark's revelation surprised her. That was not at all what she'd expected.

"She's just going through some sort of phase." Christy began to clear the table. It seemed like she wanted, or needed, a distraction.

"I'd be happy to talk to her...you know, if she wants to talk." Gray wasn't so sure that Hailey would open up to someone she hardly knew.

It was probably hard for Christy to have a daughter who clearly wasn't into hair, makeup or probably boys, but what did she know? Maybe this was something totally different. None of this explained the broken window, but Gray didn't really want to pry. A house left untended was bound to suffer small traumas—storm debris, frozen pipes, electrical problems. Compared to what could happen, a broken pane of glass seemed pretty damn minor.

"I meant to fix that window before you saw it." Mark sipped his cider. "But you know how it is...life."

"Don't worry about it. It's no big deal." But Gray wondered if it was. Not the window, but something else. It seemed like something stressful was happening just beneath the surface with Mark and Hailey. It made her think about her relationship with her father.

"Does anyone want dessert?" Christy finished clearing the table. "We have some apple pie, unless Hailey finished it off."

"I would never say no to apple pie." Gray knew she didn't have much food at her place, so she might as well score dessert while she had the option.

Christy took small plates out of the cabinet and cut three slices. Gray got up to help deliver the sweets. She didn't want Christy to have to wait on them after cooking dinner. Mark continued to lounge at the table. He was clearly spoiled. Christy fussed over him just as much as she'd always done. He had no idea how lucky he was.

"You know, if you plan to stay for a while, Lucas could use some help down at the fire station." Mark forked a third of the pie slice into his mouth.

"Is that so?" Gray wasn't quite ready to jump into anything, but it wasn't a terrible idea. The local fire station was basically a rescue squad that serviced the rural part of the county. And Lucas was a good guy. If she got bored enough, then maybe she'd stop in and see him. "I'm not sure what my plan is yet, but thanks for letting me know."

"Yeah, George Langley retired three months ago, and I don't think anyone has been hired to replace him yet."

George Langley had seemed old when she was in high school. She was surprised that he'd only just now retired. But hey, when you're in high school anyone over thirty seems old. Now that she was closing in on thirty, forty seemed young. A lot in life was simply a matter of perspective it seemed.

Faith sipped a glass of wine and slowly thumbed through an old sketchbook remembering drawings she'd been excited about. Her feet were tucked under her legs on the overstuffed sofa near the fireplace. This particular sketchbook was only half finished. She'd sketched something partway through that displeased her and as a result she'd abandoned the book and moved on to another. Now that she was seeing it again, Faith decided the drawing wasn't that bad.

Color was also a phase she went through. At the moment she was sketching a lot with red pencils. Faith wasn't exactly sure what that was about, but several pages into this new journal she'd switched from blue to red. Hmm.

She paused to study a pine cone she'd sketched from different angles. If you really wanted to challenge yourself, draw a pine cone. Not an easy thing.

Her phone pinged from the small, round table near the chair. She reached for it as she took a sip of wine.

It was another text from Sam. Faith's relaxed mood suddenly shifted. A knot began to build between her shoulders.

I know you're not in Raleigh. Let me know you're okay. Just because we're not together doesn't mean I don't still worry about you.

Faith knew this was a trap, but she also knew if she didn't respond in some way that Sam would keep reaching out. Every time Sam texted her it was like a little missile that torpedoed her entire day.

She took a deep breath, held it for a moment, and then responded.

I'm fine. Short and to the point. Faith thought, but didn't add, you don't get to cheat on me and then make yourself feel better about it. But maybe she should say that. Maybe Sam wasn't getting the message because she wasn't being clear enough.

Are you staying with Kayla? It's good for you not to be alone.

What was that supposed to mean? Now she was getting pissed.

Yes, I'm with Kayla. Please do not text me again. The second she hit send she regretted that she'd allowed herself to get sucked into an exchange with Sam in the first place. How weak and gullible could she be?

Faith turned her phone completely off and tossed it on the lamp stand near the chair. She needed fresh air. It was dark, but she grabbed a flashlight and slammed the front door behind her. She was going for a walk. If she didn't work off some steam she'd never be able to relax and definitely she'd never get any sleep. And she was supposed to be at the café super early the next day.

Sam was infuriating. Sam was also irritating and exasperating—selfish and self-serving. Maybe those were the same thing. The bigger question was if all of that was true then why had she started seeing Sam in the first place? Because Sam made her feel special. Sam was a master at making women feel special when she wanted to. And manipulating Faith when she questioned Sam's motives so that she felt like crap. Sam was a master of that as well. *Ugh!* Now she wasn't sure who she was angrier with, herself or Sam.

Faith tromped down the road at such a hard pace, as if she could stomp Sam out of her mind, that the soles of her feet began to ache. She stopped and for a moment wasn't sure exactly where she was or how far from the house she'd traveled. It was dark and probably almost eight thirty. The sidewalks in Sky Valley rolled up around eight every night, so there'd been no traffic on the road. Faith had been walking the downhill route toward the village and now realized she was going to be climbing uphill all the way back home. She'd barely begun her return trip when headlights came around the curve behind her, casting her long shadow in front of her. She stepped to the shoulder of the road to wait for the car to pass and shielded her eyes from the bright lights with her hand.

Her heart rate sped up when she realized the vehicle had slowed to a stop beside her.

"Can I give you a ride?" Gray spoke to her from the driver's seat, through the open passenger side window.

"I'm fine." She was relieved to hear Gray's voice. The knot between her shoulders loosened just a bit.

"Are you sure?" There was a hint of concern in Gray's question. "It's getting pretty dark out here."

"I'm not afraid of the dark." Why was she arguing with Gray? Gray wasn't the person she was angry with. Gray was just an innocent passerby trying to be neighborly. "I'm sorry, I didn't mean that the way it sounded."

"That's okay."

Faith paused, considering her options.

"I think I will take a ride if you don't mind." Faith opened the door and used the running board and the handle near the doorframe to climb into the high Jeep. "Thank you."

"No problem." Gray resumed driving.

They didn't talk. Faith was about to give Gray directions to her house, but then she remembered Gray had already been there. That felt a little strange. Her skin sort of tingled, but she chalked it up to the chilly night air. She'd left the house with only a light sweater and no jacket. Fury was a great warming agent.

After several more switchbacks, not much more than a mile, Gray turned into the driveway. Faith suddenly wondered if Gray expected to be invited in. Should she invite her in? No, that was a terrible idea. Faith was in the wrong head space for casual conversation or casual anything else for that matter. She opened the door and got out.

"Thanks again for the ride." Faith rotated in the open door to look at Gray.

Gray's arms were draped across the steering wheel, she was leaning forward, and looking at Faith with a thoughtful expression.

"Are you sure you're okay?"

Why did everyone keep asking her that?

"Yes, I'm fine." She closed the door.

She started toward the house but turned back before she got too far. Gray had her elbow through the open window of the driver's side door. Faith walked back to the Jeep.

"I meant to say thank you for the firewood." Without really thinking about it, she placed her hand on Gray's arm. "Have a good night, Gray."

The tingling was back, this time in her stomach and places deeper inside. She withdrew her hand slowly and turned toward the house.

"Good night, Faith."

The sound of Gray's voice when she said her name spread warmth through her entire body. Gray waited until she was on the threshold with the door open before she backed out of the driveway.

Good night, Gray. She stood at the window until the headlights of Gray's Jeep were swallowed up by the darkness.

As she readied for bed, pulling on a cozy T-shirt and slipping out of her jeans, she realized that for the first time in a long while, she wasn't thinking about Sam at all. That realization made her smile. Faith snuggled under the thick, quilted comforter. A few minutes after she switched off the bedside lamp, she sensed the weight of Otis as he jumped onto the soft mattress. He curled up near enough that she dozed off to the comforting sound of his soothing purr.

Chapter Eleven

*G*ray *stood at the edge of "the green," acres of unburned fuel stretched in front of her. A stand of ponderosa pines, dry shrubs, dead limbs, and knee-high native grasses lay as far as she could see. Behind her, something howled and popped. The crisp snap and whoosh of a roaring blaze filled her ears as dying branches and twigs gasped for their last blackened breaths in her peripheral vision. And then came the heat at her back, searing and relentless—she was gasping, drowning in smoke. But she was frozen in place among the standing dead, unable to move as the heat engulfed her.*

Gray bolted upright in a coughing fit. Another bad dream.

Her hand shook as she reached for the glass of water on the nightstand. She gulped too fast, instigating another coughing fit. The neck of her T-shirt was damp from sweat. She set the glass down and swept her fingers through her hair, brushing damp tendrils off her forehead and away from her face.

I am here. This is now.

Would she ever sleep again without dreaming these dreams?

I am here. This is now. She repeated the phrase, which did seem to help.

She reached for her phone on the nightstand. It was three thirty. Gray flopped back onto her pillow and covered her face with her hands. For several minutes she lay there, blinking, looking up at the narrow-planked ceiling. Maybe she should just stay in bed even if she couldn't sleep. No, that was worse.

It was cold in the house. Gray put on sweatpants, a heavy flannel shirt, and some socks. There were still some warm coals on the hearth. She stirred them a bit until they glowed. The warmth of the embers gave her pause, and for a while she rested on one knee and stared into the fireplace. How was it possible that the same thing could bring both comfort and destruction? Maybe there were lots of things. But in the moment, all she could think of was fire.

Gray wadded up some newsprint and then constructed a little A-frame of kindling over it. The embers ignited the paper, and within minutes she added a few small sticks of wood. The house was dark as she hadn't switched on any lights. Maybe it was all the camping she'd done, but Gray had gotten used to doing things in the dark and didn't really mind it. There was something intrusive about electric lights in the pre-dawn time. The flickering fire cast dancing shadows around the living room as the flames softly lit the room like an oversized candle. Unlike an electric bulb, firelight had warmth—visual warmth and physical warmth. Gray left to put water on to boil for coffee and then returned. She stood with her back to the fire and watched the shadow patterns dance on the walls around her.

There were a few books nearby on the coffee table, remnants from the time when her mother lived in the house. There were lots of things around the house that Gray couldn't get rid of, without them, the house just wouldn't have that familiar feel of home. *To Kill A Mockingbird*, one of her mother's favorite books, sat on top of the small stack and underneath was a King James Bible. Her mother had received this Bible in high school, she couldn't remember from whom, but it had her mother's maiden name embossed on the lower right corner—Anne Davis.

Gray flipped through the almost translucent pages. The book naturally fell open in Psalms, probably a section her mother had particularly liked. There were passages underlined throughout the old Bible and there was even one on the page where she'd landed, Psalm thirty-four, verse eighteen. *The Lord is near to the brokenhearted and saves the crushed in spirit.*

A knot rose in her throat, and she wiped at a tear with the cuff of her flannel shirt. Her mother always used to say that the Lord spoke to her and maybe this was the way. And that the word of God could speak to Gray too, if she'd only listen.

Even though Gray didn't believe any of it anymore and church had caused more harm than good in her life, even still, scripture held a certain power of remembrance. And reading this passage now brought all of it back. The comfort of community, the certainty of belief in childhood, and the desire for acceptance. But she'd had to leave North Carolina to truly find any of those things, at least, that's what she'd believed at seventeen. After graduation she couldn't wait to get away, to be free.

She closed the book. Even the feel of it in her hand had a familiar comforting weight. How was it possible that the same book could bring both solace and destruction? As her grandmother used to say, it was all in the reading of it. It was more about the hearer of the word than the words themselves. The same book was so many different things to so many different people. Her grandmother had had the perspective and wisdom of advanced age, something her mother never quite got the chance to attain.

The kettle whistled from the kitchen. Her mind had wandered so far away that she'd forgotten she'd put it on. Sleep deprivation was no picnic. Gray yawned as she shuffled to the kitchen to make coffee.

Faith saw smoke from the chimney at Gray's place as she headed to work, but no lights were on. She was surprised that anyone was up as early as she was on purpose. If she didn't have to be at the café for the breakfast shift she'd definitely be snuggled in her warm bed. Faith would choose to sleep in every morning if given the option, but she was adjusting to the morning shift. The light was great in the earliest hours of the day. Everything was bathed in pink in the eerie half-light in those moments right before the sun breached the horizon.

She took several photos of the sky with her phone after she parked so that she could return to them later with paint. The air was crisply cold. Faith could see her breath in the chilled air as she crossed the employee parking area toward the back door.

It ended up being a typical Monday at the café. There was an early rush for the breakfast-before-work crowd. After that, the retirees leisurely dined and hung out for a third cup of decaf while they discussed how no one under the age of fifty knew what the hell was going on. It was all good-natured of course, with a smattering of politics thrown in.

"Can I get you fellas anything else?" Faith had a coffee carafe in her hand in case of refills.

"No thanks, if I drink any more I'm gonna float away." Mr. N. covered his coffee mug with his hand as if he needed to ward her off. "Just give the bill to Ray over there." Mr. N's eyes twinkled as he pointed across the table to his friend.

"The hell you say." The notion that he'd pick up the tab was obviously news to Ray.

"I'll let you boys arm wrestle for it. Just let me know who wins." She winked at Ray as she walked away.

"Have you taken a break yet this morning?" Kayla was opening a pack of quarters and dropping them into the register's change drawer.

"Not yet." Faith put the coffee pot back on the burner to warm. "I'll go now. They need the check." She motioned toward Mr. N and his friends. "They are discussing whose turn it is to pay."

"Typical." Kayla smiled. "I'm going to make a bank run, but Nancy Jo can cover things while you take a break."

Faith chose an open booth at the back of the café where she could sit quietly with her sketchbook. Her time was just about up when the bell over the door chimed. A customer she didn't recognize entered and hovered near the front register area. Nancy Jo looked busy at the counter so Faith left her sketchbook and coffee to see what the newcomer needed.

Faith took in details about the stranger as she wove her way between tables as she crossed the room. The woman was about her height, probably five foot six. She had shoulder-length light brown hair that looked windblown, not in a haphazard sort of way, more like a sexy *I just came from the beach* sort of way. Her clothing screamed California. She looked as if she'd stepped right out of the Sundance catalogue with boot cut, hip-hugger jeans and a blousy top that featured a patchwork of vintage prints, with smocking, tiny ruffles along the button front, and cuff ties on the sleeves. This woman was undeniably pretty and had the sort of skinny runway model figure that could make a flour sack dress look good. She was a bit too slender for Faith's liking and could probably stand to eat something with a lot of carbs, but who was Faith to judge.

"Table for one?" She said the words even though she had a hard time imagining that this woman ate very many meals alone, you know, when she ate something other than a leaf of lettuce or a celery stick.

"I was hoping you could help me with directions. I think I'm lost."

"Sure, I'll try. I know a little about the area."

"I wrote this down and now I'm not sure I got the street right, and my cell service isn't great once I leave downtown." The woman held a scrap of paper out to Faith. An address was scribbled in loopy script. She immediately recognized it.

"You're looking for Gray?"

"Yes, do you know her?" The woman's face lit up at the mention of Gray's name. "She's not expecting me, and I don't have her cell number."

For a split second, Faith considered delivering bad directions but reconsidered. How close could this woman be to Gray if she didn't even have Gray's cell number? And why was she so interested in safeguarding Gray's privacy anyway?

"You just need to take a right out of the parking lot. Then go about four miles up that two-lane road and you'll see her cabin on the right."

"Oh, thank you so much."

"No problem." Faith smiled and tried not to care.

Of course, Ms. California was looking for Gray. Why was she surprised and why did it bother her so much? She returned to the booth to gather her bag and sketchbook. Nancy Jo was flipping through the pages as if privacy had not yet been invented.

"Hey, do you mind?" Faith delivered more sarcasm than anger with the question.

"Why is everything so red?" Nancy Jo was still thumbing through the sketchbook as if it were part of the public domain.

"Because that's all I'm seeing lately." Faith held out her hand for the sketchbook.

"Someone woke up on the wrong side of the bed this morning." Nancy Jo arched an eyebrow and handed Faith the sketchbook. "Who was that woman?"

"Someone looking for Gray."

"Hmm, that figures." Nancy Jo stood as Faith shoved the sketchbook in her bag. "She was a hottie."

"I suppose. If you're into women who disdain carbs and have way too much time to spend on their hair."

"Have you seen you?" Nancy Jo draped her arm around Faith's shoulders.

"What do you mean by that?"

"I just mean, Faith Owen, that you are very pretty and you shouldn't let your bruised self-confidence convince you otherwise."

"Thanks. I needed that."

"That's me. Nancy Jo, teller of truths."

"What conspiracy are you two hatching?" Dan appeared from the back storeroom with a stepladder. He was wearing a Braves cap and paint-splattered carpenter pants and boots.

"Honey, as usual, we're solving all the world's problems." Nancy Jo winked.

"Finally. If anyone could do it, I'm sure you two could." Dan smiled. He stepped on the ladder to check the smoke detector in the short hallway near the bathroom door.

"I haven't heard it go off." Faith had been a little distracted, but she was fairly sure she wouldn't have missed that annoying beep.

"This model blinks before the battery dies. I meant to get to it a few days ago. But you know how it goes." He glanced down at her from the top step. "The list is long."

Why couldn't she find someone like Dan? Well, not exactly like Dan, but the lesbian version of Dan—laid-back, competent, sweet, and good-looking. Was that too much to ask?

The bell chimed. A party of four waited at the front. Nancy Jo picked up menus to get them seated while Faith stowed her bag in the office off the kitchen.

She took a moment to reflect on what Nancy Jo had said.

Was she pretty? She sure hadn't felt like it lately. Nancy Jo's heartfelt compliment lightened her step just a little and she couldn't help smiling. It was true. She never used to get so down on herself before Sam. Why had she let Sam plant the seeds of doubt in her mind? She needed to be thankful that Sam left when she did. Faith deserved better. She needed to keep reminding herself of that truth.

Chapter Twelve

Gray was just about to open the car door when a beat-up Nissan Pathfinder pulled into the driveway. It took a few seconds for her to mentally process exactly why this vehicle looked familiar. Alissa stepped out of the car and Gray's stomach did a little flip. This was familiar and completely unexpected. She hadn't seen or spoken to Shane's girlfriend, Alissa, since the funeral. It had been a big gathering of friends and family. They'd scattered his ashes along his favorite bit of shoreline along Lake Tahoe.

How the hell did Alissa find her? Not that Gray was hiding, but Sky Valley wasn't anywhere near the Sierra foothills.

"Hi, Gray."

"Hi." Gray took a few steps toward Alissa.

"I hope it's okay that I just stopped by. I got your new address from Dave."

That made sense. Dave was really the only person who knew where she was, except for their crew chief.

"What are you doing in North Carolina?" They were standing a few feet apart. Alissa made the first move. She crossed the space between them and gave Gray a hug.

"It's good to see you, Gray."

After a few seconds of initial hesitation, Gray returned the embrace. "It's good to see you too." Although, was it? Seeing Alissa brought everything she'd left in California right to the doorstep of her little mountain hideout. She choked down her feelings.

She released Alissa and took a step back.

"Do you want to come in?"

"Sure, but were you about to leave? I don't want to keep you from something."

"Oh, I was going to get some food. I haven't quite stocked the kitchen yet. Are you hungry?"

"I could eat. My stomach doesn't even know what time zone it's in." Alissa rested her slender hand over her midsection.

"Well, then join me for a late lunch." Gray motioned toward the Jeep. "I can drive."

Alissa moved her car and Gray drove them back down to the main square of town. There weren't tons of options and she didn't really want to go to the café and risk running into Faith with Alissa on her arm. Not that there was anything happening on either side of that equation, but small towns had lots of eyes—and opinions. Now that she'd parked along the square, in plain view of the world, she regretted they hadn't just scrounged for something to eat at the house. But the smell of pizza lured her to stay the course. She held the door for Alissa as they entered the dark interior of the old-school Italian restaurant.

"Table for two?" A perky teenager greeted them at the door with menus in her hand.

Gray nodded and they followed the waitress to a booth. There was a game on the TV near the bar so no one really paid Gray or Alissa any attention. It only took a moment for them to order pizza and beer. Gray settled against the back of the leather bench seat and studied Alissa. A single light hung over the table. Gray had leaned back so that she was partially in shadow. When Alissa leaned forward it was almost like she was in a spotlight.

"So, what brings you to North Carolina?" Gray circled back to her original question.

"Change of scenery I guess, and also, my sister and her husband just moved to Fort Bragg, right outside of Fayetteville."

The waitress delivered drinks and Gray took a swig. The draft beer was perfectly chilled. It tasted good.

"I guess I didn't realize your brother-in-law was in the Army." In truth, Gray didn't know that much about Alissa's family. She had only been dating Shane for a few months before he died, and they hadn't gotten to spend that much time with each other. When Shane was off duty, he wanted Alissa to himself, which Gray totally respected.

"Yeah, they've moved a lot since he enlisted so I'm going to stay with Sarah for a little while, maybe longer if he gets deployed."

The pizza arrived and the server asked about drink refills.

"Yes, thanks, I'll have another beer." Gray nodded. She'd made quick work of her first one. Seeing Alissa was hard. After only a few swigs, Alissa switched to water. She looked tired and Gray wondered if Alissa was having as hard a time sleeping as she was.

"Are you driving the rest of the way today?" Gray asked.

"How far is it from here?" Alissa seemed a little lost. Maybe what had happened made it hard to focus on details like drive times.

The trauma of what had happened screwed with time. Sometimes hours would drag slowly by; other times she'd lose focus and the next thing Gray knew she'd lost an hour.

"Um, I think a little over four hours…I'm not sure." Gray paused to take a bite of pizza. She chewed slowly, trying to decide whether she should invite Alissa to stay the night. She wasn't really in the mood for a visitor and figured she wouldn't be great company anyway. But Alissa was alone and far from home, so Gray felt compelled to extend an invitation. "You're welcome to stay at the cabin tonight."

"That would be really nice, but if it's only four hours I'll probably just keep going." Alissa dabbed at her lips with her napkin. She'd taken a few bites but hadn't even finished one slice of pizza yet. "I tried to do the drive from California in three days, but I'm kind of exhausted to be honest. I just want to get there and not have to move again." She sat back and sipped her water. "You know what I mean?"

"I think I do."

They'd ordered a medium pizza, but it seemed neither of them had much of an appetite because they'd hardly made a dent in it.

"Do you think about what happened that day?" Alissa tugged a thread at the edge of her cloth napkin.

"Yes." How much should she say? Gray was afraid that if she started talking about it she'd break down.

"I miss him so much." Alissa's voice cracked.

Gray covered Alissa's hand with hers.

"So do I."

Gray wanted to say more. She wanted to tell Alissa how Shane came back for her. She wanted to say that she'd have done the same for him. But she didn't say anything. The words were all choked up in her throat making it hard to swallow.

"I have something for you." Alissa searched in her bag.

She set an antique brass compass on the table.

"And also, this." She handed a photo to Gray.

The photo of Shane and Gray together on a forested slope made the lump in her throat impossible to hold back. She covered her mouth to muffle the sob, as tears she'd tried her best to hold back trailed down her cheeks. They'd had some good times. He was too young to die. All of it just made her so sad.

"I know he'd want you to have this compass." Alissa's gift was so thoughtful. "And I thought you might like the photo too."

All she could do was nod. She wasn't able to speak.

"It's okay, Gray." Alissa wiped at tears too with her napkin.

After an awkward few moments passed, the server offered them a box for the rest of the pizza. Gray was so touched by Alissa's gift. She almost didn't know what to say as they headed back to her cabin. She turned in and they stood facing each other in the driveway.

"Are you sure you don't want to stay?" Gray worried that Alissa was as unsettled as she was and maybe shouldn't get back on the road.

"It's still early. I think I'll keep driving."

"Are you sure?" she asked again, even though she was a little relieved to be off the hook. It would be hard to avoid talking more about things if Alissa stayed the night.

"Yes, it'll be good to land somewhere and have someone to focus on besides myself."

She fell into Gray and they held each other for a few minutes.

Then Gray stood in the driveway and watched Alissa leave.

Maybe Alissa was right. Maybe she should think of someone besides herself for a while. Gray decided to go to the fire station and talk to Lucas about a job. The least she could do was put her skills to use while she was here. She was sure that's what Shane would have done if he were in her shoes. If he'd had the option.

Losing a friend so close and almost her age gave her a sense of urgency about not wasting time. She'd never waste time again.

As she turned to go into the house she realized she'd completely forgotten her original errand—groceries. Thanksgiving was in a couple of days and she'd been invited to Mark and Christy's for dinner. She was tasked with bringing dessert.

Gray put the pizza box in the fridge and then trotted down the steps to the Jeep. The market was just past the square and it was still early so it shouldn't be too crowded as the after-work crowd wouldn't be on the loose just yet. But there likely would be a pre-Thanksgiving swarm for baked goods so she figured it was best to go now and get it over with.

The visit with Alissa had unsettled her more than she'd expected. She just hadn't really talked with anyone about what had happened and why she was back. She and Alissa had barely touched on it even though it was probably the only thing either of them thought about. Gray just wasn't the share-your-feelings type.

Gray parked and sat in the car for a few minutes trying to feel normal. It was weird to be in a crowd of strangers when you felt off balance.

Sky Valley Market was buzzing when she stepped through the automatic sliding doors, busier than she'd expected. She'd parked at the far edge of the lot and braced for the worst—holiday shoppers. Mark was having a few other cousins over, in addition to her, so she probably needed to get more than one pie. Maybe she'd also pick up some hot chocolate for the kids. She wasn't completely sure she could even do a family dinner with more than just Mark and Christy. If things got weird she'd just have to bail. She didn't want to talk about her life in California and certainly not the reason she was back.

Gray was standing in the aisle, staring at boxes of instant cocoa when she heard someone say hello.

"Hi." Gray gripped the basket loaded with pies more tightly.

"I hope someday I'm comfortable enough with myself to just eat pie and nothing else." Faith smiled as she looked down at Gray's basket full of boxed pies.

"All I was missing was a hot chocolate chaser." Gray held up a box in Faith's direction. "I just want to make sure I get the one with the most marshmallows."

"Absolutely, I get it. I'm totally with you. Life's much better with marshmallows."

Faith's delivery of dry humor made Gray laugh, despite her earlier mood.

"It's not as bad as it looks."

"Did I say pie was bad?" Faith put one hand on her hip and the other rested on the handle of her grocery cart. She had one of the small ones. It was piled with salad greens and cans of soup and some delicious looking bread from the bakery section. "I was actually on my way to the pie counter when I saw you, lost in a sea of hot chocolate."

Faith reached past Gray. The closeness stirred the air and sent a little electric charge along Gray's neck.

"This one has the most marshmallows." Faith held a bright red box out to Gray.

"Thanks. I'm sure you just saved me from making a horrible mistake." Gray took the box from Faith and tossed it into her basket. Then she reached for a second box just to make sure she had enough.

The initial bantering subsided and Gray wasn't sure what to say next. There was something special about Faith. She seemed to warm the air just by standing there, as if she carried a little bit of sunshine around with her at all times.

"Do you have big plans for Thanksgiving?" That was lame, so lame.

"I'm spending the day with my brothers. You?"

"Yeah, I'll be at my cousin Mark's place." She held the basket up. "I'm in charge of dessert."

"Oh, you're not spending it with your friend? I met her at the café earlier."

"Who? Alissa?" Gray was surprised that Faith knew about Alissa's visit.

"Yes, she was lost and stopped by the café for directions." It seemed like Faith had questions, but she wasn't asking them outright. Maybe it was all in Gray's imagination.

"Alissa had to drive to her sister's place in Fort Bragg."

"Oh, that's too bad." But Faith didn't really sound like she meant it.

"Yeah, it was a short visit." Gray almost felt like she should explain herself, but she wasn't sure why. She decided the best defense was a subject change. "Where do your brothers live?"

"Charlotte. My older brother is hosting at his house."

"That sounds nice." Her conversational skills were waning. "Well, I don't want to be the reason you miss out on the pies." Gray was feeling stretched a bit thin and wanted to escape.

"Have a good holiday." Faith smiled and began to slowly push her cart. "It was nice to see you."

"Yeah, nice to see you too." Lame, again.

Gray shook her head after Faith walked away. Why didn't she just ask Faith for her number? They could go get a coffee or go have dinner like normal people. Oh yeah, because she wasn't feeling normal. She was all churned up, fragile, and unfocused.

Speaking of unfocused, Gray did need to get some actual food. She was out of coffee too. She headed down the aisle in the opposite direction Faith had taken in search of essentials.

Faith looked back once to see Gray walk toward the other end of the aisle. There was a bit of a line at the sweets counter, so she queued up to wait. Maybe she should abort dessert and just bring alcohol. She had a stash of good wine gathering dust in Raleigh. But she really didn't want to drive all the way to Raleigh and then back to Charlotte. It seemed the most direct route between two points in this case, was pie. She settled back in to wait her turn.

So, Ms. California hadn't stayed over. In fact, she hadn't stayed very long at all. What did that mean? Probably nothing and for the hundredth time, why did she care? Gray was probably only visiting Sky Valley. It wasn't like she lived here year-round, and neither did Faith.

Hold on. If they were both only here on a short-term basis, then why was she avoiding spending time with Gray? Why didn't she just invite Gray over for dinner or drinks? They'd have a casual meetup and then Faith could stop obsessing over her. So what if Gray was a player, she could play too.

No, she couldn't.

Why was she even kidding herself? She was an absolute terrible player, at both sports and love.

"What can I get for you, hon?" A gray-haired woman with a Southern accent regarded her from behind the glass pastry case.

The line had moved more quickly than expected and Faith had been so lost in thought she hadn't even decided what she wanted. She was beginning to see a similarity between the pie counter and her love life. There was only one solution.

"Which pie has the most chocolate?" Faith surveyed the glass case.

"I'd say, death by chocolate is our top seller." The woman smiled.

"I'll take two." Faith decided on one for Thanksgiving and one for herself for tonight. Now all she needed was a glass of red wine and a spoon.

Chapter Thirteen

Gray had considered spending Thanksgiving on her own, but Christy had been insistent and, in the end, she'd given in to the friendly pressure. Thanksgiving was about family, Christy had said. Living so far away for so long, Gray had forgotten what it was like to be close to relatives for the holidays. Everyone usually meant well, but sometimes being alone was appealing. Events with family involved having to answer a lot of random personal questions, and at the moment, Gray wasn't sure she could handle very much intrusive small talk.

She'd braced herself for a cousin invasion, but when she got to Mark and Christy's Gray happily discovered that she was the only guest. A holiday flu had raged through Christy's cousin's family requiring that they stay home so as not to share the bug. The knot between Gray's shoulders loosened the moment she heard the news.

The kitchen was warm and smelled of savory dishes. A sweet potato casserole sat cooling on a trivet on the counter, probably her grandmother's recipe, and one of Gray's personal favorites. It was a treat to be back in the Deep South where a dish could be simultaneously dinner and dessert. Any nutritional value was likely lost because of the marshmallows melted into a gooey, lightly toasted layer on top of the baked sweet potatoes. But Gray appreciated this time-honored recipe and was really glad that Christy hadn't tried to modernize it by making it too healthy.

Christy had enough food to feed ten people, so Gray offered to do her best by eating seconds and taking leftovers if that was an option. The two pies she'd brought were sitting on the island counter. That seemed like a weak offering after all the work Christy and Mark had done to prepare the holiday meal.

"Would you mind going out to get Hailey?" Christy glanced out the kitchen window. She was holding a tray of cornbread stuffing with two oversized oven mitts. "She's out at the swing set."

"Sure thing." Gray left the glass of iced tea she'd been sipping and zipped her jacket. Sky Valley had gotten an early taste of winter just in time for the long holiday weekend.

Hailey was sitting in a swing seat with her back to the house. The hood of her jacket was up so Gray couldn't see her face until she'd rounded the swing and stood facing her. She wasn't really swinging, simply using the swing as a seat.

"Hey, your mom sent me to fetch you." Gray realized her statement fell on deaf ears. Hailey was looking at the ground and had ear buds in. Gray bent down and waved to catch Hailey's attention. Hailey tugged the corded headphones out of her ears and looked up with sort of a dazed expression.

"I think lunch is almost ready." Gray took a step back. "Your mom sent me out to let you know."

"Okay, thanks."

"You don't use wireless ones?" Gray touched her ears as she asked the question. She didn't think anyone under sixty wore corded ear buds.

"I prefer these." Hailey tucked the earbuds in her pocket. "They're cheap and they let people know when you don't really want to talk."

"I get it. Sometimes I don't like to talk either." Gray nodded. Maybe Hailey was trying to say she didn't want to talk to her even now. But Gray understood the not wanting to engage with people. And sometimes when she wore the cordless ones people didn't notice. It was hard to tell when people were wearing the cordless ear buds, especially if the person had long hair. The white cords were impossible to miss and did set up a visual barrier.

Low-fi tech was in these days. Corded earbuds weren't that different from preferring a turntable to CDs. The corded earbuds had sort of a 2010 Tumblr vibe. Gray missed those simpler days, hell, she remembered a time before Twitter even and weren't those good days?

"Are you going back to California?"

"Probably…I mean, yeah." The question surprised Gray so she fumbled her answer.

"I'd like to go there."

"It's a long way from here."

"Even better." Hailey was staring off into the distance, not looking at Gray.

Gray rotated to follow Hailey's gaze to the woods that bordered the lawn but couldn't really discern what she was looking at.

Maybe Hailey wasn't looking at anything. Gray did the same thing when she was feeling down. She'd stare into the woods allowing her stare to lose focus until the leaves and shadows transformed into abstract shapes of light and dark.

"Is there a reason you want to leave?" Gray tried to sound nonchalant, although now she wanted to press Hailey about how she was feeling. She had her hands in her pockets and was standing a few feet away from the swing.

"You left."

"Yeah, but I was a lot older than you." Gray wondered how Hailey knew that. "We can talk about that sometime if you like." Seeing Hailey now made her wish she'd had someone like herself to talk to when she'd been a teen. Instead of having to figure things out on her own by trial and error.

"Whatever." Hailey got up from the swing and gave Gray a sideways look.

"Hey, I meant that. We can talk later if you want."

"Sure." Hailey started walking toward the house.

Gray followed a few steps behind. Hailey had said *sure*, but it seemed that she wasn't really in a talking mood. Teenagers were tough. This kid was only twelve. Gray had only spent ten minutes with Hailey and she was totally stressed out, worried she'd say or do the wrong thing. She didn't envy Mark and Christy. How did two such likeable, easygoing parents spawn such surly offspring?

Hailey let the screen door slam behind her, rather than hold it for Gray. *Nice.*

Well, at least she knew the food would be good.

❖

Kayla and Dan had invited Faith to spend the holiday at their house, but she'd gone to her brother's place in Charlotte for the actual turkey feast instead. Her plan was to reconnect with her brothers for an acceptable amount of time and then drive to her condo in Raleigh afterward. Charlotte was halfway to Raleigh so it would break up the drive too.

She figured four or five hours with family would be her limit and then she'd use the drive to Raleigh as her excuse to leave. Her brother had told her not to worry about bringing anything but the death-by-chocolate pie had been a big hit.

If someone had told Faith in high school that her brother would grow up to be a Republican working in finance she'd have laughed in their face. But people changed, boy, did people change. Her parents would call and ask about her brother because they were too afraid to ask him directly about his politics. How did two such open and liberal parents raise such a conservative son? It was a mystery. Faith was at the liberal end of her family's spectrum, but she was by no means the most liberal. Her younger brother, Jason, taught theater to high school students. She'd always suspected that he was gay too, but as they got older she began to realize he might just be asexual. He seemed truly happy being single. He was married to his work, which gave him plenty of time with children. Teaching kids was his tactic to avoid having any of his own. Good for him.

But singleness wasn't for Faith. She liked all the accoutrements of coupledom—lazy Sundays, dinner out, movie nights, holding hands, sex. She missed all of them, even the mundane ones like laundry day.

The drive from Sky Valley to Charlotte had been fairly quick. She arrived at her brother's house around eleven. Holiday mayhem was in full swing.

She'd arrived just in time to rescue Jason. With Faith there he no longer had to pretend to care about college football, instead they could sit on the sidelines, sip wine, and talk about Broadway shows they hoped to catch.

Her older brother Mike was holding court near his enormous backyard grilling station. He'd announced to Faith two weeks earlier that he planned to smoke the turkey. Faith tried to sound excited, but secretly hoped for lots of side dishes, maybe even a salad. Turkey wasn't her favorite and she suspected that even smoked it still wouldn't be her first choice. Mike's wife, Lily, and their eight-year-old daughter, Maggie, were there, but her slightly older brother, Patrick, had decided to take his family skiing in Utah instead.

Faith was pretty sure that Patrick's wife, Amber's idea of a sport was walking the length of Nordstrom's to find the perfect pair of heels. Amber would probably never even leave the lodge. But Patrick's boys would no doubt have a blast. Poor Amber, she had two sons and a husband who loved sports and she couldn't tell the difference between baseball and football and wasn't bothered by that in the least.

Faith's siblings could be divided into two groups: the jocks and the creative types. They good-naturedly put up with each other's differences as long as no one brought up politics. Jason never seemed to mind showing up at family events without a plus-one, but as her two older brothers married and started having kids, the urge to have her own family unit began to grow.

There was nothing that made Faith feel more inept at dating than holidays with family. Thanksgiving was the worst because you put up with all the usual family nosiness and free advice and didn't even get to leave with presents. Faith wanted to create her own family unit. Her brothers couldn't possibly be any more well-adjusted than she was and yet somehow, they held down jobs and had wives and even kids.

What the hell was she doing wrong?

Maybe what she needed was a permanent change of scenery. She loved Sky Valley, why not live there year-round. She didn't need the job at the café, but it would be nice to do a couple shifts a week just to ground her in the real world, force her to manage her time. And worst-case scenario she'd interact with people a few times a week. Faith had discovered that having too much time didn't necessarily make her more productive. Somehow, the less time she had the more she could get done. The physics made no sense, but she'd proven them to be true time and again.

Four hours turned out to be her cutoff.

"Save yourself," she jokingly whispered to Jason when she hugged him good-bye.

The drive to Raleigh from Charlotte was a welcomed respite after a chaotic holiday lunch. She'd been feeling the need to check in at her place in Raleigh. Her neighbor had been taking in her mail and watering her plants, but she felt like she needed to see the place for herself to confirm it was still there.

The answer was yes, everything was just the way she'd left it, a mess.

She took some time to clean out the fridge and shuffle through her mail. Maybe she needed to sell the condo and move. Raleigh suddenly felt big and noisy. All the reasons she'd settled there after college didn't really fit for her any longer. All the trappings of a college town, the ability to get to DC and NYC within hours by train, and lots of great restaurants. That had been the initial allure. But she was older and maybe now she was looking for something different.

Maybe she should find a place closer to Asheville. Asheville offered lots of gallery space and tourism was a booming industry there. Folks loved to buy art when they were on vacation. Exhibiting in a wine bar was even better. Alcohol definitely inspired a love for art like nothing else. Hours of art history couldn't hold a candle to the influence of a full-bodied merlot.

It felt good to be back in her space in Raleigh, but at the same time it felt oddly foreign. Had too much happened here? Everything about the place reminded her of things she didn't really want to focus on. Faith needed to make a change for real. She needed, no, she *wanted* to be more deliberate about her life and her choices moving forward.

She needed to update her online portfolio and reach out to her contacts for more agency work. She'd never attract a mate wallowing in her dark condo eating chips and wearing sweatpants.

Then, as if her smartphone had read her thoughts, a text message pinged. For a minute she worried that it would be from Sam, but thankfully it wasn't.

Sorry to text over the holiday. Do you have time for a job?
The text was from a publisher she'd worked with before. Or, more specifically, a designer who worked for a publisher in Chapel Hill. *I wouldn't ask, but it's an emergency.*
Yes, I'm available. Especially since rush jobs always paid more. *I'm driving home tomorrow. Can I call you in the afternoon?*
Perfect! Thank you! You've saved my life!
Faith doubted anything was that dire, but it was nice to feel appreciated. She'd pack a few more art supplies before heading back to Sky Valley because it sounded like she was going to need them. But first, she'd figure out dinner, maybe pizza. Pepperoni was a good chaser for turkey. She flopped onto the sofa and scrolled through local eateries on her phone for delivery options.

Chapter Fourteen

The week after Thanksgiving, Gray decided to put thought into action and pay a visit to Lucas Johnson at the Sky Valley Fire Station. The building was basically a large, metal warehouse on the south end of downtown. A red fire engine was visible through the bay doors when she parked out front.

Although major cities had paid firefighters, most small towns and rural America were served largely by volunteer departments. Sky Valley was no different. She knew from talking to Mark that the station supported two paid positions, one of whom had just retired, and the rest of the crew was made up of volunteers—local folks who had day jobs and other lives but enjoyed lending a helping hand when needed.

Sometimes it was hard to think about her life before she became a wildland firefighter. In the *before* time, Gray saw life as if she were wearing blinders. Things that happened in the world or to other people were an abstraction, things that happened at a safe distance. Stuff she read on her newsfeed or heard from friends. Getting involved, struggling against forces larger than herself—forces out of her control—had changed her. Gray wasn't sure she could articulate exactly how if called upon to do so, she just knew she was different. In a crisis, she'd learned to put her own fears aside and just help. But the events of that last fire had shattered her calm confidence. What had happened with Shane was a lot more personal and so far, she hadn't been able to regain her footing. She hoped diving into work would help her get back to where she'd been.

The main door was open so she walked in. She passed through a front room with a couple of sofas and a coffee table. There were random magazines and newspapers strewn on the table and a very sad, drooping potted plant in the corner. The office was down a short hallway past the kitchen. She tapped lightly on the half-open door.

"Hey, come in." Lucas was seated at a desk in a rolling chair. He spun around and motioned her in. He stood and offered her his hand.

"Thanks, Lucas." Gray smiled.

If a handshake could be trustworthy, then Lucas's was exactly that, firm and friendly. He wasn't quite as tall as Gray, but he was stockily built, all muscle. He was wearing a navy uniform shirt and work pants. His sandy hair had a touch of gray at the temples. Lucas looked older, but definitely the same guy she remembered from high school. He'd been a year ahead of her.

"Have a seat." He rolled a second chair over for her.

Gray sat down and surveyed the room. The office had an unorganized lived-in sort of feel. Not dysfunctional, but definitely comfortable. There were training notices on the bulletin board, along with the truck inspection roster. And a white board with random notes that probably only made sense to those who worked in the office every day.

"How've you been?" Lucas stood up before she could answer. "Oh, hey, you want coffee? I just made a fresh pot." He pointed toward a small break area just outside the office.

"Sure." It was still early and Gray hardly ever said no to coffee. It wasn't like it mattered if it kept her awake at night. Her brain kept her up all on its own.

Lucas returned with two faded Western Carolina University mugs and handed her one.

"Do you need cream or sugar?"

"No, black is fine. Thanks." She took a sip. It was nice and hot.

"So, back to my original question…How've you been?"

"Okay." She didn't really want to get into all of it, especially when she was still sorting it out herself. "I'm back for a little while and Mark thought you might need some help. I'm no good just hanging around the house." Gray paused. "I figured I might as well do something, you know, use my skills while I'm here."

"Yeah, absolutely." He took a swig of his coffee. "I could definitely use your help, especially heading into the holidays. It'd also be nice to get a day off now and then."

He laughed, but she knew he was probably serious. A rural fire chief was probably never off duty. Being such a local, people probably even showed up at his house when they needed help.

"Are you ready for this?" Lucas asked.

"What do you mean?" She wasn't sure how to interpret his question.

"You grew up here. I know it's been a while, but you still know folks and they know you." He sipped his coffee before he finished the thought. "Sometimes it's hard to keep it together when you know the person in need of help."

"Yeah, I guess I hadn't really thought about it that way." Somehow, she didn't consider herself a local any longer, but he was probably right. Maybe this wasn't such a good idea after all. But she tamped down her flight instinct and decided to hear him out. "How does this work?"

"Most calls come from the 9-1-1 operator, although some local folks have my number and they'll just call my cell directly." Lucas set his coffee aside and picked up the daily call logbook. "This station handles everything…forest fires, car wrecks, injured hikers, whatever…Most calls aren't about fires though." He emphasized the last part about fires.

Gray was glad to hear it. She wasn't sure how she'd react to being in a fire just yet. Surely her training would kick in and she'd be on autopilot, relying on muscle memory and experience. But how could she know for sure until she was in the burn zone again.

"That all sounds okay." She shifted in her chair. "Do I need any special certification or anything?"

"No, you're good. As a wildland firefighter you're more qualified than George was. Maybe even more than me in some ways, but I've got medical training that you probably don't have." He set the logbook on the desk and rotated again to face her. "I'm a registered nurse now."

"That's great." She stood as she sipped her coffee and surveyed the guides and handbooks on the shelves along the back wall. "I've only had the basic emergency field medical training, you know, the stuff they teach you at survival school. So, I can't set a broken bone or anything, but I promise not to pass out on you at the sight of blood."

"That works for me. As firefighters, we just do the basic CPR training. We cover the basics until medical personnel get to the scene because response times can vary. If a case is serious we transport them by ambulance to the hospital in Asheville."

Asheville was probably twenty-five minutes away by car, so stabilizing an injured person on the scene made sense.

Gray sat back down and finished the last sip of her coffee. The radio came to life with a code and call number. She was prepared to jump up and get out of Lucas's way.

"That's not ours." He sank back in his chair. "Each station has a specific tone, an EMS tone and then a fire code. You get used to which tone to listen for."

Gray nodded and relaxed back into her seat.

"Have you had any bad calls?" Gray really had no idea.

Lucas grew serious.

"Suicides are bad. We get out-of-towners who come to the mountains to end it. To be close to God or something." He took a deep breath and exhaled. "They sometimes leave a note in their car, or just lay by the road until someone finds them."

Gray didn't respond. His answer had surprised her. She couldn't imagine being some random hiker who happened to discover a suicide victim. How did you recover from that?

"There was a plane crash a few years back with children involved. They were flying too low in the fog, hit the side of a mountain. The kids burned to death holding onto each other in the back seat." He cleared his throat and looked away. "That stays with you."

Gray wasn't the only one carrying around a horrible experience. How could people walk around holding this much inside them? She had a new respect for Lucas.

"When can you start?" He changed the subject.

"Um, now, tomorrow...whenever."

"Let me show you the trucks." He got up and started toward the office exit. She followed him out into the huge garage where two fire trucks were parked.

"We'll get you a radio. There's also an active 9-1-1 app you can download for your smartphone. Once you open a call you can respond and say you're on your way or can't take the call. But all that is dependent on cell service. Which as you know, can be spotty up in the mountains so it's good to keep the radio with you for backup."

Lucas walked around the truck. He was very proud to show it off. He pointed to a panel of gauges behind the truck cab.

"That's the pump panel. This truck can pump a thousand gallons of water in and out. And those are nozzles and floats for sucking up water from lakes, ponds, and streams." The nozzles were mounted on the side of the truck below the pump panel. "Out here, you have to pull water from wherever you can find it."

He opened more cabinets around the truck to reveal the gear stowed in each space—fire rakes, shovels, a portable generator, extra hoses, a chainsaw, ladders, and air packs with spare bottles. This vehicle even had a handheld thermal imaging device to check for people or hot spots. Gray was impressed.

"We'll get you some turnout gear."

He didn't explain, but she knew that meant coat, pants, helmet, gloves, boots, and a self-contained breathing apparatus. That was an awful lot of equipment for a fire station that didn't get many fire calls. She knew from experience the gear required physical agility because it was heavy and made it hard to move.

"Your timing is great. Do you know why?" Lucas smiled and there was a definite twinkle in his eyes suddenly that made her worry.

"I'm afraid to ask."

"The annual Christmas fundraiser for the volunteer fire staff is next week." His grin widened. "You get to help me plan it."

Oh no, a Christmas fundraiser? This was not what she'd signed up for. But what could she say now? She'd already told him she had plenty of time on her hands and could start work tomorrow.

Chapter Fifteen

L ate in the afternoon, Gray decided to take a walk. A path had been worn by deer that lead from the cabin up toward the top of the ridge. The trail had once been a wagon road before the turn of the century and since had been reclaimed by wildlife and probably the occasional hiker. This was the known country of her childhood, where Gray used to play and explore as a child. The twenty-acre place had seemed enormous to her when she was young. The farthest end of the property bordered national forest land, so the forest seemed to go on forever, untamed and uncharted. At least that's how she remembered it from her childhood.

Some days seemed longer than others, and even though this one resided in December and was shorter than some, it felt particularly long. The seconds piled into minutes, which then drug on into hours and in all the fractured segments of this very long day there were too many thoughts. She'd decided to take a walk to clear her head.

Maybe she'd rushed into things by going to talk to Lucas. What if she'd gotten in over her head with this fire station job? What if she truly wasn't ready? At the same time, she definitely wasn't feeling any better sitting around the cabin. As Alissa had said, she needed to focus on something other than herself.

Dry leaves crunched beneath her boots. The familiar sound was soothing. She occasionally dragged the bottom of her shoe through the leaves to make as much noise as possible. The sound echoed in the silent forest that surrounded her. Gray was looking at her feet as she crested the ridge, so she didn't notice Faith until she was almost on top of her.

Seeing Faith here was unexpected, but it really shouldn't have been. The property that had belonged to Kayla's grandparents curved around so that one section of it bordered Gray's property line, just at the edge where it met the national forest. The red blazes on the trees marked the beginning of the government owned public lands. And just beyond that line was an overlook, a great spot to watch the sunset. That's the spot where Gray found Faith. No doubt all the scuffling dry leaf noises signaled her approach long before Faith saw her, because Faith didn't seem nearly as surprised to see Gray.

"Hi." Gray held her hand up in greeting.

"Hello." Faith was sitting on the sloped granite outcropping several feet away. She didn't get up as Gray approached, but Faith did smile as if she was happy to see her.

Gray's insides warmed, despite the chilly air. The sun was dipping low along the blue ridges that rippled like successive waves in front of the overlook. The survival training in Gray made her wonder if Faith had thought to bring a flashlight, because once the sun dropped below the ridgeline this heavily wooded area would get dark fast.

"You found my favorite spot." Gray sat down on the stone surface, keeping a cushion of space between them.

"Mine too." Faith was facing the setting sun, not Gray. "I only recently discovered this spot and I don't come up here nearly often enough." She paused. "You know, every day ends with a sunset, and we so rarely take time to savor them."

"True." Gray had expected Faith's presence to make her nervous or unsettled, but Faith's proximity had the opposite effect. She took a deep breath and exhaled slowly. Faith made her feel calm. That was a surprising discovery.

"Is that a journal?" Gray noticed a book on the ground beside Faith.

"It's a sketchbook."

Faith smiled at Gray again and warmth spread through her chest.

"You're an artist." It was a statement, not a question.

Faith watched the expression on Gray's face change as if she'd just solved some puzzle she'd been struggling with.

"Could I see your sketchbook?" Gray seemed to reconsider the request. "Or is that more like a diary and I shouldn't have asked?"

"It's just a regular sketchbook." She handed the book to Gray. "Just keep in mind that a lot of what you'll see in there are just thoughts…pieces of ideas." She watched as Gray thumbed slowly through the pages. It was hard to read her expression. "I usually keep a sketchbook with me all the time to jot things down that I'm afraid I'll forget."

"You're really good." Gray spoke without looking up.

Gray held the book open to one page longer than the others. Faith leaned closer to see which drawing had captured Gray's attention.

"That's a drawing of the old tree that fell. The one that you and Mark cleaned up. Before it fell, obviously."

"I love trees." Gray's expression was wistful. "Your drawing makes it seem so real."

"It was real."

Gray smiled, probably realizing how her comment sounded.

"What I meant was, your drawing is so good I feel like I could reach out and touch this tree…it comes off the page." Gray held the book at arm's length and studied it. "The lights and darks are so subtle." She looked at Faith. "And you did all of that with only a pencil?"

"Never underestimate the power of a pencil."

Gray laughed.

"I'm now thinking it might be mightier than the pen." Gray closed the book and handed it to her. "Thank you for letting me see your book."

Faith was happy that Gray seemed to be so pleased with her sketches. They were nothing, really, the seeds of something bigger, she just didn't know exactly what yet.

"What sort of work do you do, Gray?"

"I'm a firefighter."

"Wow, really?" That was not the profession Faith had expected and Gray had said it in such a low-key voice, as if she'd just told Faith she was an accountant or something. "Is that what you were doing in California?"

"Yeah."

Gray's eyes betrayed a sense of dread or darkness. Faith couldn't help feeling she'd accidentally hit a nerve. Initially, Gray's mood was light, almost happy, now it was as if a heavy curtain had been drawn that blocked out the sun. Faith wanted to bring the light back, but she wasn't sure how. They sat quietly side-by-side watching the orange of the sun sink lower. The air cooled and Faith zipped up her jacket, turning the collar up around her neck and ears.

"It'll be dark soon. Did you bring a flashlight?" Gray asked.

"Oh, no, I totally forgot." Faith felt stupid. "I didn't even think of it."

"Come on, I'll walk you home." Gray stood and extended her hand to Faith.

"Thanks." Faith clasped Gray's hand and electricity sparked through her entire nervous system. She was sure her cheeks were red because they felt suddenly hot. After she got to her feet she focused on dusting plant debris from the seat of her pants rather than focusing on Gray. Whew, it took a moment for her fluttering heartbeat to settle.

"You okay?"

"I'm fine. Thanks." Had Gray noticed how flustered she was just from one touch? How embarrassing.

Faith tucked her sketchbook under her arm as they started back down the trail to her house.

"I really love these woods." She wanted to regain the lighter moment, when Gray had initially walked up. "Everything looks like art to me, things I'd like to paint."

"Everything looks like fuel to me." Gray smiled thinly and scuffed her boots through the dry leaves as she walked. "I suppose that's a firefighter's curse."

How differently they saw the world. Faith wondered if while they strolled through the forest together they were actually moving away from each other, instead of closer to each other, each step carrying them farther apart. Gray did seem to be far away, somewhere in her head. Gray's hands were in her pockets. Instinctively, Faith slipped her arm through Gray's. The physical contact seemed to bring Gray back. If she was bothered by the closeness she didn't pull away. This pleased Faith. She relaxed and let the weight of her arm rest in the crook of Gray's.

Darkness overtook them before they reached Faith's house. The walk hadn't seemed that long, but the weight of nighttime was upon them before she realized it. Pinpricks of starlight were visible as the wind shifted the naked branches overhead. This had turned into an accidentally, unexpectedly magical evening stroll.

Gray held the flashlight so that the path was illuminated, an island of light in the darkness. The trunks of the trees were black, their limbs reaching skyward against the purple of the heavens. How small they were in contrast to the intangible cosmic drama of the stars.

She stopped again. Looking up, she thought of Van Gogh and about how he worked from memory especially when he painted nocturnal environments. His nighttime scenes had a particular luminous power. Faith both envied and admired his kinetic landscapes. She'd experimented with the method of painting from memory with mixed results and in this instance was torn between rushing inside to make visual notes in her sketchbook and never wanting to leave Gray's side.

Gray watched Faith look skyward and wondered what she was thinking. Faith had a radiant expression, made even more so by the moonlight breaking through the trees. She switched off the flashlight.

"Thank you." Faith was still looking up at the night sky. "Sometimes it's good to become lost in the darkness so that you can really see the moon."

How beautiful the forest would be for her if she could alter her thoughts and see the world as art instead of as fuel. Fire didn't care how the forest was before it came. It took everything.

Gray focused on redirecting her thoughts. She settled into the moment, in no hurry for their walk to end. Being with Faith made her feel good. The branches created a spiderweb of shadows on the ground as the moonlight passed through the empty branches. She stood in the broken light, feeling more whole than she had in a long time.

Was that because of Faith?

After a few moments they continued on. She could see a light from the house punching a hole in the darkness ahead. As they drew closer Gray wondered what would happen next. She'd had the impulse to pull away earlier, but now, she wasn't so sure. Faith's arm was still draped through hers and the connection felt nice. Did Faith find her attractive? Was her attraction real, or nothing more than shadows cast on a cave wall?

Faith tried to read Gray's expression. Was she okay with the light contact of their linked arms? Gray hadn't withdrawn, so that was a positive sign. The more encounters she had with Gray, the more Kayla's description of Gray as a player didn't seem accurate. But was that simply her libido talking? Gray had exhibited none of the self-promoting ego displays that Faith usually associated with someone who actually was a player, and she'd known a few. Her ex-girlfriend in the top position on that list.

Gray stopped near the porch and stepped away from Faith, ending their physical connection.

"Would you like to come in?" Faith made a snap decision to invite Gray to stay for a little while. "I might have some wine, or I could make hot tea." Faith tossed out options, afraid that if she stopped talking Gray might use the opening to decline the invitation.

"Okay." Gray nodded her head as if she were convincing herself. "That would be nice."

CHAPTER SIXTEEN

Faith sensed Gray's closeness as she unlocked the door. As she fumbled with the keys, she was grateful she'd left the porch light on. She crossed the threshold and then held the door for Gray to follow.

"Can I take your coat?" Faith took Gray's jacket and hung it on a coat tree near the front door. It was the same jacket she'd seen Gray wear the first time they met. It was brown corduroy with pile lining, and it smelled like the outdoors, but in a good way. It smelled like juniper with just a hint of wood smoke. Faith had to fight the impulse to hold the jacket against her face to breathe it in before draping it over the peg hanger.

"This place hasn't changed much." Gray stood in the foyer and surveyed the room.

Of course, she'd forgotten the connection between Kayla and Gray.

"Oh, that's right, you and Kayla knew each other in high school." How well they knew each other was still a mystery that Faith needed to solve.

"Yeah, we weren't super close, but I came to the house a few times when her grandparents were still living." Gray stopped to study a photo hanging at the base of the stairs. "I always really liked them. Kayla has a nice family."

Did Gray mean her own family wasn't nice? Faith couldn't help thinking there was something else behind the comment.

"What sounds better? Wine or hot tea?" Faith hung her coat up also and started to walk toward the kitchen.

"Maybe wine if that's okay with you."

"Absolutely." In fact, if Faith had anything stronger she'd have offered that. She was a bundle of nerves. She poured two glasses and carried them back to the living room. Gray was still standing with her hands in her pockets as if she was afraid to touch anything. Her flannel shirt was untucked, with a dark T-shirt underneath and jeans that looked like they'd been worn to perfectly highlight her lanky frame. Gray was like a butch dream girl, standing in Kayla's grandparents' parlor. Faith took a breath, "Please, sit. I hope red is okay." She handed a glass to Gray and tried to calm down.

Gray sat on the couch and Faith debated whether to join her or take the flowery-printed, overstuffed chair on the other end of the coffee table. Maybe the chair was a safer choice.

"Is this a jam jar?" Gray examined the small glass.

"Yes, I hope that's okay." Faith took a sip and tried not to stare at Gray's hands.

"I love using jam jars as glasses. It reminds me of my grandma." Gray smiled.

"It does?"

"Yeah, my grandma used to make homemade wine when I was a kid. She'd store it in jam jars and mason jars in the spring house."

"Is your grandmother still alive?" Talking about grandmothers was a safe topic.

"No, she passed when I was in high school." Gray relaxed against the back of the sofa and sipped the wine. "That seems like a million years ago now."

They were both quiet for a moment. Faith considered that she'd made a mistake choosing the chair because she really wanted to be close to Gray. She wanted to recapture the casual contact they'd shared during the walk. She wanted to find out if Gray's flannel shirt was as soft as it looked.

"What are you doing here?"

"Excuse me?" Gray's question caught her off guard.

"I'm sorry, I don't think that came out right." Gray sat forward and cleared her throat. "What I meant was, why are you in Sky Valley?" Gray paused. "I'm assuming staying in this house is a temporary thing, because this furniture doesn't really look like…you. And you just don't seem like a local, no offense."

"None taken." Faith almost laughed. This was the most she'd heard Gray say at one time since she'd met her. "It is sort of a temporary thing."

Gray took another sip of wine and waited for Faith to continue.

"I had a bad breakup a while ago and, well, Kayla offered this place to me as a change of scenery, which I definitely needed." Understatement of the year. "My ex lives in Raleigh, which is where my place is."

"Oh, I'm sorry about your breakup."

"It's okay, really." Faith didn't want to talk about her ex with Gray. "It was way over, actually, long before I knew it was over. We'd need a lot more wine for me to get into all of that." She air tipped her glass in Gray's direction.

Gray regretted bringing up any sad topics. She hadn't expected Faith to say she'd just gone through a breakup. Who in their right mind would leave Faith? She was beautiful, and funny, and she had a warmth to her that Gray just wanted to snuggle up to. And now she'd gone and brought up Faith's ex-girlfriend.

"Sorry, I didn't mean to bring up a sore subject."

Faith shook her head and took a big swig of her wine. There was probably only one sip left. Her hair cascaded around her face and shoulders, slightly ruffled from the wind during their walk. She was wearing a fuzzy gray cardigan over a scooped-neck T-shirt. The sweater was only buttoned partway up, just tight enough to accentuate Faith's curves. Gray tried to focus on Faith's eyes as she sipped her wine.

"It's not a sore subject and it's not your fault." Faith paused. "As for work, I mostly do freelance art and illustration so I can do that from anywhere."

"That's great."

"And Kayla needed some seasonal help at the café, so that gets me out of the house, you know." Faith shifted, slipped out of her shoes and tucked her legs up in the chair.

"I just sort of took a job to get out of the house myself and now I'm regretting it."

"Really?" Faith seemed pleased with this bit of news. "I guess we both needed a change of scenery, huh?"

"Something like that." Gray smiled thinly. "I mostly needed to be somewhere everything wasn't on fire."

Faith didn't respond and Gray worried that she'd killed the mood.

"Fire season starts earlier and lasts longer every year." People who lived on the East Coast never thought of forest fires as having a season, but they did.

"I guess I didn't realize that."

Most people read about climate change and drought, but for them it was more of an idea, something abstract that happened elsewhere. It wasn't like they were living it. People who didn't live on the edges, where things were visibly changing, couldn't really grasp the reality of what was happening.

"That's good. It's nice that you don't have to think about it." Gray's gaze was direct, but Faith didn't look away. "Sky Valley is a safe place to be. It's good for you to be in a safe place."

She really meant it. Faith deserved to feel safe, to be protected.

"Would you like a little more wine?"

"Sure."

Faith returned after a minute with the bottle and poured some in Gray's glass. Then she set the bottle on the coffee table and sat on the couch. Gray shifted so that they were almost facing each other.

This was beginning to feel a little bit like a date and Gray wondered where this might lead. How long ago did Faith's breakup happen? Was the slight flirtation Gray was picking up on real or was Faith simply being friendly? Sometimes it was hard to tell with Southern women and Gray was a little out of practice. She hadn't dated in a long time and had only ever had one relationship that didn't last much more than a year. The seasonal work and moving around didn't exactly make for lasting relationships. Plus, during fire season all she did was work, there was no such thing as a social life, except for hanging out with other firefighters from her crew.

"Hey, where'd you just go?"

Faith's hand was on her thigh. She stared at it for a few seconds savoring the warmth of connection, even a small, fleeting connection.

"Sorry...nowhere." Gray covered Faith's hand with hers. "This is nice."

"What?" Faith tilted her head.

"Being here with you is nice." Gray smiled. That wasn't the most romantic statement, but at least it was true.

Faith withdrew her hand and Gray thought maybe she'd misread the gesture. It was hard to know for sure based on Faith's expression. She was terrible at this *feelings* stuff.

"I should go. You probably have an early day tomorrow." Gray had no idea what time it was, but she wanted to give Faith an exit if she wanted one. Gray set the empty glass on the coffee table.

"Let me drive you home."

Faith hadn't tried to talk her into staying so she'd obviously read the mood correctly.

"I can walk. It's not that far." Gray stood up and retrieved her jacket. "Plus, I have my trusty flashlight." She removed it from her jacket pocket and waved it.

"I insist." Faith slipped on her shoes and then her coat. "You rescued me the other night on the side of the road. I'd like to return the favor. Besides, there's no shoulder along that road. It's too dangerous."

"Says the woman who went for a walk after dark along the same road just the other night."

"Shush." Faith wagged her finger at Gray playfully. "I had my reasons."

Gray's cabin was very close, less than a five-minute drive. They didn't really talk during the ride. Gray wasn't sure what to say. She wasn't even sure what had really happened between them tonight. It seemed like *something* had happened, but maybe only from Gray's perspective.

Faith pulled into the driveway behind Gray's Jeep.

"Well, thanks for the ride." Gray's hand was on the door handle, but she didn't really want to get out.

Faith's hand on her thigh had been like a hot ember and the heat of her touch had spread. Gray wanted more. She looked at Faith and considered kissing her. She wanted to kiss Faith. They held each other with their eyes, only the dim glow from the porch light filtered in through the windshield highlighting the soft curve of Faith's cheek.

Before Gray could figure out what to do or not do, Faith touched her face, leaned across the console and lightly kissed Gray.

"I'm sorry, was that too much?" Faith whispered, inches from Gray's lips.

Gray slipped her fingers into the hair at the base of Faith's neck and drew her close and kissed her back. At first, tentatively, politely and then her tongue found Faith's and the kiss deepened. Faith tasted of red wine and sweetness and light. Faith broke the kiss after a few blissful moments.

"Good night, Gray." Faith smiled.

"Good night." Gray knew this was her cue.

She stood on the porch until the taillights of Faith's car disappeared and then turned into the house as if in slow motion. Had the entire night been nothing more than a lovely dream? She hoped not.

CHAPTER SEVENTEEN

A ll day the next day, Faith could think of nothing else but that kiss. First off, she'd kissed Gray. The one person she'd been trying to convince herself *not* to feel any attraction to. But who had she been kidding? Some things were beyond a person's control, and besides, it was just a kiss—one kiss, nothing more. Luckily, she'd driven Gray home and Gray hadn't tried to tempt her with more.

But that kiss.

Wow.

Faith closed her eyes and savored the memory.

Kayla had left work for the afternoon to run some errands. Faith was hoping to catch Kayla at home, alone, so she could finally get some clarity on what exactly had happened between Kayla and Gray so long ago.

She was in luck. When she turned into the driveway, only Kayla's Subaru was there. She knocked, but then didn't wait for a reply before letting herself in.

"Kayla?" She tossed her coat across the back of the sofa.

"I'm in here." Kayla's voice came from the kitchen.

Kayla and Dan had a comfortable house. It had probably been someone's vacation getaway. It wasn't large, but with two bedrooms and two baths it was the perfect size. The walls were varnished wood, as were the floors. Kayla had added sectional rugs to break up all the hardwood and make the place cozier in the winter. There was a huge stone fireplace, the sort of hearth you'd expect in a ski lodge. Kayla had confided to Faith that the fireplace was what sealed the deal for her. And so, it became the heart of the entire place with sofa and chairs set in a half circle so that everyone could bask in its warmth.

"Hey, what are you up to?" Kayla was putting veggies in the fridge. Two bags of groceries sat on the island countertop waiting to be unloaded.

"I have a freelance job to do. I was on my way home to finish it, but I had to ask you something." She probably sounded more serious than she meant to because Kayla immediately turned to look at her.

"Is something wrong?"

"Oh, no, nothing like that." Faith distracted herself by taking groceries out of the bags and placing them on the counter for Kayla. Was that actually helpful? Probably not, but it gave her something to do with her hands. "I wanted to ask you about that thing you told me about...the thing with Gray."

"Oh. My. God. You slept with her."

"No! Please, give me a little credit." Faith frowned. Thank goodness they hadn't slept together because there's no way she'd have been able to lie to Kayla about it. "We...kissed."

"I knew it." Kayla grinned. "I knew it was just a matter of time."

"How did you know?" Faith certainly wasn't that predictable, was she?

"Because you are you and Gray is Gray. It was inevitable." Now Kayla sounded smug, but not in a mean way, just way too sure of herself.

"Well, before this thing with Gray goes any further, and I'm not saying it will, I want to know what happened between you two." Faith sat on one of the barstools in preparation for a long story.

"There really isn't that much to tell." Kayla leaned against the counter, facing Faith. "Gray and I were at summer church camp, you know, the camp at Ridgecrest."

Faith nodded.

"And we were assigned to share a room." Kayla crossed her arms and looked thoughtfully at the ceiling as if she were trying to remember. "Gray was really fun, we had a good time that week...and one night, there was a huge lightning storm and I was scared to sleep on the top bunk."

"I'm surprised you were on top anyway." Faith couldn't help the joke.

"Not my first choice, as you well know." Kayla quirked the side of her mouth up in a half smile, her tone sarcastic. "Do you want to hear this story or not?"

"Yes, please continue."

"Anyway, we decided to share the bottom bunk until the storm passed. And, I don't really know what happened, but, we kissed…and sort of made it to second base."

"Kayla! You never told me about this."

"I told you when we were roommates that I'd kissed a girl once."

"Yes, but never the part about getting to second base," Faith teased her. She propped her elbows on the counter and her chin in her hands like a little kid preparing to hear an amazing tale.

"Don't look at me like that." Kayla waved her off and reached for the tea kettle. "It was just the one time and we never talked about it after that." She filled the pot with water and lit the front burner.

"What do you mean you never talked about it?"

Kayla shrugged. "It just happened and it's not like it was going to happen again…and I don't know, we were probably embarrassed about it." Kayla paused. "Camp ended the next day and then I didn't see Gray for the rest of the summer, until our senior year started. Like I said, it wasn't like we were close friends or anything."

"But Gray mentioned she'd been to your grandparents' house before, so, you must have sort of been friends?"

"I suppose we were when we were younger. Her parents' property wasn't that far from my grandparents' place and we did see each other at school…but we ran in different circles when we got older. You know, I don't really remember."

"You made out with Gray and then you ghosted her." Faith's stomach hurt at the thought of a young version of Gray, probably barely at the beginning stages of coming out, having an encounter with a girl and then never being able to process it. Not just any girl either, a young version of Kayla. And all the while, living in a small, church-centric town where everyone knew everyone. Gray had probably been terrified that Kayla would say something.

"It wasn't like that. You make it sound like I did a terrible thing."

"Not for you, Miss Homecoming Queen, but I'll bet it *was* terrible for Gray."

"Really?" Kayla seemed genuinely surprised.

"Yes, think about it from Gray's perspective. It wasn't as if Sky Valley was a hotbed of liberal, LGBTQ-friendly thought more than a decade ago. It probably still isn't. It's just that we're all adults now and we have each other and we don't care what the church ladies think."

"I never thought about it that way."

Straight people rarely did unless their gay friends pointed it out to them. Faith loved Kayla dearly, but sometimes she really did have blinders on.

"Sure, Asheville is a little island of blue liberalism in a sea of red, but Sky Valley isn't Asheville." And what was Sky Valley really like nearly fifteen years ago. "I recently drove back here from Raleigh after Thanksgiving, and I can personally confirm that there is still a huge ass Confederate flag flying right next to I-40 not too far from Statesville."

"I know. It's terrible." Kayla shook her head. "Times are changing, but in some ways, not fast enough."

"And in some ways, not at all." Faith nodded for emphasis. "Can I just ask you one more question?"

"I'm really scared right now."

"You're hilarious." She scowled at Kayla.

"Okay, what do you want to know?" Kayla crossed her arms as if she was bracing herself for a hard question.

"Why, based on that one encounter, did you tell me that Gray was a player?"

Kayla was quiet, clearly mulling the question over.

"Gray hung with kind of a wild crowd in high school, and I guess I assumed I wasn't the only girl she'd gotten to second base with. I mean, she was always very attractive and confident and people liked her...girls liked her." Kayla took the kettle off and poured two cups for tea. "And I guess I didn't want you to get hurt so soon after Sam."

"You know that I'm a grown woman, right?" She sipped the warm tea. "I'm not as fragile as you think I am, or as naive."

"I know." Kayla sat on the barstool next to Faith and rotated to face her. "I'm your best friend and I worry, that's all."

"Thank you, it's nice to be fussed over." Faith feigned seriousness. "But listen, it's my professional lesbian opinion that Grayson Reeves is not a player." She slurped the tea loudly in Kayla's direction for emphasis.

"I stand corrected." Kayla laughed. And then she studied her teacup for a moment. "I feel awful. Maybe I should invite Gray over for dinner." She turned to Faith and her expression brightened. "We could have a double date." She grinned broadly.

"Okay, sister, pump the brakes...it was only one kiss."

They both laughed and Kayla reached to give Faith a hug.

"I love you, Faith."

"I love you too." Faith smiled. "Now, what other tantalizing camp stories have you been hiding from me?" She quirked an eyebrow.

Kayla laughed.

"What's so funny?" Dan joined them in the kitchen from the back door.

"Well, definitely not those boots." Kayla frowned. "Honey, look at all that mud you just tracked in."

"Oh, sorry." He looked down like he was noticing his feet for the first time. "I don't suppose you'd get me a glass of water?"

"If it keeps you from tracking up my kitchen, then yes, please just stay there."

Dan smiled broadly as Kayla filled a glass, then handed it to him.

"So, what were you two talking about? I feel like I missed something interesting." Dan gulped half the glass.

"We were talking about Kayla's wild church camp days." Faith loved to make Kayla squirm.

"My timing is perfect then." Dan's expression was expectant.

"Oh no, the trip down memory lane is over for today." Kayla wagged her finger at Faith. "Besides, I thought you said you had work to do."

"You're right, but you know how I loathe deadlines." Faith sighed.

CHAPTER EIGHTEEN

Gray was lounging on the beat-up sofa in the front room of the fire station reading a day-old *Asheville Citizen-Times* newspaper. Her first two days on the job had been deathly quiet so far, but at least she was out of the cabin and catching up on local news. It seemed Asheville had grown and changed a lot in the past decade. She'd also helped Lucas wash the two trucks on site in addition to laundering the turnout gear in a giant washing machine in the garage. The machine was especially gauged for removing contaminants from the suits after exposure to carcinogens that could cause cancer to the wearer. There was also an entire handbook in the office about the handling of toxic substances. Gray tried to read some of it, but it was reminding her a bit too much of high school chemistry, which she'd barely passed.

"Hey, you ready for your first call?" Lucas leaned around the corner from the office.

"Sure." Gray quickly got to her feet, expecting an actual emergency. Although, she hadn't heard anything except the phone ring. The radio at her hip was silent.

"You remember Erwin Dinkler?"

"You mean Dink?" Everyone called him Dink in high school.

"He had a heart attack and his wife drove him to the hospital in Asheville. I guess they were on the edge of town at the Walmart Christmas shopping when it happened."

"Is he okay?" Dink was a big fellow in high school. He probably still had the same thick-through-the middle physique now.

"Yeah, he's fine, he called 9-1-1 to have someone come get his wife because she's scared to drive in the mountains at night."

"Seriously?" Gray checked the wall clock. It was four thirty and it would get dark not too long after five o'clock.

"Come on, I'll drive." Lucas tugged on his jacket.

"Can't I just go pick her up in my Jeep?" Gray was confused.

"No, someone needs to take his car home from the hospital too." Lucas slapped her on the back. "Welcome to the rescue squad."

"I guess *rescue* does cover lots of…things." Gray reached for her coat.

"You first." Lucas motioned for her to walk through the door first. "I'll lock up. We'll call it a day after this."

Of course, that was assuming they didn't get some sort of call after hours.

A half hour later, Lucas dropped Gray off at the hospital entrance. At the front desk she asked for Erwin Dinkler and was directed to the third floor. She hadn't seen Dink since graduation and wasn't sure what to expect. Gray had lit out only days after finishing high school. Maybe Dink wouldn't even remember her.

Hospitals were definitely not her favorite place. She'd spent twenty-four hours in the hospital in Senora after the burnover. That was enough to last her for a while, and yet, here she was again. Gray read the numbers next to each door as she strode down the sterile hallway until she found the one she was looking for. The door was ajar. She tapped lightly and pushed it open a little farther.

"Dink?" She peeked inside.

"Hey, I know you." Dink's voice was faint and raspy. He squinted as if he was thinking hard on something.

A woman sat in an uncomfortable looking chair near the bed.

"It's me, Gray Reeves."

"I'll be damned." He motioned to the woman for water and took a sip before saying more. "I ain't seen you in forever."

"Hello, I'm Erwin's wife, Enid." Enid stood up and smiled nervously.

Erwin and Enid, cute. Enid had a scattered, disheveled air about her. Gray figured she'd had a good scare. Enid clutched a small black purse with both hands and dabbed at her eyes with a tissue.

"Dink, um, I mean, Erwin and I knew each other in high school." Gray stood a few feet away from the bed. There was a second bed in the room, but luckily it was unoccupied at the moment. "I haven't been back home for a while." She'd felt compelled to explain why she was there. Maybe Lucas had already told them to expect her. She paused before continuing. "Lucas said you needed a ride home, so that's why I'm here. I'm helping him out at the station for a while."

"Gray's a bigtime firefighter out west." He looked at his wife.

She was surprised that Dink knew anything about her life.

"You should stop talking and rest." Enid touched his shoulder. "I'll go home and feed the dogs and get Daddy to drive me back tomorrow to check on you."

"They're makin' me stay the night." Dink was clearly weak, but also probably in denial about his condition. "It weren't no heart attack. It was arith...ahrith..." He was short of breath and couldn't finish the word.

"Arrhythmia." Enid finished his thought.

That made more sense. It seemed unusual for someone his age to have a heart attack. She and Dink were the same age, but he looked a lot older for some reason. Possibly it was due to lack of exercise and poor eating habits. He had the look of a man who didn't often decline a plate of fried food. Maybe life had also not been kind to him. That showed on some people. She'd seen it before. Even his hair had thinned.

"It was nice to see you, Dink. You get some rest." Gray waited for Enid to gather her coat and sweater.

"Don't forget about the car door." Dink was talking to Enid, not Gray. Enid nodded and patted his arm and then bent down and kissed his forehead.

Gray and Enid walked to the elevator and waited.

"What did he mean about the door?" Gray let Enid step in first as the doors slid open.

"The driver's side door is stuck so you have to climb over from the passenger seat."

"Oh." Gray nodded.

"Also, if you give it too much gas going uphill the engine will die." Enid said this earnestly as if they weren't about to drive up the mountain in the dark. It would be uphill almost the entire way.

No wonder Dink called 9-1-1.

Dink's car was a Pontiac, maybe from the nineties. Gray wasn't sure about the age of it, but if she'd seen it parked anywhere she'd have been surprised to find out it was actually road worthy. Following Enid's directions, she climbed into the passenger seat and then shifted one long leg at a time onto the driver's side, almost impaling herself with the gear shift in the process.

She waited for Enid to get settled before she cranked the car.

"Are you hungry?" Gray asked. "Or do you need to pick up anything on the way home?" She figured it might be smart to ask since Enid was afraid to drive in the dark.

Which was actually no surprise given the weakness of the headlights. She'd have sworn one of them pointed straight up at the sky. That wasn't very helpful if you were actually trying to see the road.

"No, thank you."

They were quiet for a moment, with only the loud hum of the heater fan to keep them company.

"Are you back home to visit family?" Enid politely asked.

Enid seemed nervous, and Gray wondered if Enid had ever been alone with a lesbian before. Or maybe that had nothing to do with it. Maybe Gray was just paranoid.

"Sort of." Gray wasn't sure how much she wanted to reveal. "My folks don't live here anymore, but I still have cousins here."

"That's nice." Enid sounded like she meant it.

"So, you don't like to drive?"

"Not this hunk of junk." Enid shook her head. "I've been after Erwin to get us a new car forever. A car with doors that work."

"Well…" Gray looked over at Enid. "I really don't think that's too much to ask."

They both laughed.

❖

There was one flaw with Lucas's plan. Once Gray drove Enid home, she was stranded. She had to call Lucas to give her a ride back to the station to claim her Jeep. A half hour later, she was back at her cabin with a burger and fries she'd picked up at the only fast food spot in Sky Valley, the Black Bear Drive-in. The menu was pretty limited, but a hamburger would hit the spot after the trip to Asheville and back.

Gray ate standing at the sink, staring out the window at the dark woods. A hoot owl called from the darkness and another owl answered. It was an eerie sound.

She thought of building a fire to warm things up, but then she had another thought, a thought that kept circling in her head, especially at night, which also made her feel warm. It was definitely more of a feeling than a thought. It was remembering the kiss from Faith. That kiss was just out there, like a promise, making her want more.

Gray had stupidly not gotten Faith's number, so if she wanted to see Faith again she was going to have to either go to the café, or pay a surprise visit at Faith's house. There would be too much of an audience at the café. Gray checked her phone. It was just now seven o'clock, still early. She grabbed her coat and headed for the door.

The drive up the mountain to Faith's place took only a few minutes. Not nearly enough time to formulate a clever opening line for when Faith met her at the door.

Luck was on her side. When she turned into the driveway, no one was home. Even better. Gray could simply leave a note. She rummaged in the console for something to write on and something to write with. Maybe she should have thought of that before she left the house.

Should she try and think of something clever? No, just stick to the basics.

Hi, Faith,

Would you like to have dinner sometime?

That was about as basic as you could get. Gray signed the note, added her cell number, and folded the paper so that she could wedge it in between the door and the doorjamb right next to the deadbolt. Now, she'd have to wait for the response. But at least she'd taken a step forward and made the next move.

The minute she was back home Gray second-guessed leaving the note.

That was a stupid idea.

She quickly climbed back in the Jeep and returned to Faith's place. It would be much better to stop by sometime when Faith was home. Then she'd get an answer right away, instead of waiting for Faith to respond, or not respond, to a random note left at her door. And what if the note blew away and Faith never got it and Gray waited indefinitely for an answer to an invitation Faith never even received. The whole situation was stupid. Gray had the note in her hand and was about to leave when Faith pulled up.

"Hi." Faith seemed happy about the surprise visit.

"Hello. I stopped by to leave you a note." Gray held it up as proof.

"But the note is in your hand, so you didn't leave it."

"Um, yeah, I dunno, it seemed silly to leave a note, you know, like we're in junior high and I'm shoving a note into your locker or something." That almost sounded worse; now she was rambling.

Don't just stand there staring, say something.

"I want to see you again and find out what happens next." Whoa, that sounded a little too honest. It had sounded much better in her head.

"Dinner would be nice." Faith smiled and held out her hand. "I'd like to find out what happens next too."

"It's got my number on it." Gray handed Faith the note.

"I'll text you mine." Faith slid the note in her jacket pocket. "What night is good for you?"

The air was cold, crisp and dark. Somewhere, not too far away, Gray heard the owl again and wondered if she'd been followed.

"Well, I have to be at this fundraiser on Friday evening, what about Saturday?"

"Is that the event at the fire station?"

"Yes."

"Kayla mentioned it to me. I think she's donating a bunch of pies."

"Everyone is helping out. I think it'll be a nice event."

"Saturday works for me." Faith finally responded to the original question and Gray relaxed, having gotten an answer. "I have a freelance job to finish up by Friday, so that's perfect."

Standing outside in the driveway, it was starting to feel colder.

"Well, I guess I should let you go." Gray took a step toward her Jeep but turned back. "Maybe I'll see you at the fundraiser on Friday?"

"Maybe so." Faith was teasingly vague.

Gray waved then backed out of the drive and onto the main road. She had a date with Faith for Saturday night. A little surge of adrenaline shot through her body. She had a date with Faith. Repeating the thought still didn't make it seem real. No doubt the rest of the week would move at a snail's pace.

Chapter Nineteen

Gray had been wrong about time moving slow, it literally dragged. Most of the week was uneventful, which gave Gray and Lucas time to get the station prepped for the fundraiser.

It was lucky that they'd gotten a head start because Friday, the day of the event, ended up being a very busy day. The station got an emergency call shortly before lunch that a hiker needed assistance. Lucas worried that they might have to carry someone down off the mountain, and if that was the case, they probably needed two more sets of hands. The two volunteers who answered the call were new to Gray. A couple in their early forties who'd moved to the area from Prescot, Arizona. From the look of them they spent a lot of time on the local trails. That's probably why they'd been at the top of the call list for this particular rescue.

Jen and Henry were both very fit and clearly, seasoned hikers. The four-person response team left the parking lot at the trailhead carrying the rescue stretcher. Jen shouldered the med pack, while Gray and Henry carried the litter which basically looked like a flat canoe with handles all the way around at the top so that it could be gripped from any angle. Jen set a quick pace as she led the crew up the switchbacks along the trail ascent. This particular path was a spur trail that crossed the Appalachian Trail at the ridgeline.

The AT ran north and south from Georgia to Maine. Before she'd discovered wildland firefighting, Gray had dreams of hiking all two thousand miles of it, but life had sort of derailed that plan. Maybe she should put that back on her goals list.

The injured hiker was very lucky to have been in an area with cell service when she needed help, and lucky not to be hiking alone. In different circumstances this whole scenario could have turned out much worse, especially if the injured party was a novice hiker or ill prepared for the dropping temperatures. Getting stranded in the mountains in December without the right equipment was no joke.

After forty-five minutes of walking along the rocky, sometimes icy, trail full of switchbacks, Gray could hear the sound of rushing water; the falls were just ahead. Gray and Lucas were wearing orange vests with the fire station insignia on the left pocket so they were easy to spot in the bare, wintry landscape.

"Over here!" a woman called to them from the side of the main trail. "She's over here." The woman motioned them over to the base of the falls.

Another woman was on the ground covered with a down jacket.

"I don't know if it's broken, but she can't stand or walk." The woman was clearly upset. She hugged herself against the cold. She had obviously given her jacket to her injured friend.

Gray and Lucas knelt beside the woman on the ground.

"Hi, I'm Lucas." He introduced himself. "We're with the rescue squad and we're here to help. Can you tell us what happened?"

Both women appeared to be in their mid-twenties, or maybe they were college students from Asheville, but both struck her as not locals and probably not experienced hikers.

"What's your name?" Gray asked the woman on the ground, who grimaced in pain as Lucas explored her ankle. Her friend answered for her.

"I'm Alice and this is Nicole. We were just trying to get a photo closer to the top of the falls when Nicole slipped. She slid straight down into those rocks." Alice pointed toward large boulders at the base of the narrow falls.

"I tried to stand on it, but it hurts." Nicole winced as she tried to shift her position on the damp ground.

Ice had formed along the edges of the falls. And probably the black rocks that looked wet were also icy. A dumb place to snap a photo, thought Gray. Nicole was shivering despite the extra coat.

"It was smart to try to keep her warm." Lucas rocked back from his forward, kneeling position. "I think this needs x-rays. I don't think she should try to walk out. Let's get her loaded so we can carry her down."

Lucas radioed to have an ambulance meet the group at the parking lot.

They eased Nicole onto a warming blanket and then lifted her using the blanket into the stretcher. Jen covered Nicole with a second warming blanket before fastening the straps in place.

Seeing the woman's body on the stretcher, under the thin, reflective fabric caused an unexpected flashback. All Gray could see was the shape of Shane's motionless body beneath the fire shelter. They'd come out of the burnover, climbed out of the shelters into the black—but not everyone, not Shane.

Gray lurched to her feet, swayed, and blinked to erase the memory.

"Hey, are you all right?" Lucas put his hand on her shoulder.

It took a moment for the knot of memory to ease.

"Yeah, I'm fine." But was she? That was a question she found herself asking a lot.

The stages of grief began with dreams, then numbness, memories of the event had become intense and fragmented. Moments came back to her and she wasn't always prepared for them. Gray knew that grief was a well-traveled path, and she wasn't exactly sure how far along it she'd traveled. Or how far yet she had to go.

Gray shouldered Nicole's daypack. Jen returned the jacket to Alice. Nicole moaned from the litter on the ground. Each of the four rescuers took a corner of the litter and began the descent back to the trailhead, with Alice following behind. It wasn't easy to maneuver with the litter on the narrow trail and a few times they were forced off the trail to go around large trees growing too close together.

The ambulance arrived only moments after they returned to the parking lot. And in another few minutes, lights and sirens blazed as the white van headed down the mountain toward Asheville.

This call hadn't been too bad, and yet, Gray couldn't quite shake the flashback. Luckily, Lucas didn't press her to talk about it as they drove back to the station.

Tonight was the volunteer firefighter Christmas fundraiser, which Gray really wasn't in the mood for. But maybe the distraction would be a good thing. It was hard to know for sure.

❖

It took Faith almost an hour of prep time to settle into the book cover project. The request from the art director was for an atmospheric, coastal scene with a rocky shoreline, but not a recognizable location. She decided to do the image on a vellum surfaced illustration board with a palette knife. Using the knife rather than a brush would force her to create something moodier and abstract, with less detail. She mixed several shades of blue, blue-green, and gray along with a dollop of white and pure cerulean blue for highlights.

First, she blocked out the rocky coastline. She was working from a photo on her laptop but changing some of the shapes. Even doing something more abstract, it was best to work from life so that the perspective and lighting was correct. Faith liked to start with something real and then deconstruct it until all that remained was color and mood. A base color, a middle tone, and highlights.

Having worked out the basic structure of the landscape, she took a break to make some hot tea while she waited for it to dry a bit. She'd applied the paint with heavy strokes to create texture that she would use later to increase depth as she built up the environmental elements, especially the rocks on the shoreline. She checked the time on her phone. She'd need to leave this project soon to help Kayla at the Christmas fundraiser. In fact, she should probably stop now and get changed. She sipped the hot tea as she climbed the stairs to her bedroom.

Normally, she wouldn't be concerned with what to wear because she knew she'd be working, but she also expected to see Gray. So, casual but elegant? Perhaps elegant was a bridge too far for a local fire station fundraiser. But a sheer, floral-print scarf with any sweater would raise the bar a little without seeming like overkill, and then a touch of dark red lipstick. Not bad for a workday.

"Don't wait up." Faith turned to Otis before opening the door. She laughed at her own optimism about the evening.

Faith arrived at the café just in time to help Kayla load the van.

"I was about to text you. I was afraid you forgot." Kayla seemed a bit frazzled.

"Forget my best friend in her hour of need? Never." Faith took a tray from Kayla and placed it in a secure shelf inside the van.

"And I'm sure knowing that Gray will be there has nothing to do with it?"

"The thought hadn't even occurred to me." Faith grinned.

"I'll bet."

The parking lot at the fire station was already filling up when they arrived. A huge pine tree had been decorated with white lights at the edge of the parking area. Festive colored lights were strung all along the gutters at the front of the otherwise, boring warehouse. Music seeped into the night air from inside, along with the hum of voices.

Kayla and Faith loaded the pies onto a rolling food dolly and eased across the paved parking area. Faith steered at the front while Kayla pushed. Gray spotted them the minute they crossed the threshold and she waved.

"Hi, thanks so much for bringing all these." Gray surveyed the cart loaded with various fruit and berry pies. "Here, let me help you. We have a table set up over here."

Gray helped steer the cart as they crossed the room. The two big red fire trucks had been moved out of the garage and the party had taken over. There were several tables of handmade goods being sold to benefit the volunteer firefighters, and a live band was playing from a raised stage at one end of the huge, open space. There were also bins set up for the fire department's annual toy drive and food bank. There were booths selling wreaths and a table of handmade Christmas ornaments crafted by the entire third grade class from Sky Valley Elementary School.

Faith watched for any awkward uncomfortableness between Gray and Kayla, but there seemed to be none. Whatever had happened between them had faded, or been dealt with, either directly or indirectly, years earlier. They acted like acquaintances from long ago when they were both very different people, not yet the people they would eventually become.

While they transferred the pies to the table, Faith took a moment to study Gray. She wore a navy uniform shirt, jeans, and boots. Nothing spectacular about the attire itself, but more about how Gray wore the clothes. Faith thought Gray could definitely be on one of those fireman calendars. Actually, Gray could carry all twelve months without any complaints from Faith.

Lucas called to Gray from across the room.

"Let me see what he needs help with and I'll check back."

"No worries." Faith tried to seem nonchalant. "We'll just be here…selling pies."

Gray smiled, then turned and strode toward Lucas who was struggling with a cart of folding chairs.

"Here." Kayla held a tissue out to Faith. "You're drooling."

"Ha-ha, very funny." She swatted Kayla's hand away.

Forty-five minutes later, most of the pies were sold and boxed, waiting to be picked up by patrons on their way home from the event. Faith had slipped out from behind the table in search of drinks. She bumped into Gray near the hot apple cider stand.

"Hey, sorry I got hung up." Gray also bought a hot cider.

"I was taking one of these to Kayla." Faith raised her two steaming cups.

"I'll walk with you."

They wove through the festive crowd, back to the pie table.

"Oh, I forgot to bring you a chair. Hang on." Gray set her drink down and disappeared into the crowd for a moment, before returning with a chair.

"Thank you." Kayla was grateful for the drink and the folding chair.

"I should have brought chairs over sooner." Gray stepped back and retrieved her drink from the table.

"No problem." Kayla tasted her drink. "You two should mingle. I'm happy to just sit and rest."

"Are you sure?" asked Faith.

"Please, go…spread some holiday cheer." Kayla waved them off. "Dan is supposed to be here soon anyway."

Gray and Faith wandered around, looking at different booths and tables, ending up not too far from the bandstand. The band played mostly bluegrass, infused with some modern folk tunes. Faith thought they were quite good. She sipped her cider and swayed gently to the beat of the music.

"I'm really glad you're here." Gray sounded so serious all of a sudden.

"Me too." Faith smiled, and then Gray smiled back.

"We're still on for tomorrow night, right?" Gray's moment of insecurity was endearing.

"Yes, I'm looking forward to it. Where should we go—"

"Don't look now, mistletoe!" Nancy Jo had appeared out of nowhere and was holding a green sprig tied with a red ribbon over Gray's head.

Nancy Jo stood on tiptoes and kissed Gray quickly.

"Nope, still not gay." Nancy Jo shook her head.

Gray laughed.

"Hey, aren't you going to kiss me?" Faith felt left out, but not really.

"Honey, *if* I was gay, you would *not* be my type." Nancy Jo sashayed away from them in search of her next victim.

"It's nice to know that some things never change." Gray finished her cider.

"So, she's been this way all along?" Faith suspected as much.

"Forever."

Gray was in search of a place to toss her empty cup when a young woman approached. Faith didn't recognize her, but she definitely seemed to know Gray.

"I just wanted to say thank you for today." The woman braced herself on crutches. "Can I give you a hug?"

"It's not necessary, but—"

"Hi, I'm Alice." Another woman standing nearby introduced herself to Faith.

"I'm Faith."

"Oh, I'm sorry to interrupt. My name is Nicole." She seemed to suddenly realize that Faith was with Gray. "I fell at the falls earlier today and these guys rescued me."

"Are you sure you should be up on your foot this soon?" Gray seemed genuinely surprised to see Nicole at the event, so Faith forced herself not to feel jealous about the hug.

"It's only a bad sprain. We had planned to stay for one more night before heading home so we thought we'd stop by and support the cause. The folks at the lodge told us about the fundraiser." Nicole seemed in great spirits, despite the crutches and the oversized Velcro-strapped boot on her foot. "Well, I didn't mean to interrupt. Thank you again."

"You're welcome." Gray was bashful from the attention, which made Faith feel a little guilty about the spike of jealousy.

The two women walked away and Gray seemed suddenly restless.

"Would you like another cider?" Gray asked. "I think I might even get a hard cider."

"That sounds great."

"I'll be right back."

Faith turned her attention back to the band. A minute later, Nancy Jo was at her elbow.

"You know, eventually players stop playing." Nancy Jo's tone was serious, in direct contrast to the fake antlers hair band she was wearing. "Don't you want to be there to catch that ball?"

Nancy Jo was gone again before Faith could respond.

"Was she back with the mistletoe?" Gray offered a chilled bottle of hard cider to Faith.

"No, just giving me a hard time about work stuff." Faith wasn't about to share Nancy Jo's comment with Gray.

Gray had watched the exchange between Nancy Jo and Faith from a few strides away. Whatever Nancy Jo had said, Faith's expression had completely shifted. By the time Gray reached her, Faith had regained her holiday cheer.

"Hey, are you guys taking off?" Gray spotted Mark and Christy in the nearby crowd.

"We've got to get the kid home before it gets too late." Christy rested her palms on Hailey's shoulders.

"I could stay out later." Hailey scowled.

"This is Faith Owen." Gray made introductions. Mark and Faith had already met, but not Christy. "This is Mark's wife, Christy; and their daughter, Hailey."

"It's nice to meet you. And nice to see you again, Mark."

Christy gave Mark a questioning look.

"Dan asked Gray and I to cut up a big tree that fell at the house where Faith is staying...Kayla's grandparents' place." Mark explained the connection.

"Oh, right...I remember now." Christy smiled at Faith. "It's nice to meet you."

"Well, we're gonna head out." Mark put his arm around Christy. "We'll catch you later, Gray. Nice to see you again, Faith."

Gray and Faith lingered near the band for a few more minutes, but she was getting a little tired of all the people and noise.

"Would you like to get some fresh air?" Gray motioned with her drink toward the open bay door.

"Sure, that'd be nice."

The air was crisp and cold, in contrast to the heated interior. The light from the large door cast light halfway across the parking lot. Gray angled away from the light, into the cool blue shadows of the trees along the boundary of the lot. She took a deep breath, savoring the smell of pine in the air. The moon was almost full, casting strong shadows on the dry grass at her feet.

"I love the wintertime here." Faith was looking up at the moon.

"Me too." Gray took a swig of her drink. "They're saying we might have a white Christmas this year too."

"Oh, that'd be nice." Faith turned to Gray. "I love the snow, although, I'm not great at driving in it."

They were quiet for a moment, enjoying the night sky.

"I was thinking about tomorrow night. There's this brewery Lucas was telling me about on this side of Asheville. Does that sound good to you?" Gray wasn't sure how much of a big deal to make of their date. Part of her was anxiously looking forward to it and another part of her worried she would blow it because she just wasn't feeling herself.

She didn't want to come off as too serious. It was just dinner. But she also didn't want to not seem serious enough. Wherever they went, it couldn't be a place with any sort of dress code because she didn't have anything other than flannel shirts and jeans.

"They have food and a bar and porch seating under heaters." Faith hadn't responded, so Gray kept talking. "It might be a little trendy, but Lucas said the food is really good."

"That sounds perfect." Faith seemed like she meant it, which made Gray relax.

She was anxious for Saturday to arrive.

Chapter Twenty

Gray turned into the driveway a little before six thirty for their seven o'clock dinner reservation. She knocked and then stepped back from the door. She was too nervous and coached herself to calm down. This was just dinner and a few drinks, nothing more. Don't make a big deal out of it, or you'll freak her out. Gray really hated the idea of appearing needy.

"Hi, let me just grab my coat." A tantalizing hint of Faith's perfume filled the air when she opened the door. It was a delicate and pleasing smell. It made Gray want to take in a slow, deep breath.

Faith was dressed for the weather in a fuzzy sweater with a deep V-neck over a silky camisole, her lovely neck was wrapped in a cashmere scarf of deep green. A beautiful color next to the red highlights in her hair. Her skinny jeans were tucked into tall boots with a low heel.

Gorgeous. Gray immediately began to sweat under her Carhartt jacket. She felt underdressed and out of her depth.

"You look amazing." Gray held the door for her as she nimbly and gracefully climbed into the Jeep.

"Thank you."

There was that smile again, like sunshine, warming the air around them. Gray rounded the Jeep to the driver's side and got in. Just focus on driving.

"So, where are we going?"

"I made a reservation at that place I mentioned, Nocturnal Brewing Company."

"Sounds great."

Gray tried to make small talk on the way down the mountain toward Asheville, but she felt like she wasn't doing very well. Maybe Faith was nervous too, but if she was, she hid it well, which only made Gray feel more so.

The brewery parking lot was almost completely full when they arrived. There was one spot left, half paved but mostly dirt. Luckily, almost any parking spot could work when you had four-wheel drive. Gray parked so that Faith could climb out on the paved side.

Large silver distilling equipment could be seen from the entrance. The area just past that, around the bar, was nice, but super loud and crowded so they opted for the covered porch. Temporary plastic walls had been erected to cover the open spaces around the porch and it was nice and toasty as heat seeped outside from the large open doors of the interior. There were also a couple of heaters at the edges near the areas that were more exposed to the night air.

The menu looked good although she was a little suspicious of all the taco offerings. After living in California for so long and getting to try authentic Mexican food, she had her doubts. But she threw caution to the wind and ordered beef brisket tacos, while Faith got a kale Caesar salad. The waitress brought them each a beer and an appetizer of chips and salsa while they waited for their food.

"The fundraiser seemed like a big success last night." Faith sampled the beer. "This is good. I like it."

They'd each tried a different offering from the draft menu.

"Do you want to try it?" Faith offered her glass to Gray.

"Sure." Gray had gotten a darker ale. She slid her glass toward Faith. "You're welcome to try mine too."

Both were good, but Gray preferred her dry stout to Faith's amber ale.

"I think the event went really well. At least, according to Lucas." Gray circled back to Faith's original comment. "That was the first one I've attended." She sampled a bit of the salsa on a chip.

"This may be a dumb question, but doesn't the county support the fire station? I mean, isn't that why people pay taxes?" asked Faith.

"They do fund the trucks, the building, and two full-time positions. But all the volunteers have to pay for their own gear. And it's expensive."

"I had no idea."

"Yeah, it seems crazy that if people are willing to donate their personal time to be a volunteer firefighter that the least the county could do is pay for their turnout gear." It did sort of make Gray angry, given how demanding and dangerous the job for a volunteer could be.

"Turnout gear?" Faith didn't know what she was talking about.

"That's what we call the protective clothing and the breathing gear."

"But this is a different sort of job from what you were doing in California, right?"

She knew Faith was just trying to get to know her, but Gray desperately wanted to change the subject.

"Yeah, I was a wildland firefighter, so, mostly forest fires in remote areas." Gray didn't want to make it sound exciting or glamorous in hopes that Faith's interest in the topic would go away. "But what about you? You said you're an artist. What's that like?"

"Nice way to change the subject." The corner of Faith's mouth tipped up in a knowing half smile.

"I guess I don't really want to talk about my last job."

Faith could see the mood shift instantly, like a shadow over Gray's whole aura. She sensed Gray might be moments away from shutting down, and the food hadn't even arrived.

"My last job was a disaster, but only because my client had absolutely terrible taste in art." Faith pivoted to a lighter subject. Gray's expression brightened and she visibly relaxed. "You know, they don't tell you this in art school, but everyone thinks they are an art director…trust me when I tell you they aren't."

Gray laughed.

"I don't really know a lot about art, and I promise never to try to art direct."

"Thank you."

The waitress delivered the food order and refreshed the basket of chips. Faith was happy that she'd ordered a salad. Not only was she still trying to climb back from the pile of stress snacks she'd consumed in the past few weeks, but she preferred to eat with a fork on a first date. It was hard to look graceful while eating a taco, although, Gray was so far making it look easy.

"What sort of projects do you work on?"

"Right now, I'm working on a painting for a book jacket." Faith paused to take a sip of her beer. "It's sort of a rush job that came in over the Thanksgiving holiday. I actually need to finish it this week."

"Do you work on a computer?"

"I do most everything on canvas or paper. Then I scan the work to finalize it in Photoshop on the computer. I don't really enjoy digital painting, although, I can do it if I have to."

"I suppose working with materials in the real world feels more... organic?"

It was cute that Gray seemed to genuinely be trying to talk about a subject she didn't know much about.

"Yes, besides, when you work digitally it's a constant fight against perfection."

"How so?"

"Well, working digitally allows you to correct every mistake." Faith paused. "When you work on paper or canvas sometimes things happen that you didn't plan for. Some of those happy accidents make the overall piece stronger. That's the alchemy of creation that you can't quite control. I love that part of the process."

"Here's to a little bit of happy chaos." Gray hoisted her glass.

"To joyful chaos." Faith touched her glass to Gray's and smiled. They were quiet for a few minutes while they both ate.

"So, did you put up a Christmas tree?" Gray had been to her house, but Faith hadn't yet been inside Gray's place. She wondered what it was like.

"No, I have a hard time cutting down a living tree." Gray shook her head. "I suppose that's another side effect from fighting forest fires."

"I guess I didn't think about it that way, but that makes sense." In an attempt to talk about something happy, like Christmas, Faith had still managed to bring the conversation back to Gray's previous work. "I sometimes like to buy a potted tree, a tiny one, and then replant it." That was definitely her plan for this year, especially if she wanted to invite Gray over.

"That's a really nice solution for the holiday." Gray smiled. "Let me know if you need any help planting it."

"Careful, I might take you up on that offer."

Dinner was enjoyable, once Faith stopped asking Gray about her life in California, things lightened up. That didn't mean Faith was going to let the topic go forever, she just hit pause for now. This was their first outing together, there was no pressure to get into anything heavy. She was trying her best to keep things easy and casual, although, it was hard to maintain the cushion of space between them that Gray seemed to prefer. During the drive home, Faith deliberated silently about the best approach to breaching that space.

Gray parked behind her in the driveway and walked her to the door.

"Would you like to come in?"

Gray stood beside her as she searched in her bag for the housekeys. Faith couldn't tell if Gray wanted an invitation or not. It was impossible to read her demeanor at the moment. Gray hung back a little, with her hands in her jacket pockets, as if she were afraid to set them free. She took more time than she needed with the keys to give Gray room to consider the invitation. Faith had forgotten to leave the porch light on, so she only had the ambient light from a lamp in the front window to aid her search.

"Um, I should probably go." Gray bit her lower lip as if she was thinking hard about something. "Lucas is off tomorrow and I'm on call."

"Okay." Faith turned to face Gray. She'd unlocked the door but hadn't opened it. A car drove past. The headlights illuminated the porch for a few seconds. She was glad the porch light was off. She didn't want Gray to feel like she was on display. "I had a really nice time."

"Me too." Gray took a step closer.

When Gray took one hand out of her pocket, Faith reached for it. Seizing the brief opportunity to make physical contact. She'd been thinking about the kiss they'd shared so many days ago and hoping Gray would kiss her again. Gray couldn't exactly make a run for the car if Faith was holding onto her hand. The thought that she'd captured Gray made her smile.

"What's funny?" Gray shifted a little closer.

"I was just thinking it'll be hard for you to escape if I don't let go of your hand."

She looked down at their joined fingers. When she angled her face upward to meet Gray's gaze, Gray had closed what little space remained. Her lips were so close. Faith tilted her mouth up to meet Gray's. She felt Gray's other hand at the small of her back, just under her coat. Faith let go of Gray's hand and draped her arms around Gray's neck as the kiss deepened.

Faith's back was against the door as Gray pressed into her. Her hand was at the back of Gray's head. She filled her fingers with Gray's hair. Gray shifted, changing the angle of the kiss, practically lifting Faith off her feet with her strong hands at Faith's waist. Faith had never been kissed like this. The intensity made her head swim, her insides liquid. She wanted more.

In this moment of acute awareness, Faith felt as if she was recovering her will to love. All the hurts she'd suffered from others, her loss of faith in romance and the human race, faded into the background. With time in Gray's embrace she was certain it would drop away completely. Despite her watchful heart, she found herself letting go.

Gray broke the kiss, but continued to hold her, gently brushing a strand of hair off her cheek and looking at Faith as if she was seeing her for the first time.

Then Gray stepped back, and the absence of her touch forced Faith to rest against the solid firmness of the door.

"Good night, Faith." Gray's words were breathy and a little unsure.

Faith couldn't quite believe Gray would leave her after that kiss. She blinked a few times and tried to regroup.

"Good night, Gray."

And with that, Gray was gone, leaving Faith standing on her stoop in the dark trying to understand what had just happened.

Gray sat in her car, in the dark driveway of her cabin for quite a while before going inside. Faith had asked her to stay. She wasn't even sure what that meant, but Faith made her feel things, and feeling anything real would lead to other feelings that she was striving to keep down, as far from the surface as possible.

She'd wanted to stay.

Part of her wanted to be held, to be comforted, but in order for that to happen she had to let Faith in. Gray knew she'd try to sleep and wake into hurt, on fire, trying to climb higher, just like she'd done so many nights since the big fire. Would having Faith in her arms make that any different? She was almost too afraid to find out, too embarrassed for Faith to see all of it.

Gray knew that experiencing loss was a messy, nonlinear process. If you cared about anyone and lost them, then grief was inescapable. And it wasn't just losing Shane, she'd almost died in that fire herself. Gray knew she was in this until she wasn't, and there was no point dragging Faith down with her.

She climbed out of the driver's seat and trudged up the steps of the cabin. The interior was dark and cold, but she didn't turn on lights or build a fire. She simply crawled into bed with all her clothes on and pulled a pillow over her head. If she was lucky, the world would just go away and leave her be.

CHAPTER TWENTY-ONE

The days that followed the date with Faith were a blur for Gray. Every so often, she thought of calling Faith. She knew she should call Faith, but she hadn't. Faith had texted her Sunday to say she'd enjoyed their dinner out and she'd responded with *me too*. *Lame*. Gray was annoyed with herself.

Gray had initiated the kiss, panicked, and then not followed up. Talk about mixed signals. She felt terrible about it and wanted to make it right somehow.

Gray held her phone in her hand. She'd pulled up Faith's number and was just about to hit call when a code echoed through the fire station—cardiac arrest.

Lucas ran toward the smaller rescue squad truck with the medical gear and gurney in the back. Within seconds, they were in motion, sirens wailing. They could do on-scene triage until the ambulance arrived for transport to the hospital.

It turned out that the holiday season was a magnet for accidents and crisis calls. With each call, Gray resigned herself to feel less, to do the job, to help, but not to feel the pain. At this point, she was convinced that feeling anything meant feeling everything, and she just couldn't deal with it.

Sunday, a sports car nut had wrapped his Porsche around a tree speeding along the Blue Ridge Parkway. Two teams had been dispatched because the incident occurred along the county line. Lucas was off duty. Henry had responded to the call with Gray. Luckily, the only serious injury was to the vehicle and the unlucky maple tree that broke its fall. The driver walked away with a banged-up shoulder, a testament to modern air bags.

Monday, a seventy-year-old man had fallen while trying to hang Christmas lights, breaking his arm and wrist. The fall could have been much worse. The verbal chastise he received from his wife might have been as painful as the fall.

True to Lucas's words during their first meeting, there had been no fires.

This was the first cardiac call Gray had been on, and she was basically on scene to assist Lucas as he was the one with the nursing degree. Gray considered herself not much more than a field medic. Lucas parked on the grass in front of the rundown house. The unpainted boards of the front porch sagged under the weight of a threadbare loveseat. A chicken ran for cover as they drove in. The siren was off but the lights were on when they trotted up the front steps. A woman met them at the door. The scruffy interior of the living room was like a monochromatic soft-focus image to Gray as she focused solely on the man lying on the floor near the sofa. She hoisted the coffee table aside to make room for Lucas to work. A stack of magazines slid off, along with an ashtray.

"He just fell over all at once, with no warning." His wife hovered and filled in details as they worked. She fisted the front of her apron nervously, her fingers aged and red from years of labor.

The patient was in his late sixties, with untreated diabetes, high blood pressure, and a history of heart trouble. Not good.

Gray ripped his shirt open and started compressions. Lucas placed the defib pads on the man's chest and started an IV in his arm. Beside them, his wife prayed softly as Lucas started the drugs.

"Charged." Lucas was calm in a crisis. It was great to work with someone who knew what they were doing.

Gray rocked back on her heels. Lucas defibbed once, twice, and a third time. No response. He checked the man's vitals one last time.

Lucas shook his head, his mouth a thin, grim line.

The man's wife dropped to her knees beside her unmoving husband and sobbed. Gray was nearer to her and without feeling sadness herself, put her hand on the woman's shoulder as some small form of support, a simple gesture to say *you aren't alone*. The woman put her head on Gray's shoulder and cried.

There was nothing Gray could really say to comfort the woman, whom she didn't know. Sometimes the only thing to do was just be there, be still, and sit with someone.

Gray had a strange remote feeling about the entire scene. She had witnessed this woman's darkest hour and was untouched by it beyond polite sympathy. What was wrong with her? Would she ever be herself again?

"Gray, find out if there's someone we can call for her." Lucas spoke softly and then got to his feet.

Gray nodded. Lucas walked away from the scene and quietly spoke into his radio. After calling the woman's sister to come over, Gray waited outside by the truck until the coroner arrived. This family's holiday had now been ruined forever. Every year, Christmas would remind them of this tragic loss.

An hour later, Gray was back at the station, pacing back and forth in the parking lot out front, not really wanting to be alone with what had just happened. She dialed Faith's number and waited for her to pick up. The call went to voice mail.

"Hey, I'm sorry I haven't called." Gray took a breath. "It's been sort of a crazy day." She wanted to say, today was especially rough and it would be nice to see you. But she didn't want to say that much to a recording. "Give me a ring later if you get a chance."

Gray clicked off and slid her phone into her pocket.

"I'm going to lock up." Lucas called to her from the office door. "Do you need anything from inside?"

"No, I'm good." It was cold so she already had her jacket on and her keys were in her pocket.

Lucas walked in her direction after locking the door.

"Are you okay?"

"Yeah, I'm fine." She gave her standard response.

"Sometimes we can't bring them back." Lucas was thoughtful. "It was just his time, you know."

Gray nodded. She felt like she should say more or feel more, but she was literally numb.

"Have a good night. I'll see you tomorrow." He turned toward his truck.

She waved good-bye and climbed into her Jeep.

Before she put it in drive, her phone rang. She was happy that Faith had returned her call so quickly, and for a moment, her mood buoyed, but it wasn't Faith.

"Hey, Mark, what's up?"

"Hi, Gray. I'm hoping you can do me a favor."

"Sure."

"Christy and I are both stuck at work, and I was wondering if you could pick Hailey up. She's still at school." Mark sounded stressed.

"She's there kinda late." Gray remembered when the school day ended at three o'clock. It was well past four thirty.

"She had detention today after school."

"Oh."

"Yeah." Maybe he wasn't stressed, maybe he was annoyed.

"No problem, Mark." She put the Jeep in gear, turned the wheel with one hand. "I'm leaving the station now. I'll go pick her up. Just text me when you want me to drive her home."

"Or we can come by your place and pick her up." There was a rustling sound on the other end of the phone and loud voices in the background, possibly some hammering. He was obviously at a job site. "She thinks she can be home by herself, but I don't think that's such a good idea at the moment."

"I understand. It's not a problem, really."

"Thanks, I owe you one. I'll let the school know you're coming to pick her up."

Mark clicked off. Five minutes later, Gray turned into the half-circle drive in front of the main building. The junior high and high school were combined on one campus. Gray had not been back to this place since graduation, and driving past the gymnasium and the ball field brought back a flood of memories, not all of them bad. She'd had some good times in high school and the thought of it made her smile.

Hailey was sitting on the curb outside the office when she pulled up. Hailey stood up and approached the Jeep.

"Hi." Gray spoke to Hailey through the open passenger window. "Your dad asked me to pick you up. He and your mom are stuck at work."

Hailey didn't say anything. She just got in the car. She was wearing her usual jacket with the hood up and a baseball cap under the hood, but no headphones this time.

"Are you hungry?" Gray waited for an answer, but Hailey didn't respond right away. "We could get some food before we go to my place." Gray paused. "Because, in all honesty, there's not much food there."

"Sure."

This was going to be fun. An evening of single syllable responses. Yay. This long day was feeling even longer, but Gray tried to rally. At least helping Mark and Christy out was a distraction from going home and thinking too much.

❖

They drove past the pizza place, but it was packed, with a line out the door. The only other appealing local option was the café. Maybe Faith would be working. Maybe that's why she hadn't picked up when Gray phoned earlier. It would be nice to see her. And having Hailey in tow would keep everything nice and casual.

The café was moderately busy when they walked in. Nancy Jo waved them to an open booth near the back. She didn't see Faith. Gray was a little disappointed, but maybe this was for the best since she had a non-communicative preteen with her.

"Y'all want something to drink while you look over the menu?" Nancy Jo set two folded menus on the table.

"I'll take a sweet tea." Gray motioned toward Hailey.

"I'll have a Sprite."

Nancy Jo nodded and left them to make dinner decisions. Gray had only had breakfast at the café and wasn't familiar with the dinner menu, so it took a few minutes to decide. She was surprised when Kayla came back to take their order.

"Hi, Hailey...hello, Gray." Kayla had a small spiral notebook in her hand. "Nancy Jo got swamped so I thought I'd get your order started."

"Hi." Gray set the menu aside. "It was really nice of you to donate those pies to the fundraiser."

"It was my pleasure." Kayla smiled. "Also, Faith isn't working tonight, in case you were wondering. She had some art project to finish."

Small town, right.

Everyone knew what everyone was up to, and she was sure Faith had confided things to Kayla about their date. Now she felt a bit exposed by the not calling thing. It was also a separate sort of thing to be talking to Kayla about her friend Faith in general. Gray had known Kayla in a different life, when she was a different person. It was almost as if they didn't know each other at all any longer, as if Kayla was a near stranger. Except they weren't strangers, and yet, they weren't really friends either. They simply had the connection of their long-ago youth in Sky Valley.

"Yeah, she mentioned something about a freelance job." Gray didn't want to let on that she hadn't actually talked to Faith in a few days.

Gray ordered the fried chicken dinner with sides, and Hailey opted for a burger. After Kayla took the order, they were silent for a few minutes, just awkwardly looking at the condiments or out the window.

"Is Faith your girlfriend?"

"Um." Gray was surprised that Hailey had even been paying attention enough to ask. Maybe the disinterested teen thing was all an act, although, it didn't feel that way. "No, we're just friends." That didn't seem accurate. "I mean, we've only been on one actual date, so I don't think I can call her my girlfriend."

"She's really pretty."

Gray was reminded that Hailey and Faith met briefly at the fundraiser.

"Yes, she is."

Nancy Jo interrupted them with food.

"Here ya go. Y'all let me know if you need anything else." She lightly touched Hailey's shoulder. "Enjoy."

Hailey applied a generous helping of ketchup to both the burger and her fries.

"Do you have a girlfriend?" Gray took a guess. She figured it was only fair that she got to ask the same question, plus, maybe this would be the ice breaker she'd been looking for. Not that she thought Hailey was old enough to have a girlfriend necessarily, but definitely old enough to have a serious crush on someone. And old enough to be figuring out if she was more interested in boys or girls.

"No." Hailey shook her head. "I liked this one girl, but it didn't really go anywhere." Hailey nibbled a fry as she regarded Gray from across the table. "Besides, Mom and Dad won't let me date until I'm sixteen anyway." She didn't seem happy about that last part.

"Dating is hard. Maybe it's better to wait a few years anyway… you'll know yourself better and know more what to look for in a person." Gray was dying to ask more. She wondered how different things were for gay teens in Sky Valley now. "Do kids at school give you a hard time for…you know, liking girls."

Haley shrugged. "Some people are jerks, no matter who you like."

"That's very true."

The cabin was dark and cold when they arrived. Gray rubbed her hands together to warm them. The days were short and still she kept forgetting to leave a light on. She switched on the front porch light and a lamp near the sofa. Hailey stood near the door with her hands in her jacket pockets. The glimpse of her standing there stopped Gray in her tracks. With her short hair, jeans, boots, and lined denim jacket, Hailey looked like a ghost of Gray from the past. Hailey's hair wasn't quite as dark as Gray's, but everything else about this kid felt familiar. Gray fought the urge to cross the room and give Hailey a hug. Based on her own past, she figured this kid needed one.

"Is something wrong?"

"No." She realized she'd been staring.

Gray took her jacket off and hung it on a brass hook near the door.

"Hey, would you mind starting a fire while I go put on a fresh shirt?" She still had her uniform on from a very long day. She pointed toward the fireplace. "There's kindling in that bucket and matches on the mantel."

"Sure." Hailey's expression brightened. She wondered if Hailey liked feeling useful as much as she did.

Gray paused for a minute to turn up the thermostat on the ancient wall heater. This unit was too old to leave running during the day while she was away. If being a firefighter had taught her anything it was that old heaters weren't to be trusted. The cool air gave her chill bumps when she took off her shirt and tossed it in a hamper in the corner. Thoughts of kneeling on the carpet in that ramshackle house made her take off her jeans too. Maybe she'd just take a five-minute shower and wash the entire day away.

Several moments later, Gray emerged from the back bedroom in fresh clothes, towel drying her hair. Hailey was standing like a small statue in front of the hearth. She stared at the huge fire as if she couldn't quite gain focus. Orange light danced around the room and across Hailey's face.

An ember popped loudly and sprang free of the flames onto the hardwood floor. Gray quickly scuffed the ember back into the fireplace with the side of her shoe. She'd put on a pair of leather house shoes because the floor was cold.

"Hey, that's a little too big." Gray motioned for Hailey to step back. She used an iron poker beside the bucket of kindling to break up the stack of burning wood. Separately, each piece would burn at medium heat. Together they were an inferno. She placed the screen in front of the fire and dusted her hands.

Hailey still stared blankly at the flames as if she were in a trance.

"You have to be careful with fire." Gray touched her shoulder, keeping contact until Hailey looked up at her. "I know fire can be exciting, but it can get away from you quickly. You know that, right?"

Hailey nodded. "I'm sorry."

"Don't build such a big fire that it could easily edge out into the room." Gray paused for emphasis. "And always replace the screen." She waited for her to respond. "Hailey, do you hear what I'm saying?"

"Sure."

Hailey nodded, but Gray wasn't quite convinced that her lecture on fire safety had sunk in. People who had no experience with fire trauma were far too cavalier for Gray's liking.

CHAPTER TWENTY-TWO

Faith finished washing the last brush and set it aside to dry, careful not to fray the bristles. The final illustration sat on the small, desktop easel. The acrylic would dry quickly, and she'd be able to photograph it in a few hours and import it into Photoshop for last-minute adjustments before sending it off to the art director.

She'd left her phone in the bedroom while she worked. When she checked the screen she saw that she'd missed a call from Gray. *Finally.* She was beginning to think she'd completely misread the situation with Gray.

Faith listened to the voice mail. Gray sounded sad. Or stressed. Maybe something had happened with work and that's why she hadn't called. Faith considered calling back, but then she had a better idea. Maybe she'd drive over and surprise Gray. She'd made a Christmas wreath from greenery she'd picked up in the yard and had planned to leave it on Gray's porch anyway. Delivering it in person sounded much more appealing.

Faith tugged on her coat and opened the door. She had to hold it open for Otis, who sauntered in, rubbing her leg as he passed.

"Thank you." She frowned. Faith was wearing leggings that now were covered with white fur. Cats had no respect for static cling or dark leggings for that matter. She closed the front door and searched in the bathroom for the garment roller.

On her second attempt to depart she actually made it out the door. She was excited to see that Gray's Jeep was in the driveway when she turned it. She'd have left the wreath either way, but she really wanted to see Gray. Their date had left her feeling a bit unmoored and unsure and she couldn't help thinking that seeing Gray would put her mind at ease.

She knocked and then heard voices. Oh no, Gray had company. She panicked.

"Hi." Gray stood in the doorway, one hand still on the door.

Before she could bolt, Gray swung the door open. She relaxed when she realized the other voice she'd heard was Hailey's.

"Hello." Faith smiled. "Sorry to just pop by without calling."

"I'm glad you did." Gray stepped to one side of the entry. "Please, come in. Hailey is hanging out for a little while until her parents come to pick her up."

"Hi, Hailey." She gave a small wave. "Oh, this is for you." She held the wreath out to Gray.

"Thanks." Gray accepted it as if she wasn't quite sure what to do with it next.

"It's for your door," Faith explained. "You mentioned you weren't going to get a Christmas tree and so I made this for you. And just so you know, there were no trees harmed in the making of this wreath."

"What a relief." Gray smiled. Her response was playful.

"Yeah, I picked all the limbs up from the edge of my yard and upcycled them into a Christmas wreath." Faith felt a little silly that she couldn't stop herself from explaining more, but she was nervous. She always made jokes when she was nervous. Could spruce bows even be upcycled? Or was that only for vintage jeans?

"The plaid flannel bow is a nice touch."

"Well, I wanted it to have a little personal connection…to you." She became hyper aware that she and Gray were having a moment while Hailey looked on. Faith glanced over, aware that Hailey had been watching them intently from the minute she stepped across the threshold.

"You know, I think there's even still a nail in the door from back when my mom used to hang up a wreath each year." Gray returned to the door.

It only took a few seconds for her to locate the nail in the dim glow of the porch light. She hung the wreath then stepped back, then adjusted it once before closing the door.

"It looks great, thank you." Gray smiled.

The house was cool. Faith was still wearing her coat. She hugged herself and moved closer to the fireplace.

"Sorry, it hasn't quite warmed up in here yet." Gray shoved her hands in her pockets. She stood a few feet away, facing Faith. Hailey was on the couch. "We just got here. I took a quick shower." Gray seemed nervous as she ran her fingers through her still-damp hair.

It made Faith feel better that she might not be the only one who was nervous.

Someone knocked at the door. Faith had been hoping to find Gray at home, but this was turning into a real gathering. Maybe this was her cue to leave.

"Hi, Christy. Do you want to come in?" A draft swept past Gray standing in the open door.

"I should probably get going." Christy stepped inside, but the door was still ajar. "I'm sure Hailey has homework and I need to figure out something for dinner."

"Gray and I already ate." Hailey was at her mom's side. Christy brushed her fingers through Hailey's hair like a doting parent, which seemed to annoy Hailey a little.

"You didn't have to do that." Christy spoke to Gray.

"It was no big deal. I was hungry too." Gray seemed to remember Faith was there. "You remember, Faith?"

"Oh, yes. Hello, it's nice to see you again."

Christy seemed like a really sweet person.

"It's nice to see you too." Faith was finally starting to warm up standing by the fire.

"You should get your backpack so we can get home. Your dad is probably already there wondering where we are." Christy was in full *mom* mode.

"I left it in Gray's Jeep." Hailey started out the door.

"I'll just walk them out and I'll be right back."

Faith nodded. She was happy to be left alone in the house for a few minutes so that she could look around and get a feel for the place. The cabin was rustic, with dark walls, the plaster was a lighter color and visible between each beam. The space was warmly appointed. The ceiling in this main room was vaulted with large exposed rafters.

The sofa was an old leather Chesterfield littered with cushions and quilted throws. This looked like a sofa with a history, and probably many stories to tell. There were a few books on the coffee table and an old clock on the mantel with Roman numerals. A set of wooden skis were mounted to the wall opposite the rock fireplace. There was one painting of a forest scene. It was a pleasant composition, nothing extraordinary, but nice. The interior felt like a movie set from the forties. But it didn't feel dated, it was tastefully vintage, like an historic mountain lodge. The main room wasn't packed with furniture. Only the sofa and one rocking chair nearer the fireplace. There was a sectional rug covering the floor between the living room and the kitchen. She didn't venture into the kitchen because she didn't want Gray to catch her being nosy.

A small sofa table with one lamp also held a display of glass figurines of deer, a fawn, and a small group of rabbits. These must have belonged to someone else; they didn't fit with her impression of Gray.

The door opened and Gray quickly closed it behind her. She'd gone out without a jacket. She rubbed her hands together and blew on them.

"Sorry about that." Gray stood with her back to the fire to warm up.

"No problem." Faith smiled. "Your cabin is very cozy."

"Thanks." Gray looked around the room. "I suppose it's a little sparse compared to your place."

"Actually, I think it feels just right." Faith had hoped maybe they could grab dinner together, but now she knew Gray had already eaten. "I should go. I haven't eaten and hearing Christy talk about it reminds me that I'm hungry."

"Um, I could make something if you'd like to stay." Gray's expression was hopeful.

"Really? You cook?"

"Well, I wouldn't go that far." Gray smiled. "Let me see what I have."

Faith followed Gray to the kitchen, which had not been updated probably since the fifties. A bright yellow Formica-topped table, complete with vinyl chairs, sat along one wall of the eat-in kitchen.

The table and chairs were still in good shape. Someone had taken good care of this place.

Gray leaned into the open fridge as if she expected someone to have stocked it. The minute she glanced inside the mostly empty refrigerator reminded her that this was exactly why she and Hailey had stopped at the café. But she didn't want Faith to leave.

"Uh, I have eggs...and toast?" Gray looked at Faith.

"Breakfast for dinner?"

"Yes?" Gray tried to read Faith's expression.

"That actually sounds really good. I've been working on this project all day and haven't eaten much."

"Have a seat." She slid a chair out for Faith. "Is scrambled okay?"

"Yes, thank you." Faith sat down but didn't seem very relaxed. "Are you sure I can't help."

"Well, I suppose you could make the toast if you want to, while I do the eggs."

Faith seemed to like that plan. Gray handed over the butter and a half a loaf of wheat bread from the fridge. Then she whisked two eggs with a fork while she waited for the skillet to warm over the gas burner. It felt oddly normal to be cooking side-by-side with Faith.

Everything was ready in a few minutes. Gray scooped the eggs onto a plate beside two pieces of buttered toast.

"I have a little strawberry jam." She held up a jar.

"Perfect."

"What about a beverage?" Gray paused as she scanned the selection on hand. "I have hard apple cider, beer, one Coke...or water."

"Hmm, water sounds good."

Gray felt a little bad about her hosting skills. Was this the lamest meal ever?

"I'm sorry I didn't have more to offer you."

"You know, this actually suits me very well." Faith was holding the plate.

Gray poured two glasses of cold water from a mason jar and tipped her head toward the living room.

"Do you want to eat in by the fire where it's warmer?"

"Yes, thanks."

Gray pulled a couple of large cushions from the couch and placed them on the floor near the fire. She held Faith's food until she got settled. Faith took several bites and Gray stared at the fire so as not to stare at Faith while she was eating.

"It's sweet how much Hailey admires you."

"What do you mean?" Faith's comment surprised her.

"She hangs on your every word and her eyes follow you. I noticed it the other night at the fundraiser and again tonight." Faith paused. "You're clearly her hero. It's really sweet."

"I guess I hadn't noticed."

"It's probably harder for you to see it since you're on the receiving end." Faith touched her arm. "I hope I didn't make you feel uncomfortable by mentioning it."

"No, not at all." But if Hailey did look up to her, then she felt even more responsible for trying to help out. Maybe she could be a positive influence for the kid.

"That was great, thank you." Faith set the empty plate on the coffee table and rotated again to face the fire. She pulled her knees to her chest and sipped the water.

They were quiet for a few minutes as they both basked in the glow of the warm flames.

"I'm sorry I didn't call you sooner, you know, after our date." Gray felt like she owed Faith an apology.

"It's all right. I'm sure you've been busy."

"Work has been a little crazy." Gray hesitated, but then decided to share more. "We actually lost a patient today." She stared at the flames, not looking at Faith.

"I'm so sorry." Faith's hand was on her shoulder. "Was it someone you knew?"

Gray shook her head.

"No." She tried to organize her thoughts about it. "It's weird to think that I was with this guy when he passed, but it didn't really affect me." She thought about it more. "Shouldn't I have felt something?"

Faith didn't respond. Maybe there was nothing to say. For some reason, it could have been the sensation of Faith's touch, maybe it was the warmth of the room and the intimacy of sitting so close, but Gray kept talking.

"I lost a friend in California." She took a swig of water as if her throat was suddenly parched. "That's why I came back to Sky Valley."

Faith watched Gray's face, hoping for clues about what Gray was thinking.

"I'm sorry." She'd already said that but wasn't sure how else to respond. Faith studied Gray's profile. It seemed like their conversation had just taken a turn. Faith was getting a glimpse behind the curtain and was afraid to say too much. She wanted Gray to keep talking. She waited. Faith let her hand drift down and she began to make small circles on Gray's back.

"He and I were on a helitack crew together." Gray seemed lost in thought.

"Did he...was he killed in a fire?"

Gray nodded.

"I don't know why I'm telling you this." Gray turned to face her. Her eyes were damp, with flecks of orange from the reflected flames nearby. "I think what happened today has me thinking about things."

"It's good to talk about it." Faith scooted closer and draped her arm around Gray's shoulders. "I'm glad you're talking to me about it. I want to know about your life, Gray."

They were close now. If Gray set down her glass she could simply rotate and draw Faith into her arms. There was a split second when Faith thought that was exactly what was about to happen. But Gray was holding the glass with both hands as if she needed something to grab onto.

An alarm sounded and broke the spell. Gray reached for her cell phone.

"That was a 9-1-1 alert." Gray stood up. "I should respond to this."

"Of course." Faith got up also. The mood between them had completely shifted.

"It's a motorcycle accident not too far from here." Gray looked up from her phone, her gaze distant. "I'm sorry to rush you, but I should go."

"I understand." Faith wasn't sure if Gray had to go, or simply wanted an excuse to escape. But either way, their cozy night was at an abrupt end.

"I'm sorry to jump up and leave." Gray was already tugging on her jacket. Then she handed Faith hers from where she'd left it on the sofa. "I'll give you a call tomorrow."

"Sure." Faith put on her jacket and then gave Gray a hug.

Gray was stiff in her arms, but Faith didn't care. She wanted Gray to know she cared.

"Be safe out there." Faith followed Gray down the steps.

"It was nice to see you, Faith." Gray briefly glanced back before she climbed in her Jeep.

And then she was gone. Faith stood for a moment on the steps of the cabin. Her breath came out in white wisps in the cold air. She looked up, admiring the exceeding brightness of the winter moon. The shadows of the forest at the edge of the yard were as dark as ravens. She shivered and pulled the front of her coat tighter before zipping it up.

Gray had moved closer to her tonight. She was sure of it.

Faith smiled as she got into her car.

CHAPTER TWENTY-THREE

Gray was splitting wood at the side of the cabin. She glanced up just as Hailey rode up on her mountain bike. Gray sank the ax into the stump she'd been using to split the logs into pieces and waved.

"Hi, Hailey."

"Hey."

"What are you up to?" It was Christmas Eve, a clear and crisp day.

"Just out for a ride. There's a trail, a cut-through from down below the hill." Hailey pointed toward the woods across the road. There was mud splattered all up her jeans from the trail. "It was a little slick in places, but not bad."

"That's a nice bike."

"I got it for Christmas last year."

Gray remembered the Christmas she'd gotten her first bike. One of the best Christmases on record. This bike looked more like an upgrade than someone's first bike.

"What are you folks up to today?"

Hailey shrugged. Gray wanted to be better friends with Hailey. No one said this to her, but she couldn't help thinking that Hailey might be feeling isolated. She had a lonesome air about her even when she was doing something that she clearly enjoyed.

"Want to help me stack some of this wood on the porch?" It'd be nice not to have to trek all the way out to the woodpile first thing in the morning to start a fire.

Hailey worked alongside Gray to pile some of the small pieces next to the wall, under the window, on the porch. The rest they stacked on the main woodpile at the side of the cabin.

"Do you want to come in and warm up before you ride farther?"

"Sure."

Man, it was hard to get this kid to talk.

Gray opened a small bottled Coke for each of them and handed one to Hailey. Something about the small bottled Cokes reminded her of kiddom. They sat on opposite ends of the couch watching the fire.

"Do you ever put salted peanuts in your soda?" Gray looked over at Hailey.

"No."

"Really?" Kids just didn't know what was good anymore. Gray smiled at herself. She sounded like she was a hundred years old. "The salt and the sweetness of the Coke…and the fizz…it's a pretty good combo. You should try it."

They were quiet for a minute.

"Did you decide whether you're going back to California or not?"

"I haven't really decided yet. But I'm not going any time soon." Gray wondered if that was partly why Hailey was reluctant to open up. Why open up to someone who was going to leave.

"Could I come down to the fire station sometime and see the engines?"

"Sure, anytime." Gray would be happy to show Hailey around. Especially if she could build Hailey's interest in something larger than herself. Having a focus had helped Gray.

"I better go." Hailey set the empty Coke bottle on the small table near the sofa. "Mom will wonder where I am."

"Plus, it's Christmas Eve. You don't want to miss out on that."

For some reason, Hailey didn't seem as excited as a kid should about Christmas.

"What's the matter? Are you afraid Santa won't find you or something?" Gray lightly punched Hailey's shoulder in an attempt to lighten her mood.

"I never get what I want for Christmas."

"You got that bike out there."

"Yeah, that was great, but Mom always gets me these clothes that I don't want to wear."

Gray remembered those days well. The struggle to be the person she wanted to be started by being allowed to dress the way she felt most comfortable. And that was basically in anything but a dress. Getting her mom to let her shop in the boy's department was a huge ordeal.

"It's frustrating isn't it? Clothes shouldn't have a gender, they should just be treated as clothes." Gray could see that she'd guessed right. Hailey looked up, her expression softened. "People should be able to wear what they want."

"Yeah, that's how I feel."

Gray followed Hailey out onto the porch. Hailey started down the steps toward her bike, but then trotted back up the stairs and fell into Gray, wrapping her arms around Gray's waist. Gray hugged her back.

"It's going to be okay, Hailey. Just give your folks time to catch up." She spoke softly into Hailey's hair.

Hailey squeezed tightly for another minute before letting go. She turned abruptly and ran down the steps. Gray suspected she was crying but didn't want Gray to see.

"Have a nice ride." Gray waved from the porch.

Hailey looked back and waved once she was at the trailhead on the other side of the road. And then she was gone, swallowed up by the thick grove of trees.

CHAPTER TWENTY-FOUR

Gray served herself the last of the coffee from the ancient Mr. Coffee machine. It was a little eerie to be at the station by herself on Christmas day, but it was more important for her to cover things so that Lucas could be with his family. She knew Christmas was a much more demanding holiday for people with kids, and Lucas had three.

Speaking of kids, the only call she'd had all day was for an eight-year-old who had tried to turn his slip and slide in the backyard to a ski slope. The temps had hovered just below freezing all day, and although Sky Valley hadn't gotten snow yet, hosing down the long plastic slide turned it to ice fast. The kid learned quickly that skis didn't work so well on ice. He had a broken arm to show for his newfound knowledge.

Mark and Christy had invited her to spend the day with them. They were having Christmas lunch with Christy's parents, who Gray didn't really know. She'd learned from past years that Christmas with folks you didn't know so well sometimes made you feel lonelier. Especially if the other people gathered had a real connection.

No, she didn't feel like making small talk today. It would have been nice to be there for Hailey, but still, she thought she'd made the right decision.

The office phone rang. She abandoned her post at the front window to grab it.

"Hello, Sky Valley Fire Station."

"Hi, Gray. Merry Christmas. How's it going?"

"Hey, Lucas. It's a slow day, only one call so far." She dropped to a nearby rolling chair. "Merry Christmas, by the way. How's your day going?"

"Oh, you know, chaos and crying." The kids were yelling in the background. "I think everyone has had way too much sugar at this point."

Gray tried not to laugh.

"Listen, I got a call for assistance from Lucille Cavney. Actually, not from her directly. It came from the 9-1-1 operator."

"Why didn't they call the station? I'm sorry they bothered you on your day off." Gray was confused about why she hadn't received a code on the radio.

"Well, Lucille is gettin' up there in years and didn't remember that we've got so many folks in the county now that you have to dial the area code and the phone number to get someone. She couldn't figure out how to call the station directly so she called 9-1-1 and asked the operator to get a message to me." He sounded amused. "The poor operator had no idea who Lucas was but finally put two and two together. She thought maybe Lucille and I were family so she just rang me directly. Anyway, to make a long story short, can you go out to her house and check on her?"

"Sure thing. Just text me her address."

"She said her well pump isn't working and it's probably a fuse. This happened a few months ago and I was able to just flip the breaker to get it working. Hopefully, that's all it is because if it's really dead she won't be able to get anyone out to fix it with the holiday and all."

"I'm sure I can figure it out."

"Great. I'd rather not leave an elderly person without running water." There was a loud bang in the background immediately following by crying. "Well, that's the Bat-Signal...I gotta go."

"Good luck."

She grabbed her coat and locked the front door. This sort of house call didn't seem to warrant taking one of the trucks so she just headed toward her Jeep. The text from Lucas with the address came through as she climbed into the driver's seat.

Lucille Cavney lived on the east side of town. If she'd searched her memory banks Gray probably could have called up the address herself. Mrs. Cavney taught fourth grade math for years in Sky Valley. Every kid who'd attended public school for decades developed math skills under her astute tutelage. Except for Gray. She'd barely passed math at any grade level. Numbers just weren't her thing. She was lucky to discover work in the outdoors, where very little math was required.

The drive out to the Cavney place took about fifteen minutes. The houses along the winding two-lane road hadn't changed much. Most of the homes had been built in the teens, set back from the road the way places used to be when folks had actual front yards. Each residence had plenty of space from its neighbor. Gray wondered how many of these places were still inhabited by the original owners. Some seemed to have fallen into disrepair, which indicated that the original, now elderly owners were still there.

Mrs. Cavney seemed like she was old back when Gray was in grade school, so she must be in her eighties or nineties now. At the time, she'd probably only been in her fifties, but to a kid, every adult is old.

The house was the way she remembered it. The yard and landscaping looked a bit scruffy from neglect, and the two-story frame house could use a fresh coat of paint. But nothing looked terrible. The place just had that homey, lived-in look.

Gray knocked on the door. No one answered, so after a moment, she knocked again a little louder. Eventually, she heard someone's steps coming toward the door. The woman who answered had to be close to ninety.

"Can I help you?" She spoke to Gray through the screen door.

"Mrs. Cavney, Lucas said you needed some help with your well pump. He couldn't come because he's off today. He asked me to come instead." She opened her jacket to reveal the fire squad insignia patch on her dark blue uniform shirt. "I work at the station with Lucas."

"What's your name, young man?" Mrs. Cavney seemed suspicious.

"It's me, Mrs. Cavney, Grayson Reeves. Um, Marie Reeves. You taught me math in fourth grade. I go by Gray now."

Mrs. Cavney pushed the screen door open and squinted up at Gray as she adjusted her spectacles. She was always a short woman and now that she was stooped, she'd shrunk further.

"Well, I'm sorry, sweetie, you've cut your hair and I didn't recognize you. You'll have to forgive an old woman." She turned and motioned for Gray to follow her. "The pumphouse is out back."

"Maybe we should check the breaker box first?"

"All right then." Mrs. Cavney's glasses had fogged up because of how warm the house was. She cleaned them with the hem of her sweater and then put them back on. "The box is just outside the back door here, on the porch."

Gray stepped around her and glanced from side to side until she located the box. There was a lot of stuff piled on the partially covered back porch so it took a moment for her to find it. Sure enough the switch marked "pump" was in the off position. It must have gotten overloaded. It was possible that the entire breaker box needed to be updated. If the faded, masking tape labeling system was any indication, this box had been here for a while.

"Let's go inside and see if the water comes back on."

Mrs. Cavney had been watching from the door. Gray followed her inside to the kitchen sink. Gray turned on the water. Nothing happened at first, then it sputtered as the air cleared the line. After several seconds the water was running smoothly.

"Oh, what a relief. I don't know what I'd have done without water."

Gray's heart went out to her, elderly and living alone in this big old house.

"Well, you call me if you have any more trouble with it, okay?" Gray had a small spiral-bound notebook in her pocket. She took it out and wrote her contact info down. "Here's my name and phone number in case you need any more help. Don't hesitate to call."

"Thank you, darlin.' I do appreciate it." Mrs. Cavney carried a tea kettle to the sink. "Won't you stay and have a cup of tea with me before you run off?"

Gray looked around the cozy, but lonesome kitchen.

"Yes, ma'am, that'd be very nice."

"Now you sit down right there and we'll have us a nice chat while we wait on this kettle to heat up." Mrs. Cavney pointed to the tiny kitchenette.

Gray took off her jacket, hung it on the back of the chair and sat down across from Mrs. Cavney, who regarded her with a serious expression.

"Now, Grayson, tell me…does your mama not mind you dressing like a boy?"

Gray would have laughed, except that Mrs. Cavney's gaze was so intense, as if Gray was a tiny creature she was studying under a microscope. She was unsure if the question was rooted in small-town nosiness or simply the unfiltered honesty of age. Either way, there was no malice in the elderly woman's question.

"My mom passed away several years ago." She ignored the other part of the question. How would she explain that anyway?

"Oh dear, I'm so sorry to hear that. Now that you say it, I think I already knew that. Forgive my poor memory." The kettle whistled and she got up to fill two teacups. "Do you need sweetener, hon?"

Gray shook her head and jumped up to help deliver the teacups when she saw how much Mrs. Cavney's hands were shaking.

"Thank you. I'm just not as steady as I used to be." She settled back in her chair and Gray set one of the cups in front of her.

These were the sort of teacups her mother would have loved. Painted with a mix of flowers and tiny blue birds.

"My mother would have liked these." Gray held the cup up to examine the details.

"My sister brought them back to me from England years ago. Now there's no one to leave them to." Her gaze was far off for a moment. "Maybe you'd like to have them."

"That's very generous, but how 'bout if I just stop by some other time to have tea with you again. We can enjoy them together."

"That would be real nice." She smiled broadly and then daintily sipped her tea. "Now, tell me something interesting. I haven't had company in ages."

Gray relaxed against the back of the chair. Maybe this was what Christmas was about. Sharing a moment of kindness with someone in need of company. Gray definitely felt more in the spirit of things simply sharing a cup of tea with someone she'd known a lifetime ago. She was a different person now, but so was Mrs. Cavney. They had a lot to catch up on.

Chapter Twenty-five

Faith spent Christmas day with Kayla and Dan. Their house was an explosion of Christmas cheer, Kayla loved to decorate. The entire place looked like a set from a Hallmark holiday movie. Being in the house definitely put Faith in a festive mood.

If Kayla was homebound for the season, then she was determined to make the most of it. Ever since they'd taken over the café and lodge, leaving for the holidays had become impossible. Kayla's parents recently retired to a small town on the South Carolina coast so they were no longer local. She planned to visit them after New Year's when things calmed down a bit and Dan could manage without her.

"I should probably go check in at the lodge." The café was closed just for Christmas Day, but the lodge was partially booked by people in town to visit family or to spend the holiday in the mountains. A skeleton crew of one was manning the front desk but Dan didn't want him to have to work the entire day.

"We can clean up. You should go relieve Tyler." Faith stacked dishes near the sink to rinse them.

Tyler Caldwell, resident floater and landscaper, the guy who always forgot to lock the dumpster lid at night, but could manage the front desk in a pinch. And especially on holidays when he made time and a half at his hourly rate.

"It was fun to have you here for Christmas." Dan hugged Faith. Then kissed Kayla on the cheek.

"Thank you for inviting me." Faith braced her hand on the back of a nearby kitchen chair. "Tell Tyler merry Christmas for me."

Dan waved as he headed out the door pulling on his coat. The local weather service had been warning of a freak winter freeze that was supposed to hit the mountains by the following afternoon so she figured Dan had lots to do to winterize pipes around the old lodge.

"Thanks for letting me take leftovers." Faith scooped food from various serving bowls on the island counter while Kayla rinsed plates and put them in the dishwasher. "I can help with the dishes too."

"I'm happy for you to take some food with you. We'll never eat all of this. My eyes were bigger than my stomach. But you know how you get certain cravings around the holidays." Kayla dried her hands with a towel and rotated to face Faith. "Um, are you planning to feed an army there?"

Faith glanced down at the full containers.

"Well, I thought Gray might enjoy some yummy holiday leftovers." Faith grinned.

"I see." Kayla nodded and the corner of her mouth curved up in a playful half smile. "You know, that double date offer was still on the table. You could have invited Gray to join us."

"I know. And thank you." Faith sincerely appreciated Kayla's support. "But she had to work today at the station. I think she wanted to let Lucas have the day off with his kids."

"That was a nice thing to do."

"I thought so too." Faith licked a bit of sweet potato casserole from the serving spoon and closed the lid of the glass to-go container. She slid the spoon into the sudsy water in the sink to soak.

"But seriously, we should all have dinner some time." Kayla carried a few glasses from the table to the sink. "It's good to test these things out with your friends."

"Yeah, I know. I haven't wanted to rush things." Faith leaned against the counter and stacked the two containers. "We've only had one real date." She swept her hands through her hair and took a deep breath. "I don't really know how it's going, except slowly. I've never had an experience like this."

"Details, please." Kayla poured a little white wine into two glasses and handed one to Faith.

"Oh, where to begin?" Faith took a sip. "I'm very attracted to her, I mean...*very*. And I think she's attracted to me." Faith paused trying to organize her feelings into words. "But I feel as if there's something holding her back, she hasn't really opened up to me."

"Do you think she's seeing someone in California?"

"I don't think so." Faith furrowed her brow. "It doesn't feel like that. It feels like something else."

"Hmm." Kayla was thoughtful. "You two have so much chemistry that I'm surprised things are moving so slow."

"Really? You think we have chemistry?"

"Are you kidding?" Kayla arched her eyebrow in mock surprise. "Yes. One hundred percent, yes. And I was only around the two of you at the fundraiser for a few minutes."

"Thank you for confirming this. I was starting to feel a little crazy." Faith was beginning to fear that this thing with Gray was going to end up going nowhere. Confirmation from Kayla was encouraging. "Maybe I'll text her when I get home to see if she'd like to have dinner."

"I support this plan." Kayla held up her glass and Faith lightly touched it with hers.

❖

Faith texted Gray after she arrived home. It was close to five o'clock so she imagined that Gray would be finishing up work soon. *Hi, Gray, Merry Christmas.* She hit send and then added more. *I brought enough leftovers home from Kayla's to share. I thought you might want to have dinner once you finish work.* She typed and then retyped the message in an attempt to sound casual, but not too casual.

It only took a few minutes for Gray to respond.

That would be great. Thank you. I'm leaving at five.

And then a second message came through. *Also, Merry Christmas,* with an evergreen tree emoji.

The emoji made Faith smile. She set the phone aside figuring she had about twenty minutes at most to freshen up and tidy the living room a bit. The place wasn't a total wreck, but left to her own devices she did have the tendency to discard clothing and shoes in random places. The house didn't have a fireplace as large as the one in Gray's cabin, but she decided even a small flame would raise the coziness factor.

Faith removed the cover from the Pyrex containers and slid them in the oven to warm. Almost the same instant she closed the stove she heard a knock at the front door. Her heart did a little summersault into her stomach when she opened the door and saw Gray. It wasn't that Gray looked that different than the last time she'd seen her, but damn, Faith had forgotten how good she looked in her fresh-from-the-fire-station uniform. Gray was wearing the usual navy shirt, jeans, and boots, but she'd thrown a scarf into the mix. The scarf was blue striped and somehow it drew Faith's attention to Gray's flawless skin and her firm jawline. Gray held a small dark brown box tied with a red ribbon in her hand.

"Come in. Your timing is perfect. I just put the food in to warm."

"Thanks." Gray began to unwrap the scarf with one hand. She held the box out to Faith with her other. "I picked this up for you yesterday. It's just a little something, no big deal."

"How thoughtful." Faith accepted the gift and kissed Gray on the cheek. She set the box on the entry hall table. "Here, let me take your coat and scarf."

After she'd hung up Gray's things she once again picked up the gift box.

"Should I open it now?" Faith loved presents and in truth, she had no impulse control about waiting to open them. She was already slowly tugging the bow loose before Gray responded.

"Yes, please. Like I said…it's not much, just a little holiday cheer." Gray seemed nervous about the gift.

Faith didn't have anything for Gray. She'd been unsure about the gift protocol for where they were. She was a little anxious about what was in the box also, but delighted when she discovered it was chocolates. Six little candies with different shapes and garnishes of color were nestled in little paper nests inside the box.

"There's that little gourmet chocolate shop on the square now and I thought…well, I hoped you liked chocolate."

"I love chocolate." Faith smiled. "Especially, handmade, small batch chocolates. This was the perfect choice."

"Good."

Gray visibly relaxed. Were they ever going to get past this nervousness with each other? Faith was beginning to wonder.

"We have a medley of things…ham, sweet potatoes, creamed corn, green beans, and these really yummy brioche rolls." Faith walked to the kitchen and Gray followed. She set the box of candies on the table and checked the food. Then she took down two glasses. "I have wine or beer."

"Which are you in the mood for, because I'd be happy with either."

"I think I'm in the mood for wine." She'd started with wine at Kayla and Dan's for lunch. Why not stay the course? Faith poured two glasses of a cabernet she'd been saving. "Please, sit." She motioned toward the table. "I can bring the food over."

Gray accepted the glass and was about to sit down. "Do you mind if I use your bathroom?"

"Sure, do you know where it is? There's a half bath under the stairs near the foyer." Faith indicated the direction and then started spooning food onto plates.

Gray felt pampered to have someone prepare a meal for her. Even if the meal had already been prepared, it was still really nice not to eat alone on Christmas. She took a few seconds to savor that thought before leaving the room.

Gray stepped into the bathroom and closed the door. She briskly washed her hands and then splashed cold water on her face and willed herself to settle down. She could attend to a car accident with multiple injuries without getting the least bit rattled, but somehow every time she was alone with Faith her nervous system ratcheted up to an unsafe speed.

When she pressed the hand towel to her face she held it there for a moment, breathing it in. The cloth held the faintest hint of Faith's perfume. The scent was soothing and exciting at the same time. Gray hung the towel up and swept her fingers through her hair. She looked tired and she wondered if she should confide to Faith that she hadn't been sleeping well for weeks. She shook her head. No, tonight was for celebrating and enjoying each other's company.

Gray took note of the small potted spruce tree strung with lights in one corner of the living room. She was reminded that she'd promised to help Faith plant it after the holidays. Faith was just placing cloth napkins beside each plate of food when she returned to the kitchen.

"Everything smells so good." Gray waited for Faith to take her seat and then she sat down too.

"A toast." Faith raised her glass. "To Christmas."

"To Christmas." They clinked glasses lightly.

Gray took a few bites. She realized she was starving. She dabbed at her mouth with the napkin and tried to pace her forkfuls of food. If she didn't slow down she'd finish before Faith had barely started.

"How was your day today? Was it busy?"

Faith's question gave her an excuse to stop shoveling food for a minute.

"It was only mildly busy. One kid with a broken arm and then a call from Lucas to help an elderly woman who lives alone." Gray took a sip of wine before continuing. "She'd thrown a breaker, so she was getting no water from the well to the house. The pump wasn't working."

"Wow, you guys really do end up getting every sort of call."

"Yeah, I don't mind. It's nice to be able to help people." Gray took a bite and swallowed before continuing. "This lady, Lucille Cavney, was my teacher in grade school. I don't think I'd seen her since elementary school."

"Did she remember you?"

"She actually did, you know, after we talked for a while." Gray rested her elbows on the table, reflecting back on the conversation. "She was all by herself in this big old house, so she invited me to stay for tea after we got the pump running." Gray paused. "It was nice."

"That's really sweet." Faith set her fork down and sampled the wine. "I think about that sometimes."

"What?"

"Growing old and being alone."

"You do?"

"Why does that surprise you?" Faith seemed genuinely curious.

"Because, I mean, because you are you." Gray fumbled her words. "I don't think you need to worry about that."

"Well, I'm glad someone thinks so." Faith shook her head. "I was so sure that I'd be married with kids by now, but look at me... still single."

"Lucky for me." Gray tried to sound playful, but deep down she was serious.

"Thank you." Faith blushed. "I'm flattered."

They finished dinner and moved to the living room with a bit more wine. Faith brought the half-finished bottle and the box of chocolates. They sat on the sofa facing the fireplace. Faith set the wine and chocolates on the coffee table.

"It seems only fair that we share these for dessert." Faith held out the box to Gray.

"Okay, if you insist." She selected one that she knew was salted caramel. Her personal favorite.

"Oh wow." Faith sampled her choice. "I love chocolate truffles."

Faith slipped off her shoes and propped her feet on the coffee table.

"You can take your boots off if you like. The fire feels good on my feet."

Gray set her wine aside and unlaced her boots. It was a relief to slip out of them. Although, if she got much cozier she was afraid she might doze off. Sleep deprivation, a home cooked meal, and a cozy fire—lethal lounging combination. The initial nervousness around Faith had ebbed and now she simply felt relaxed. Although, every time Faith breached her airspace, even with the most fleeting gesture she got a tingly sensation all along her arms.

The floral print sofa was softly overstuffed, and Gray found herself slouching comfortably into it once she'd taken off her heavy boots. It was nice to just be with someone and not feel like she had to make conversation. She sipped the wine and watched the dancing flames. After several minutes Faith leaned forward for another chocolate. When she settled back to the couch, her arm and shoulder were against Gray's. Her heart rate sped up, but she didn't want to shift away from Faith, who seemed unaware of the effect she was having on Gray as she savored the chocolate.

"We could watch a movie if you like." Faith licked her lips. "And by the way, those chocolates are amazing."

"What movie did you have in mind?" Gray couldn't remember the last time she watched a movie. There was a TV in the cabin, but no cable service and the set was so old it was unable to connect to any of the streaming services. Gray had been enjoying the quiet, but the suggestion of watching a movie sounded fun. Besides, that would mean at least two more hours with Faith.

"I love to watch *It's a Wonderful Life* every Christmas and I haven't seen it yet."

"That would be nice. I haven't seen that one in forever."

Faith reached for the remote and pointed at the flat-screen TV mounted above the mantle. "I checked earlier today for it. We can rent it."

Gray watched as Faith clicked through screens until she was able to hit *play* and start the movie.

"I hope you don't mind the original black-and-white version." Faith glanced over at Gray. "I really don't like the colorized movies."

"I prefer the original version too."

Before Faith could resume her reclined position, a large cat jumped into her spot.

"Hello, big guy." Gray reached over to stroke the huge feline.

"This is Otis." Faith picked him up and shifted him to the side. "He loves to steal my seat any time I move."

Otis seemed content with the other end of the sofa. Faith snuggled back against her shoulder. This was shaping up to be the best Christmas she'd had in a very, very long time.

Faith felt a slight chill, she sleepily tugged the blanket from the back of the sofa down and over her shoulder. Only then did her foggy brain remember she was next to Gray. It had been her idea to watch the movie, but somewhere between George Bailey on the bridge and Clarence getting his wings, she'd drifted off.

She tried to sit up, but the sofa cushion moved and Gray blinked. They'd fallen asleep all snuggled up together on the couch.

"I'm so sorry." Gray tried to sit up. "I must have…I mean, I didn't mean to—"

"It's okay." Faith rested her palm on Gray's torso. "I fell asleep too."

"What time is it?" Gray sank back against the cushions.

Faith reached for her phone to check.

"I'm embarrassed to say it's not that late. Only ten o'clock. I guess it's been a hectic week." The movie had been over for a while and only the splash image showed on the TV screen. The fire had also gone out, which was probably why the room had gotten chilly.

"Should I go?" Gray seemed unsure. "I should probably get home."

"I do have a very early shift tomorrow." Faith didn't really want Gray to leave, but she also knew she had the morning shift the day after Christmas, no fun. If Gray stayed she would not want to leave quite so early. But she didn't want Gray to drive home all sleepy and after a few glasses of wine. "Are you sure you're okay to drive? You're welcome to stay here."

That didn't really sound as inviting as she'd intended.

"What I mean is, I would love to spend the night with you." She paused to gauge Gray's response. "Just not on a night when I'd have to leave so early in the morning."

"I know what you mean." Gray brushed hair away from Faith's cheek with a light touch.

They were still close enough on the sofa that Faith could feel the warmth of Gray's body, and it was very hard not to curl up again and compel her to stay. She closed the space between them, stopping just before making contact with Gray's lips. Gray angled her head and kissed Faith, gently, sweetly, luxuriously, until Faith broke the kiss, breathless and feeling flushed.

"I really should probably drive home now." The breathy delivery of Gray's statement told Faith the kiss had had the same effect on her.

"Maybe. My brain is saying that I should walk you to the door, but all the other parts of me want to walk you to the bedroom."

Gray smiled. She kissed Faith lightly then stood up. She offered Faith her hand. They walked with fingers entwined to the door. Faith hugged herself while Gray bundled back into her jacket and scarf.

"Thank you for dinner and for the movie we almost watched."

"You're welcome." Faith tucked the ends of the scarf into Gray's jacket.

"Do you have plans for New Year's Eve?" Gray rested her hands on Faith's hips.

"I do now." Faith stood on her tiptoes and kissed Gray. "I'd love to bring in the New Year with you."

"It's a date then." Gray reached for the door. "I'll call you tomorrow and we can figure out a plan."

Faith stood in the frigid air on the porch, in sock feet, and watched Gray walk to her car.

Merry Christmas.

CHAPTER TWENTY-SIX

F aith had to drag herself out of bed before dawn. Why was she
doing this again? Oh yeah, because Kayla fed her Christmas
lunch so she'd volunteered to take the early shift. But wasn't this
exactly the sort of thing she'd tried to avoid by getting a degree in art?
Yes, she was sure of it.

She brushed her teeth swearing this was the last early shift she'd
volunteer for. Faith needed to get back to work on her actual career.
She'd delivered the cover art to the publisher and the art director
mentioned she might have another job for Faith after the holidays.
One illustration project produced the equivalent of two weeks of
income from the café. That was good news on both counts. Faith was
painting again and feeling generally optimistic about the world. Was
this change of perspective because of Gray? Partly, but not entirely.

A change of scenery had also helped her gain perspective on
her past life and had given her space and the support of friendship to
move forward. Kayla had been right, not something she often readily
admitted to her. Too much *rightness* would inevitably go to Kayla's
head.

The dishes were still in the sink from the previous night, but she
decided to leave them.

She topped off Otis's food bowl and water dish. The sound of the
cat food bag called him to the kitchen from somewhere in the house.

"There you are, little man." She scratched the fur between his
ears. He angled his face up and smiled the way happy cats do, with
squinted happy cat eyes. "You should probably stay inside today. It's
supposed to get really cold."

Faith glanced out the kitchen window. Only the faintest hint of pink was visible at the ridgeline. The inky outlines of leafless trees crisscrossed the purple sky. She considered lingering to make coffee, but then just decided to get some at the café.

The windshield of her Volvo was covered with a thin glaze of ice. Living in Raleigh, which was a warmer, low altitude climate, she had no need for an ice scraper. She didn't really own any winter gear of any kind, unless you counted cashmere scarves. Now that was a collection she was quite proud of.

Faith tucked her hands in her jacket pockets and waited for the defroster to work its magic on the windshield. It seemed to take forever for the car to warm up. Waiting gave her a few minutes to remember the previous evening with Gray. They'd had a very cozy, relaxed night together—almost like a regular couple. The thought of it made her smile.

She still couldn't believe they'd both fallen asleep, but maybe the discovery that they were comfortable enough with each other to do so was a promising sign.

With the windshield finally clear, Faith put the car in reverse and then turned onto the winding road heading toward town.

By ten o'clock, snow was falling in heavy, quarter-sized flakes. By noon it was beginning to pile up in the parking lot between spaces. It was a wet snow that forecasters were warning would turn into an ice storm. The café was empty by two o'clock. Faith was standing at the window watching the snow when Nancy Jo came to join her.

"Kayla just called." Nancy Jo wore a sparkly plastic tiara with the words Happy New Year across the top. "She says if we're not busy that we should close up and head home before the storm gets any worse." She paused. "Ed is closing up the kitchen now."

"Do you think it's going to get that bad?"

"It might." Nancy Jo pointed at the parking lot. "See all that wet blacktop showing through? If that freezes under the snow, then yes, it's gonna get super slick out there." She reached for the string to close the blinds. "I need to swing by grocery store and get some stuff in case this thing lasts for more than a day."

"Oh, I hadn't even thought of that. I should do that too. My fridge is almost completely empty." She quirked an eyebrow. "Unless I could survive on wine. I mean, it's made of grapes, right? And grapes are a fruit."

"I like the way you think." Nancy Jo laughed.

But all kidding aside, Faith knew she didn't have anything edible to sustain her for more than a day. She left the café and followed Nancy Jo to the local market. It was a zoo, complete chaos. You'd have thought they were about to attempt to survive the snow apocalypse the way people were buying up water and toilet paper. Maybe she was naive, but surely it wouldn't get that bad. Didn't Amazon still deliver even in an apocalypse?

An hour later, Faith was trying to escape the chaotic parking lot to drive home. She schooled herself to leave plenty of space between herself and the car in front of her. Driving in snowy conditions was something she had very little experience with. There were no other cars visible when she turned onto the curvy road leading up the mountain to her house. She was driving slowly, keeping a steady pace so that using the brakes would be kept to a minimum. It was hard to tell exactly how slick the road was and she didn't want to take any chances.

Huge, wet snowflakes were making the wipers work overtime. She leaned forward, almost resting her chin on the steering wheel, as if that would improve visibility. She rounded a turn and flinched when she saw a dark shape against the white of the roadway. Instinctively, she hit the brakes to avoid hitting a small group of deer crossing the road.

Whew, she took a deep breath and allowed the car to idle while the animals cleared the road. But before she could accelerate, she had the oddest sensation that the car was moving, not forward, but backward. She'd braked on the high side of the curve and the car had begun a gentle slide down the incline. She tried to give the car a little gas, but the more she pressed the accelerator the more the wheels spun without gaining any traction.

Oh, shit. Oh, shit.

Faith frantically rotated in the driver's seat to see if there were any cars coming up the mountain behind her as the car continued its slow, uncontrolled slide. Not only was the vehicle gaining speed in the wrong direction, but she was now at a thirty-degree angle heading toward the snow filled ditch. This was like watching a horror movie and having to endure the scariest scene in slow motion, helpless and with no way to escape.

Gray fitted ice cleats onto her boots on the front porch so as not to scar the hardwood floors. The snow had been coming down strong all day, and the last time she'd made an attempt to get to the woodpile at the side of the cabin she'd slipped and hit the ground hard. Then she remembered there was a pair of old cleats in the mud room at the back of the house.

She was about to round the corner of the cabin when something caught her attention through the veil of white falling snow. A car was in a slow slide backward down the road.

Gray started walking down her driveway. Visibility was terrible, but she finally could see that it was Faith's car!

She reached the shoulder in time to see the Volvo slide at an angle into the ditch about fifty feet below her driveway. The wipers were swishing back and forth frantically, and the headlights were on, angled skyward because of the car's uneven landing spot. It was impossible to see Faith inside the car. Gray walked as fast as she could without falling. Faith was attempting to climb out when she arrived, but the door was probably even heavier than usual because of the angle of the car.

"Faith, are you all right?" She wedged her back against the open door and offered her hand to Faith. Gray's heart was in her throat. Helplessly watching Faith's car slide into the ditch left her with a terrible, sick feeling in the pit of her stomach.

"Oh, my God…that was the scariest thing ever." Faith sounded understandably rattled. "I had no control. It just kept sliding backward."

Faith was standing beside Gray, but suddenly lost her footing and would have fallen if Gray hadn't caught her.

"It's super slick." Gray put her arm around Faith's waist. "Here, let me hang on to you until we get to the house."

"How are you so stable?"

"Ice cleats on my boots."

"Smart." Faith nodded as if she knew what ice cleats were, but Gray suspected she didn't.

"I have my moments."

It was a painfully slow walk back up to the cabin. Faith slipped numerous times. She was definitely wearing the wrong shoes for this sort of weather. By the time they got inside they were both shivering. Gray hadn't planned on a rescue mission so she wasn't even wearing her coat.

"You're freezing. Let me get you a blanket."

Gray parked Faith in the rocking chair close to the roaring fire and then returned with a heavy quilt. Faith was wearing low-healed slip-on shoes with thin socks, which were now soaked. Gray knelt down to remove Faith's shoes and socks and started to rub her feet. She rubbed each foot for a few moments between her hands. She did this instinctively, without asking Faith if she minded. Only when she rocked back on her heels and looked up at Faith did she realize what she'd done.

"Um, I hope that was okay." Gray tried to read Faith's expression, but couldn't. "I probably should have asked first."

"No, no…that was perfect. My feet were numb." Faith's words were soft and had warmth. "Thank you."

Gray nodded. She was still on her knees, looking up at Faith. The realization that Faith was in an accident and could have been seriously hurt suddenly clenched into a tight knot in her gut. She cared about Faith, more than she'd been willing to admit. The discovery sent that tingling sensation up her arms again.

Chapter Twenty-seven

Faith studied Gray's face as she slipped dry wool socks onto Faith's cold feet. Gray's tender caretaking since she'd arrived helped her feel more settled. The freak accident had scared her badly.

"I feel so stupid. I was completely unprepared for the weather in those shoes. What if I'd gone in a ditch somewhere else?" Faith knew she'd been lucky. If Gray hadn't watched it happen and come to help she wasn't even sure she'd have been able to get out of the car by herself.

"But you didn't." Gray's calmness was reassuring. "That's what matters."

"I just realized there are groceries in the car. I was stocking up in case the weather took a turn for the worst." Faith laughed. "And hello, I think it just did."

"You wait here." Gray reached for her coat. "I'll go get them."

Gray had left her cleated boots near the front door. She tugged them on, then turned and smiled at Faith before heading out into the driving snow.

Faith was finally beginning to feel warm. She rocked gently in the chair under the quilt, thankful to be safe. How would she ever get her car out of the ditch and when? Certainly, it would have to remain where it was until the weather cleared.

It seemed like forever and Gray still wasn't back. In reality it probably hadn't been that long, but she began to worry. With the quilt still draped around her shoulders she shuffled to the front window in search of Gray. It was getting dark. She switched the porch light on and also a lamp near the sofa. The door opened just as she was returning to the window. Swirling snow swept in, along with the cold draft. She tossed the quilt on the sofa so that she could help Gray with the groceries. There were two brown paper bags, damp from the snow along with her purse that she'd forgotten in the car. Gray had the strap across her chest like a sling so that she could carry the groceries at the same time.

"You're freezing!" Gray's fingers brushed Faith's as she took one of the bags out of her arms.

"It's definitely getting colder." Gray waited for Faith to set the first bag of groceries on the table. "Can you take this one too? I don't want to come in with these cleats on." The door was half open which was lowering the temperature of the entire front room.

"Sure." Faith hurried back.

"I think I should bring some firewood in. We might need it if we lose power."

As if on cue, the porch light flickered.

Gray made three trips. She piled wood just inside the front door so it would stay dry and be easy to access. After taking her boots off, Gray added a couple more sticks of wood to the fire.

"Now you're the one who's freezing." Gray had her back to the fire. Faith held Gray's hands in hers to warm them.

The lights flickered again and then went dark.

"Don't worry, we're okay."

"Do I seem worried?"

"Yeah, a little." Gray smiled and squeezed Faith's hand. "But you did just slalom ski your car into a ditch, so you're allowed."

"Thanks."

"We have plenty of wood. The stove and hot water heater run on gas." Gray put her arm around Faith's shoulder and drew her close. As if for warmth, but also affection. "I have a couple of gallons of water in jars and if we need more I have a generator for the well pump." She paused. "And thanks to you, we have groceries."

"Too bad I didn't think to buy some candles."

"I have a few in the pantry." The house was dark except for the warm light from the fireplace. "I guess what I'm saying is, I think you should plan to stay here tonight."

Faith hadn't even thought of it, but Gray was right. There was no way to get home in the storm, even though home was not much more than a mile away.

"Will Otis be okay?"

"He'll be fine." Luckily, she'd filled his food and water dish before leaving for work. "Although, he won't be very happy if the house gets too cold. He has been known to get under the covers. This might be one of those times."

They were quiet for a few minutes. Faith stared at the flames and allowed her eyes to lose their focus. Gray's arm was still around her shoulders and her arm was around Gray's waist, as if they were a couple, and completely comfortable with this level of sustained closeness. Possibly falling asleep next to each other on the sofa the previous night had taken their relationship to the next level, whatever that was.

"I hope you're okay with this." Gray sounded serious all of a sudden. "I just want you to know that we don't have to sleep together." She hesitated. "I mean, not in the same bed. You can sleep on the sofa and I'll make a bed on the floor. With the electricity out we might need to stay close to the fire."

"I'm really okay with this." She kissed Gray on the cheek. "Thank you for coming to my rescue."

"It's kinda my job." Gray's statement was playful.

While Gray searched for candles, Faith made dinner. The menu was simple, she cut a chicken breast into thin strips and browned them in a skillet on the stove top. Since it was a gas stove she was able to light the burners she needed with a match. She also cut a couple of potatoes into tiny pieces and fried those in a second pan. Everything was almost ready by the time Gray made her way to the kitchen.

"Should we have some wine with dinner?" Gray had a bottle of red wine in her hand.

"That sounds great to me." Faith filled two plates with food. It was a little complicated to cook in someone else's kitchen, but she managed to find everything she needed.

She followed Gray to the living room where in her absence, Gray had set up a twin mattress on the floor with pillows and blankets and set several candles around the room. This whole scenario was dangerously romantic, and Faith found herself trying to remember what sort of underwear she'd worn, hopefully a sexy pair. Not that she was getting ahead of herself, but seriously. This whole scene was right out of a lesbian romance novel.

Gray held her hand until she was seated crossed-legged on the mattress. Then Gray joined her. Gray explained that there was a twin bed in the guest room and it seemed like a better idea than sleeping on the cold, hard floor. The coffee table had been moved aside so that the mattress and the sofa were as close as they could safely be to the hearth, with the mattress just in front of the sofa.

"This is really good. Thank you for cooking."

"Thank you for all of this." Faith made a small circle in the air with her fork. "You seem to take all of this in stride."

"I suppose I'm so used to camping that this feels normal. When we're working on a fire we basically camp the whole time." Gray took a bite. "It feels natural to me now."

"I've never been much into camping, but I wouldn't mind trying it sometime."

"Maybe when the weather is a lot warmer I could take you." Gray's offer sounded a little bit tentative.

"I'd like that."

Gray's expression brightened.

Faith's phone buzzed. It was a message from Kayla.

"Sorry, let me respond to this text quickly." Faith set her plate aside so that she could type with both hands. "She's just checking to make sure I'm okay because of the storm."

Faith let Kayla know she was at Gray's place but tried to be vague. She was certain Kayla was going to give her the third degree after this was over.

"Maybe I should switch this off to save the battery." Faith's phone had only a partial charge remaining.

"Probably a good idea."

"What about your work? Are you on call or anything?" Faith hadn't even considered until now that a snowstorm might create all sorts of emergencies.

"I'm off duty today and tomorrow. Lucas and Henry were actually planning to sleep at the station tonight in case they had to respond to a call." Gray sipped her wine. "Hopefully, people are smart enough to stay home."

"And not try to drive, like I did."

"You almost beat the storm."

"Next time, I'll be smarter." Faith took a swig of her wine. She was feeling very lucky at the moment that everything had worked out the way it had. Someone up there was looking out for her.

CHAPTER TWENTY-EIGHT

Gray was feeling cozy and a little aroused. She and Faith were sitting side by side, with their backs against the sofa, and their legs stretched out across the mattress so that her feet were getting warmed by the fire. They held hands and from time to time, Faith rubbed her toes against Gray's foot, which meant that their legs made contact. Her heartrate registered each fleeting touch. Once she got up to add more wood to the fire, it took all her strength to move away from Faith, even for an instant.

She offered the last of the wine to Faith upon her return to the bed on the floor. In hindsight, bringing the mattress into the front room made it impossible not to confront her desire for Faith. She'd tried to keep her cool, but their closeness only served to stoke the flame.

They'd managed to finish the entire bottle during and after dinner. Gray was so happy. She couldn't remember the last time she'd been so happy. Getting to spend two evenings in a row with Faith was like a pleasant dream.

The quilt she'd given to Faith earlier was now draped around both of them. Their intimate proximity was creating an urge that Gray was having a hard time ignoring. She didn't want to initiate something in a situation where Faith had nowhere else to go, but she finally gave in and kissed Faith. Her lips were soft and tasted of wine. She set her glass aside and drew Faith down onto the mattress beside her.

"Is this okay?" Gray softly asked. "I don't want to take advantage of the situation."

"Please, take advantage of the situation." Faith smiled and then kissed Gray lightly.

She rested her palm on the sensuous curve of Faith's hip as they kissed. She teased with her fingers at the hem of Faith's shirt. Sensing her intention, Faith tugged her blouse free from the waist of her pants. Faith's skin was silken and warm to her touch.

Faith shivered.

"Sorry, are my hands cold?"

"No, it's not that." Faith pressed against her and applied pressure with her hand on Gray's back, then even lower.

Gray swept her hand slowly up Faith's arm and then cradled her cheek with her hand. Faith rotated and kissed Gray's palm.

Gray was getting so turned on. She deepened the kiss and rolled on top of Faith, shifting so that her thigh was between Faith's legs. Faith's fingers were in her hair and on her back under her shirt. She wanted less clothing between them, but fumbled with the buttons of Faith's blouse. She felt a little inept, like a teenager having sex for the first time. Maybe she was out of practice, but also, the stakes were higher with Faith. She didn't simply want to have sex with Faith, she wanted to make love to her. She wanted Faith to want her.

Faith must have sensed her uncertainty because she switched their position. Faith rolled Gray onto her back, straddling her at the waist. Gray watched as Faith slowly unbuttoned her blouse, like a flower dropping one petal at a time until all were gone, and then she tossed the blouse aside.

Gray swallowed. If she wasn't nervous before she certainly was now.

Faith was gorgeous.

Gray rested her palms on Faith's thighs as Faith unbuttoned her shirt, then she lifted the hem of her undershirt and trailed light kisses across Gray's torso. Her abs involuntarily tightened in response to Faith's sensual touch.

"You are so hot," Faith whispered against her skin.

Her eyes were closed, but she felt the tug at her waist and knew that Faith had loosened the top button of her jeans. Her heart beat against her ribs like a savage lovely beast trying to escape.

She sat up, with Faith still on top of her midsection and quickly got rid of her shirt. She yanked the T-shirt over her head with one swift movement and tossed it away. Then, shirtless, facing each other, she wrapped her arms tightly around Faith and kissed her, deeply. With one hand she unfastened Faith's bra then it was also gone. Faith's breasts were pressed against her chest and yet still, she couldn't seem to get close enough. A riot of sensations fought for dominance in her system, every nerve raw, burning like liquid fire.

Faith allowed herself to be lifted and then gently laid onto her back. She gripped Gray's muscled arms as Gray shifted her body as if she weighed less than air.

Facing each other, lying together without barriers of clothing or even air, Gray breathed Faith in. The lightest scent of rose and vanilla and something else that she was coming to know as simply Faith.

She trailed her fingertip along Faith's arm and the elegant curve of her neck and shoulder. Gray wanted to take Faith and yet didn't want to rush these moments of discovery. Her head and her body were like two notes octaves apart, one wanting to rush to sex, one wanting the moment to last forever. Short days ago she could not see this, yet here she was.

"Is this too much?" Gray brushed the back of her fingers along her cheek as Faith nuzzled her neck.

"This is perfect," Faith whispered.

She appreciated that Gray kept checking in with her, but the truth was this wasn't nearly enough. She wanted more. She arched against Gray, taking Gray's hand and moving it to the throbbing place between her legs. Faith worried she might climax before they were even completely undressed. She sensed Gray's reserve so she tried to assist by unzipping her pants to give Gray easier access, and to send a signal that she was definitely okay with this turn of events.

Gray was on her knees. Her mouth was at the lowest curve of Faith's stomach. She gripped Gray's strong, broad shoulders as Gray eased her pants down and off, leaving only her underwear. Then Gray did the same, except Gray was completely naked now. Gray drew the quilt back over them and covered Faith with the full weight and warmth of her body.

Faith managed to wriggle out of her underwear and kick it away.

There would be no hiding it now. Gray's rock-hard thigh was pressed against her wet center as Gray began to slowly move on top of her. Was Faith ready for this? When Gray had whispered the question she'd said yes, but now control was slipping away. She was unveiled and open, completely at Gray's mercy, the measure between them shrinking until they were one. She clung to Gray, sinking her fingernails into Gray's back unmoored by ecstasy.

Their intense dance continued until the candles faded and the fire dimmed to glowing embers. Outside, the cold wind howled. Inside, Faith had no thoughts beyond the sensuous touch of Gray's mouth and the insistent caress of her strong fingers. She was awash in the surging sea of her own desire.

Gray relished the gentle rise and fall of Faith's breathing next to her. So close, so spent. Her beautiful long hair cascaded across the pillow and lightly tickled her arm. Gray shifted and Faith sleepily adjusted so that her head rested against Gray's shoulder. The blanket that covered them was coifed in moonlight, with an orange glow at the edge closest to the fireplace.

Holding Faith in her arms, she felt a sense of peace, perfect and complete. Her tired brain had no more thoughts and she drifted off with hopes of lesser dreaming.

Chapter Twenty-nine

Faith sensed movement beside her. The room was dark and it took a few seconds for her to clear the cobwebs of sleep and remember where she was and who she was with. She'd been in a dead sleep. Beside her, Gray twitched and moaned softly. Then she began to thrash about as if she was in distress.

"Hey, Gray, wake up." She touched Gray's arm.

Gray cried out and lurched away from her, blinking rapidly as if trying to clear her vision. Gray sat up and pressed her palms over her face.

"Gray, it's okay. You just had a bad dream." Faith pulled Gray's hand away from her face. She could see the paths of tears reflecting the dim glow from the fireplace. Faith wrapped her arms around Gray and held her. "It's okay. I'm here."

"I'm sorry I woke you." Gray's words were raspy.

"Let me get you some water." Faith fumbled her way to the unfamiliar kitchen to fill a glass.

She knelt beside Gray and offered her the drink. Gray drank as if she was dying of thirst. The house was cold. Faith gathered the blankets around them and held Gray again. She was shaking. This had obviously been a horrible dream. Gray looked stricken and forlorn.

"Do you want to talk about it?"

Gray was quiet for a minute. The shivering subsided and she took a deep breath.

"Remember how I said I lost a friend in California?"

"Yes."

"His name was Shane. He was my best friend."

"What happened?" Faith didn't want to press, but Gray seemed tortured by something.

"They are always with me—always—the memories of that day." Gray was staring at nothing, not looking at Faith as she talked. "Days are bad, but nights are worse." Gray clenched the fabric of the quilt near her heart. "I have these memories, flashbacks, aching moments of sadness…"

Her words trailed off. Faith waited for Gray to reveal something more. Slowly, Gray began to tell the story, as if she were reliving it.

Gray was exhausted and she couldn't stop the words, they fell out of her like so many stones. She didn't know if Faith wanted to hear what she was about to share, but she kept going. Faith regarded her with an expression of silent support. Faith entwined her fingers with Gray's. They sat, wrapped in blankets facing each other.

"It's okay, Gray, you can talk to me about anything."

Gray leaned against the front of the sofa, gazing at the glowing embers in the hearth.

"The fire took us by surprise. We had some very seasoned fire-fighters in our crew, and even they didn't expect it." Gray used her hands as she talked, making small movements in the air. "The wind shifted. Dave had gone back up to the road to get a water pump. Before he could get back to our position the whole thing just blew up."

She could visualize the scene so clearly, so clearly that she could almost smell the smoke.

"We started running as fast as we could trying to out-climb the fire." She looked at Faith. "That's when we deployed fire shelters. We weren't going to be able to outrun it. The fire was like a dragon bearing down on us."

Gray swallowed, reliving the fear of those tortured moments under the shelter.

"Time passed, maybe forty-five minutes after the second wave hit us, everything was so quiet…I was just listening. Waiting for the sounds of the fire to stop." She paused, remembering. "I climbed out of the shelter."

She called up the scene in her mind. She'd emerged from the shelter with the rest of the crew to take stock. Like dim, ghostly figures moving through a thick fog in a blackened landscape.

"It was hard to know if we were alive or dead, except that every muscle in my body ached from trying to hold the shelter in place when the fire passed over us, so I knew I was still alive. And I was thirsty. God, I've never been so thirsty."

She felt tears gather and one slid down her cheek.

"Everyone seemed okay, with only a few minor burns. But when I scanned the small group of sooty faces for Shane he wasn't there."

The image was as clear as a photograph in her memory. The air was still thick with smoke, but she'd seen the collapsed shelter several feet away. She'd tried to get to him, but Dave had blocked her path.

"I tried to reach him. Maybe he was asleep there under the shelter. It sounds stupid to say that now. But in that moment, my mind couldn't grasp what I was seeing." She wiped at the tear with her free hand. "Dave had to keep telling me that Shane didn't make it. I fought against him, I just couldn't believe it. I didn't want it to be the truth."

She took a shaky breath.

"He'd been right behind me. I'd heard him tell one of the junior firefighters to stay calm and not make a run for it. My head just couldn't make sense of it."

She'd swayed on her feet and almost passed out. Somewhere over the background noise inside her head she heard her commander, Vince, order a ground ambulance. *There's been a fatality.*

"Vince called for ground support. I heard him say there'd been a fatality. He said the words so calmly. As if he didn't know Shane and care about him just as much as I did."

Vince had given the coordinates for the burnover site. The reply squawked loudly over the radio, Copter 402 would leave the spot fire on their left flank to pick up water before responding to the site where the crew was located. The entire ravine was still hot and smoky.

She'd heard the request, and the response, she was standing in the aftermath—she'd experienced the burnover personally—and still she couldn't grasp what had transpired.

"After that, everything became sort of a dreamlike blur. The forest service helicopter airlifted me and Jake to Shaw Mountain Airport to meet an ambulance. From there we were transported by ground ambulance to the hospital in Sonora."

"I found out later that Shane's body was recovered by a search and rescue team and then transported to Sonora too. But I never got to see him." She looked at Faith. The tears were coming and she couldn't stop them. "I never got to see him again."

"Oh, Gray, I'm so sorry." Faith tried to console Gray. She moved closer and held Gray in her arms. "I'm so very sorry."

"Shane came back for me." She was sobbing, her words uneven and choppy. "I fell and he came back for me." She gulped air. "I made it and he didn't."

Faith wanted desperately to console Gray. She pressed Gray's cheek to her chest and caressed her hair.

All this time Faith kept trying to convince herself that Gray was the person Kayla had first warned her about, but in her heart, she knew that wasn't true.

Gray wasn't that same confused teenager that Kayla had known. It was clear now that Gray's initial distance was rooted in grief. She'd suffered a great loss and had come home to heal. Faith knew that Gray couldn't see it now, but things would get better. This wound might never heal completely, but with time it would become less painful.

"You're the first person I've told about any of this." Gray had settled a bit. She was snuggled against Faith in a half-reclined position. "I couldn't even tell Shane's girlfriend, Alissa, when she was here. I should have told her what happened."

Faith instantly felt a sharp pang of guilt for misreading the situation with Alissa. It had been too easy to assume the worst of Gray and now she felt bad about it.

"It's not too late. I'm sure she'd be willing to listen whenever you feel ready to talk to her about it." Faith pressed her lips to Gray's forehead.

After a little while, Gray got up and put more wood on the fire. Then she returned to the warmth of their shared bed and nestled again in Faith's arms. They drifted off holding each other, cozy and safe from the winter storm outside.

Chapter Thirty

G ray woke before Faith, who was still sleeping soundly. The fire had died down completely so she could see her breath in the air even inside the house. She'd slept comfortably snuggled against Faith under the pile of quilts and blankets, but once her bare skin made contact with the cold air her skin pebbled. She searched for her T-shirt and then gingerly slid from beneath the covers to retrieve sweatpants and a sweatshirt. As she pulled the hoodie over her head she realized that she felt a lightness in her chest that hadn't been there in weeks, maybe even before that.

Faith stirred as Gray attempted to rebuild the fire as quietly as possible. Faith squinted at her from the bed, her hair adorably tousled in every direction.

"What time is it?" Faith's voice was raspy from sleep.

"It's early." Gray was kneeling by the hearth. She replaced the screen as the wood caught fire. "To be honest, I haven't checked. I think it seems brighter in here because of the snow. It's like a winter wonderland outside." She shifted from her kneeling position to sit at the edge of the mattress.

"You're dressed. And I'm—" Faith peeked under the covers. "Not."

Gray laughed.

"I'll find you a sweatshirt or something."

"I can wear this, if you have some sweats I can borrow." Faith slipped into Gray's discarded Flannel shirt.

It was oversized on Faith and sexy as hell.

When she returned from the bedroom, Faith was standing at the front window looking out, the flannel shirt hung down to the upper part of her thighs. Faith gratefully put on the sweatpants over the socks Gray had given her the prior evening. Gray stood behind Faith and encircled her with her arms.

"It's magical." Faith sank against her and she rested her chin on top of Faith's head.

The first snowfall of the season always was. And this one was unusually deep. Every detail of the outside world was softened by several inches of pristine white snow. The temp was obviously still below freezing because nothing had begun to melt. It was as if the entire world was frozen in place.

"How are you feeling?" Faith rotated in her arms and nestled her cheek against Gray's chest.

"Better." Gray was reminded of how she'd told Faith everything. She'd known on some level that if she got close to Faith she would be unable to hide the hurt for very long. Feeling one thing deeply meant feeling all of it. She could be vague now and try to pretend it hadn't happened, but she decided instead to stay the course and be honest. It was much less exhausting, and besides, why retreat now. "I think I believed I could outrun it, or leave it behind."

Faith tightened her embrace but didn't say anything. Faith clearly had a sixth sense about knowing when not to talk.

"That was a stupid idea. I know that now." Gray held Faith's face in her hands so that she could see her eyes. "Everything was here with me all along, weighing me down, until now...until you." She kissed Faith. "Thank you."

Faith studied Gray's face in the light from the window. Gray's countenance was so changed. There was a closeness between them now that was almost painful, but it was a pleasant pain. The sort of painful ache you felt deep inside, maybe it was more desire than pain. It was hard to formulate words to describe the sensation. All Faith knew was that she'd never felt this with anyone else, ever. The feeling was exhilarating and more than a little scary.

"Are you hungry? Do you need coffee?"

Faith was grateful for the mundane questions.

"Yes, and yes." She squeezed Gray, then released her.

"I can start the generator too so we can take showers." Gray's fingers entwined with hers as she shuffled behind Gray in sock feet to the kitchen. "The generator has a small gas tank, so I try to only run it for short periods of time."

Faith knew next to nothing about generators, but a hot shower sounded heavenly.

Breakfast consisted of things that could easily be cooked in a skillet on the stovetop, eggs and toast. She'd never had toast pan-fried in a skillet. Maybe that was a skill you learned camping. At any rate, it was delicious, or possibly she was simply famished from their evening of lovemaking.

After breakfast, Gray found some fresh clothes for Faith. Warmer clothing than what she'd worn from work the previous day so that they could venture out into the snow. Everything was two sizes too large, but she didn't care. Wearing one of Gray's flannel shirts would feel perfect. Unfortunately, Gray couldn't offer any pants that fit, but she did have a pair of rubber boots that Faith could manage if she stuffed the toes with extra socks.

Faith stood in the shower for as long as she dared, standing motionless in the hot stream. Steam filled the tiny room. She toweled off and finger combed her hair. She opened drawers in the vanity until she discovered an ancient hair dryer. She held it in her hand for a moment trying to decide if plugging it in might be a fire hazard. Faith decided to chance it because she certainly couldn't play in the snow with wet hair, she'd freeze. Or worse, catch a cold.

Luckily, the hair dryer worked well, despite its advanced age.

Gray was next in the shower. She kissed Faith on the cheek as she passed by.

Faith was wrapped in a towel. She slipped into Gray's bedroom to dress. The temperature in the room was cool, but her skin was so warmed by the shower that the coolness felt refreshing. It was odd to realize that they'd made love, but this was the first time she'd actually been in Gray's bedroom. She gave in to her curiosity, slowly touring the space, picking up things to study them. Like a book of essays by John Muir on the nightstand, or the wallet on the dresser darkened by use. She rubbed the soft leather with her fingertips. Next to the wallet was a brass compass that looked like an antique.

She opened the top dresser drawer and lifted one of the shirts to her face, inhaling deeply. Under the shirt, she discovered a photo of a rugged looking guy and Gray. Faith assumed the man was Shane. They had their arms on each other's shoulders like returning war heroes. Gray had an ax in one hand and both of them looked dusty. The background looked like photos of the Sierras she'd seen. She wondered why the photo was in the drawer rather than on top of the dresser. Maybe seeing the photo every day made Gray too sad. She refolded the shirt, covered the photo and closed the drawer.

She stuck her head into the guest room also. Nothing seemed personal to Gray in that room. There were two twin beds separated by a nightstand and lamp. One of the mattresses was now on the floor in front of the fireplace.

There were family photos in the hallway. A few of them looked vintage. There was more than one that featured younger versions of Gray with her mother and grandmother. She studied each one briefly as she made her way back to the warmth of the living room.

She'd plugged in her phone to charge it while they showered, taking advantage of the generator. She checked the screen. She had a few messages from her brothers because of the winter storm. She texted them back, assuring them she was okay. In fact, she was better than okay.

Faith texted Kayla next. She was sure Kayla was dying for an update. She kept it simple. She'd save the details for an in-person chat.

Still at Gray's. Didn't want you to worry.

Kayla responded right away. *Me? Worry?*

Faith texted back. *LOL*

Is the power on at Gray's place? It's still off here.

No, Gray has a generator.

I'll bet that's not all she has. Faith could almost hear Kayla's playful tone via her text. She couldn't help smiling.

I'll fill you in tomorrow. That was assuming this didn't turn into the never-ending date. Which wouldn't be the worst thing in the world.

I can't wait. There was a pause and then a second text from Kayla came through. *The café is closed today, in case you wondered. Can't run a restaurant without electricity.*

Thanks for letting me know. I'll check in later.

"Is everything okay?" Gray entered the room, towel drying her hair. She was wearing a zipped hoodie over a heavy flannel shirt, with jeans. How did she make the simplest attire look so good?

"Just Kayla, checking in to let me know the café is closed today. I guess the power is still out in town too." Faith set her phone on the coffee table. "And my brothers were checking in to make sure I survived the storm."

"How many brothers do you have?"

Faith realized they'd sort of skipped some of the usual get-to-know-you questions.

"Three."

"Wow, three brothers." Gray arched her eyebrows. "That's a lot of brothers."

"It wasn't that bad. Being the only girl, well, I think I was more than a little spoiled...probably...you let me know." She wrapped her arm around Gray's waist.

"I'll get back to you about that." Gray smiled. "So, should we go build a snowman?"

"Absolutely."

The temperature outdoors had gone up just enough to make the snow stick together as they rolled large balls of it across the yard. They didn't quite finish the snowperson though. Throwing snowballs was far too tempting and after one of the icy balls slid down Faith's collar she felt compelled to respond in kind. She playfully shoved a handful of snow down the back of Gray's shirt.

"Ah!" Gray danced to dislodge the snow. "You're in trouble now!"

Faith tried to run, but her oversized boots weighed her down. She lunged forward, leaving one boot stuck in the deep snow. Now she had one boot and one wet sock. Gray lifted her up by the waist and swung her around as if they were dancing. She wriggled causing Gray to become unbalanced. They toppled backward into the snow, laughing.

"Is it hot chocolate time yet?" Faith rolled over on top of Gray, dusting snow off her chest.

"I don't think I have any."

"Luckily, I bought some yesterday." Faith hopped up and balanced on one foot. "My treat."

"I think you lost a shoe." Gray got to her feet and turned around so that her back was toward Faith, arms out, offering a piggyback ride. "Climb on. I'll carry you to the porch."

Faith wrapped her arms around Gray's neck. Gray held onto her with one arm and retrieved the errant boot with the other. And then carried her to a dry spot on the porch.

"I'm going to grab a few more sticks of wood. I'll join you in a minute."

Faith went inside and put water on to boil. She rummaged in the brown grocery bag for the box of instant cocoa. This was turning out to be the best Christmas ever. She stood at the kitchen window waiting for the kettle to whistle. Unlike the front yard, the back lawn outside the kitchen was undisturbed. Not a mark was visible on the smooth white that blanketed her entire view. A layer of snow frosted the dark, naked limbs of every tree she could see from the window. It was a lovely monochromatic scene. Faith retrieved her phone and snapped a photo so that she could paint it later. She heard Gray at the front door just as the kettle began to sing.

"Thanks." Gray accepted a steaming mug from Faith as she warmed by the fire. "I staked a flag near the rear bumper of your car while I was out there. But given the road conditions I don't think we need to worry about too many cars passing by."

"Thank you for thinking of that."

"If the weather holds, it would probably be safe to take the Jeep and go check on Otis if you'd like." Gray sampled the hot beverage.

"That would be great."

Faith was touched that Gray would be so thoughtful as to know she might be concerned about Otis. This, and many other tiny, considerate actions told her that Gray was a genuinely nice person. Something she'd suspected all along.

CHAPTER THIRTY-ONE

The snow lingered for two days and even by late in the week there were still spots of white where the sun could not reach and which the nighttime chill preserved. The dark asphalt on the roads magnified the sun's warmth so that the highways were clear. Like the lingering dollops of snow, there were still spots of ice in shady areas, but even those were beginning to dissipate. Faith's car was extracted from the shallow ditch with only minor scratches.

Midweek, Gray discovered that Faith had left the box of cocoa behind. A cup of hot chocolate with marshmallows would forever remind Gray of her first sleepover with Faith.

And what about Faith?

What about California?

What about everything?

Time with Faith was causing her to question everything she thought she'd wanted. The thought of heading back to California and not seeing Faith was pretty unbearable. But it wasn't as if Faith lived in Sky Valley full-time. She'd mentioned on more than one occasion that she planned to return to Raleigh. Faith's life was there, she even owned a condo in Raleigh.

Gray's situation was completely different. She actually could choose to stay in Sky Valley. But would she want to without Faith? Even though they hardly knew each other Gray had to force herself not to ask Faith to stay. The notion was still a little vague even to Gray. Did she want Faith to stay for a week, a month, or forever?

That seemed like a crazy leap from their first meeting at the café so many weeks earlier.

But wasn't that how life happened? If losing Shane had taught her anything it was that time was beyond anyone's control and it should never be taken for granted. If Shane had known that day in the ravine would have been his last would he have done things differently? It was impossible to know, but Gray couldn't shake the feeling that she'd been granted a second life after the fire and she was determined not to take it for granted.

If any day was to be her last, then she wanted to know she'd lived it, without reservation. The catch was to live every day as if it might be the only one. This was a new way of being in the world for Gray. Firefighters were always looking for planned escape routes and safety zones. Well, that wasn't her any longer. She didn't want to escape. Gray wanted to play this thing out with Faith and find out what happened next for real.

They'd agreed to spend New Year's Eve together and the plan hadn't changed simply because of their snowbound sleepover. In fact, Gray had driven into Asheville after work a day earlier and purchased a new shirt and dress pants. She'd even splurged and added a blazer and cap toe leather shoes. As she made one last pass in front of the full-length mirror on the back of the closet door, she hardly recognized herself. She swept her fingers through her hair, pushing a few wild, damp curls off her forehead.

She felt nervous, excited, and happy all at the same time.

On the way out the door, she grabbed the gift she'd picked up for Hailey. She was hoping Faith wouldn't mind if they dropped it off on their way to dinner.

Faith checked the time on her phone. Gray would be on her way soon.

She leaned toward the mirror for a closer look as she applied lipstick. She squeezed her lips together and decided the color was good. She fluffed her hair a little with her fingers and then twisted it so that she could hold it up at the back of her head. She'd been trying all day to decide whether to wear her hair up or down. Not a life-altering, world-changing sort of decision she realized, but a valid New Year's Eve query nonetheless.

If she wore her hair up then she'd be able to show off her earrings, gold with chalcedony stones. Not to mention wearing her hair up would call attention to the plunging neckline of the little black dress she'd borrowed from Kayla for their evening out. She was pleased with the fit.

When she'd packed to leave Raleigh for her weekend visit that had turned into weeks, she never thought to pack anything *special*. Faith had been certain she'd spend the rest of her life in pajama pants, binge-watching old episodes of *Sex in the City*. And look at her now. How swiftly life could turn into something truly wonderful. Just like her favorite Christmas movie.

Faith released her hair and it tumbled to her shoulders. It was a chilly night. She'd just keep it simple and wear it down for warmth and ease.

She heard her phone ping and assumed that it was a text from Gray. She was very disappointed to see a message from Sam.

Thinking of you. Happy New Year.

Faith took a deep breath and exhaled loudly. Three weeks ago, a text from Sam could ruin her entire day, now she simply found it annoying. She took a moment to block Sam's number without responding. No more texts from Sam. Good-bye and good riddance.

Taking charge of her life was exhilarating and liberating. She smiled into the mirror.

Faith heard a knock at the door just as she slipped into her heels. They created a satisfying clicking sound as she crossed the landing to the stairs and descended to the foyer. She'd had a moment earlier in the afternoon when she'd worried she was overdressing, but when she opened the door and saw Gray she knew she'd made the right choice.

Gray looked practically edible in her dark suit. The starched collar of her dress shirt was open just enough to give Faith a tantalizing view of the soft indentation at the base of her throat.

"Wow." Faith didn't even try to play it cool. Gray was gorgeous.

"Wow yourself." Gray crossed the threshold and invaded Faith's personal space.

Gray's kiss was soft yet confident. When Gray broke the kiss, she was wearing some of Faith's lipstick.

"Is it not a good color for me?" Gray smiled.

"Oh, yes, actually it's perfect." Faith gently wiped it away with her thumb and then lightly kissed Gray again, just because she couldn't help herself.

"I hope you don't mind if we make one stop on our way to dinner." Gray held Faith's long, emerald wool dress coat so that she could slip her arms into it. "Today is Hailey's birthday."

"That's terrible."

"Come again?"

"I mean, it would be terrible to have your birthday right after Christmas." Faith scowled. "And on New Year's Eve nonetheless. I'm sure the poor kid gets shortchanged every year."

"Exactly what I was thinking." Gray held the door for Faith. "So, I bought her a gift and I want to drop it by the house. I called Mark earlier to let him know. They celebrated with a pizza lunch, Hailey's choice, and now he and Christy are at a New Year's party." Gray offered her hand to assist Faith into the Jeep. "Hailey is at home with a babysitter."

Gray circled the Jeep and climbed in. It was cold, so she cranked the heater the minute she started the ignition.

"What did you get her?"

"This." Gray produced a small plastic case with a ribbon on the handle.

"Tools?" Faith couldn't hide the surprise in her question. "I know we've barely started dating, but can we make a pact right now that you will never give me tools for my birthday?"

Gray laughed.

"I like that you're planning ahead. And yes, I promise never to buy you tools. As if." Gray smiled at her before returning her attention to driving. "Here's the deal." She paused. "Let's see, how do I explain this?"

Gray's hesitation made her even more curious.

"When you're a kid like Hailey, like I was, there's this moment when the people in your life finally begin to see you for who you are." Gray's earnestness made Faith's heart ache. "They stop trying to force you to wear dresses and play with dolls and they begin to give you things that actually match with your true identity."

"I'll never think of tools the same way again." She was joking but found Gray's story quite touching. She put her hand on Gray's thigh. "You're very sweet, you know that?"

"I think it's time for Hailey to have her first set of real tools."

"She's going to love this." Faith held the small tool case on her lap for the rest of the drive, happy to be part of this little birthday caper.

CHAPTER THIRTY-TWO

Gray expected to make a quick stop to deliver the gift to Hailey, then they'd be on their way. But as they rounded the curve of the long driveway and got a glimpse of the house she immediately felt as if something was wrong. She climbed out of the Jeep but stood for a moment in the open door. There was smoke in the air, something she was highly attuned to. This wasn't simply smoke from the fireplace though; this was something else. There were no outside lights on and the clouds hid the moon, but even still, she could see that something wasn't right.

"Gray, what is it?" Faith asked from the car.

"I don't know."

Gray took a step forward, paused and then an instant later, a young woman burst from the back of the house. Gray didn't know her but assumed she was the babysitter. The young woman ran into her arms. Then pointed frantically toward the house.

"Fire!" She was out of breath.

"Where's Hailey?" Gray held the woman's arm, forcing her to make eye contact.

"I don't know! I don't know!" She was crying. "Smoke was everywhere. I couldn't get up the stairs. I ran out the back door from the kitchen."

Faith put her arm around the girl and regarded Gray with wide eyes.

"Call 9-1-1!" She ran toward the house, shouting to Faith over her shoulder. "Tell them there's someone in the house and one firefighter at the scene."

"Gray!"

She heard Faith call her name, but there was no time. Gray worried she might already be too late. There was not a moment to lose.

Gray focused on her training. Never open a closed door without feeling it first. She placed her palm on the front door, it wasn't hot so she threw it open. Smoke billowed out. She dropped to a crawl, trying to stay close to the floor where the air was cooler, under the smoke. She fought back her fear. Gray needed to get under it too to gain clarity. Fear would immobilize, and what she needed right now was forward motion.

There was a thermal imaging camera in the fire truck that would have allowed her to see inside the house, to find Hailey's location, but she didn't have any of her gear and there was no time to wait for it.

In a typical house fire, it was hard to see anything when you first entered the building. Usually the smoke was just too thick. Normally, she'd have a breathing apparatus with a face mask, but that only kept the smoke out of your lungs and eyes, it didn't help you actually see.

Gray was suddenly back in that rocky ravine remembering the heat. She hesitated at the foot of the stairs.

I am here. This is now.

I am here. This is now. She was determined to push through her fear. She balled her fists, summoning every ounce of drive she had, willing herself to move forward.

Flames licked the walls near the fireplace, drapes ignited and flames swept upward toward the ceiling. Billowing plumes of darkening smoke roiled in her direction. The fire was about to breach the landing on the second floor where the bedrooms were, probably where Hailey was.

"Hailey!" Gray shouted, but the smoke set off a coughing fit. "Hailey!"

The sound of the fire drowned her out. The familiar crackle and whoosh sound of something bursting into flames reached her from the living room.

Move. Move! She crawled swiftly up the carpeted stairs. Timbers creaked and groaned from heat contractions.

There was no time. If flames reached the second floor and the roof, she was done and whether she got to Hailey or not, they would never make it out.

Smoke picked up the smell of whatever was burning. Walls and wooden furniture had sort of a campfire smell at first. Those scents were soon blended with an acrid smell, probably something plastic, that stung her throat. She lowered her face for a second, trying to get as close to the fresh air near the floor as possible. Even that narrow breathable space wouldn't last long. As the fire grew, so would the smoke.

Gray made it to the second floor, but which room was Hailey's?

Luckily, all the doors were open, except one. That had to be because Hailey had closed it. Gray ran toward the door. After checking the temp, still cool, she threw it open. She swept the room with her eyes. It was filled with all the stuff of childhood. Finally, in the dark, she spotted Hailey huddled in the corner.

She knelt beside Hailey and hugged her. Hailey was stiff in Gray's arms, frozen with fear.

"Hailey, we need to leave now." She lifted Hailey to her feet. "I'm with you and I'm going to get you out of here. Stay close and do what I tell you."

Hailey nodded.

"This wasn't my fault." Hailey clung to Gray. "I wasn't even near the fireplace. I was up here."

"It's okay, Hailey. Let's focus on getting you out of here."

The flames were bigger and the smoke was heavy in the hallway. They were near the bathroom. Gray quickly took off her blazer and doused it with water in the sink. She draped the wet jacket around Hailey as they made their way to the stairs. The flames were climbing and had begun to blacken the railing along the upper floor but had not quite reached the stairs.

"Stay low, Hailey." Gray tightened her arm around Hailey. "We're going to stay low and move fast."

Outside the house, Faith was in a near panic. She could hear faint sirens in the distance, but no one had arrived to help Gray. Gray was alone and the flames were getting bigger. She covered her mouth with her hand to smother her cries. She clung to the distraught teenager in her arms, Emily. They didn't know each other, but in this crisis, they were some small comfort to one another.

Faith was adrift.

She could do nothing to help Gray and the not knowing was like a knife through her heart. All she'd wanted was a little more time. This had not been nearly enough time.

More smoke poured from the open front door and she could see its white-gray coloring against the purple of the night sky.

How long had Gray been in there?

Too long. Something was horribly wrong.

Lights and sirens pierced her thoughts as two engines drove across the lawn to staging positions that would give them good access to the house. Fireman leapt from the trucks and immediately started pulling hoses toward the front of the house.

Faith recognized Lucas and ran toward him.

"Gray is in there!" Faith had to shout above the noise. The heat increased the closer she got. "She went in to find Hailey!"

"Hey, we've got people in the house! Move fast!"

Lucas didn't respond to her. He was shouting directions to the rest of the crew to get water to soak access points to the house. He and another guy donned air tanks and masks and moved swiftly toward the front door.

"Are you injured? Were you in the house?" A paramedic was at Faith's side. She was so focused on watching for Gray to reappear that she hadn't even noticed the ambulance arrive.

"No, I'm fine." Faith began to back away, making room for people to work the scene.

And then, miraculously, Gray came through the front door. She and Hailey were flanked by Lucas and the other fireman. Gray's dress shirt and face were covered with soot. She collapsed on the wet grass, soaked from the hoses, coughing. She signaled for the medics to tend to Hailey first.

Lucas knelt beside Gray and slipped his mask over her face. She sat back, nodding her head. Faith ran to Gray and threw her arms around Gray's neck. Tears streamed down her face. Gray removed the breathing mask and handed it to Lucas. He patted Gray on the back and then returned to his fight to save the house.

"I'm okay…It's gonna be okay." Gray's voice was raspy. She started to cough again.

"I was so scared." Faith held onto her.

"So was I." Gray got to her feet and helped Faith up. "Where's Hailey?"

"We've got her on some oxygen." The female paramedic was back. The same woman who'd asked Faith if she was okay. "Let's get you taken care of too."

They walked toward the open back doors of the ambulance. Faith kept her arm around Gray. There was no way she was letting go.

Gray stood with a blanket around her shoulders against the cold, watching as the crew did their last sweep.

"What are they doing now?" Faith asked.

Gray opened the side of the blanket so that Faith could join her warmth.

"They're checking for hot spots," Gray explained. "The fire could smolder but then start up again if they don't get every bit of it."

Mark and Christy had arrived moments after the ambulance. Christy had gone to the hospital with Hailey, who was fine, but probably needed to stay overnight for observation just to be safe. Mark stayed to meet with the fire inspector.

Gray had stayed to watch, but was no help. She was spent.

She'd faced the fiery dragon and lived. Until tonight, she wasn't sure she'd ever be able to overcome her fear of it, but she had. For Hailey's sake, she'd faced her fears and pushed through them. Gray felt as if she'd conquered a giant, slain the beast, and lived.

Overconfidence hadn't claimed her completely though; she still had a healthy respect for what no one could control—fire.

This was the sort of disaster that reminded her of the beliefs she'd grown up with. Belief in a higher power you could call on in times of crisis and need. She remembered the passage from Psalms that she'd come across when she'd first returned and the verse she'd learned as a child from the book of John that said God was love.

If God was love, then it was true that love had mended her broken heart. And so much more than that. She enveloped Faith in her arms inside the blanket and rested her chin on Faith's hair as they stared at the smoking husk.

How was it possible that she could have come home with nothing and somehow found everything? A life lost and then found. The warmth of Faith's arms around hers kept her tethered to the Earth or she might have floated into the air like the gray tendrils that rose from the charred remains.

Finally, there were too many sensations. Everything blurred at the edges and she no longer had the will to resist her feelings for Faith. If losing Shane had taught her anything, if surviving tonight had any larger message it was seize your life, don't waste the gift of living.

She pulled away only a little and rotated so that she could see Faith's eyes.

"Faith, I need to tell you something."

Faith waited, her expression hopeful.

"I'm in love with you." Gray paused. "I love you."

Faith's embrace tightened and she rested her cheek on Gray's chest.

"I love you too."

EPILOGUE

W ell, that's done." Gray flopped onto the sofa next to Faith, facing the warmth of the flame on the hearth.

"How did it go?" Faith rested her palm on Gray's thigh.

"Vince took the news pretty well. He said he was sorry to lose a seasoned firefighter like me, but I think he understood." She propped her sock feet on the coffee table.

The bright winter sun filled the room with light.

"I think he was glad I was going to use my experience and skills here."

"He's not the only one," Faith teased her.

Gray smiled; liquid warmth flooded her system.

It had been a whirlwind couple of weeks since the fire.

The inspector had determined that a cigarette was to blame. Emily had gone outside to smoke, something she'd been trying to hide from not only her parents but also Mark and Christy. She'd put the cigarette out in the snow and thoughtlessly dropped it into her coat pocket, with plans to flush the evidence once she was in the house. But then she'd gotten a text from her boyfriend and completely forgotten about it. The cigarette butt was still warm and had burned through the pocket of the highly flammable fleece jacket and dropped to the floor. The jacket burst into flames and climbed the wall.

Faith had been staying with Gray so that Mark, Christy, and Hailey could move into Kayla's grandparents' place while they rebuilt. But Gray wasn't expecting Faith to stay in her space forever. Even still, she'd been putting off asking because she wasn't anxious to hear the answer. She didn't want Faith to leave, but she also didn't want to pressure her to remain.

"I have some big news too." Faith smiled as if she was about to reveal the biggest secret.

"You do?" Gray glanced over. "What is it?"

"I listed my condo with a Realtor."

"What? When? Why didn't you tell me?" She sat up and shifted to face Faith. This news was like Christmas all over again.

Faith began to play with the buttons of Gray's shirt.

"Well, see, I met this sexy firefighter and I thought I might just stick around." Faith angled her head and gave Gray a sheepish look. "You know, in case she needs to be rescued."

"I *do* need to be rescued. Every minute of every day." Gray kissed Faith. She rolled onto her side and tugged Faith with her so that they were lying facing each other on the couch. She drew Faith close and kissed her again. "In fact, I need to be rescued right here, right now."

"I don't ever want to leave your side." Faith whispered the words against her lips.

"Stay forever." Gray kissed Faith slowly and deeply.

Her phone vibrated in her pocket, surprising them both. Gray fished it out of her pocket with the intention of tossing it aside, but then she saw that the call was from Hailey. Faith saw it too.

"You should get that." Faith toyed with the hem of Gray's shirt.

"Hailey, how's it going?" Gray partially sat up. "You want to come over?" Gray repeated the request so that Faith could hear. "Yeah, I can show you how to use those carving tools for sure. I've even got some stuff you can practice on."

Faith snuggled closer and kissed Gray's neck.

"How about you come over in an hour?" She felt Faith's fingers under her shirt. She tried not to react over the phone, but Faith was driving her crazy. "Hmm, better make that two hours." She smiled at Faith as she tried to wrap up the call. "Okay, see you then."

Gray clicked off and tossed the phone onto the coffee table. She drew Faith close.

"Now, where were we?"

The end

About the Author

Missouri Vaun spent a large part of her childhood in southern Mississippi, before attending high school in North Carolina and college in Tennessee. Strong connections to her roots in the rural south have been a grounding force throughout her life. Vaun spent twelve years finding her voice working as a journalist in places as disparate as Chicago, Atlanta, and Jackson, Mississippi, all along filing away characters and their stories. Her novels are heartfelt, earthy, and speak of loyalty and our responsibility to others. She and her wife currently live in northern California.

Books Available from Bold Strokes Books

Cherry on Top by Georgia Beers. A chance meeting leaves Cherry and Ellis longing for a different life, but when Ellis's search for truth crashes into Cherry's insta-filter world, do they have any hope at all of a happily ever after? (978-1-63679-158-6)

Love and Other Rare Birds by Angie Williams. Ornithologist Dr. Jamie Martin and park ranger Rowan Fleming are searching the Alaskan wilderness for a bird thought to be extinct and they're about to discover opposites really do attract. (978-1-63679-108-1)

Parallel Paradise by Mayapee Chowdhury. When their love affair is put to the test by the homophobia of their family, community, and culture, Bindi and Rimli will need to fight for a chance at love. (978-1-63679-204-0)

Perfectly Matched by Toni Logan. A beautiful Cupid named Hannah, a runaway arrow, and just seventy-two hours to fix a mishap that could be the best mistake she has ever made. (978-1-63679-120-3)

Royal Exposé by Jenny Frame. When they're grouped together for a class assignment, Poppy's enthusiasm for life and love may just save Casey's soul, but will she ever forgive Casey for using her to expose royal secrets? (978-1-63679-165-4)

Slow Burn by Missouri Vaun. A wounded wildland firefighter from California and a struggling artist find solace and love in a small southern town. (978-1-63679-098-5)

The Artist by Sheri Lewis Wohl. Detective Casey Wilson and reclusive artist Tula Crane are drawn together in a web of passion, intrigue, and art that might just hold the key to stopping a killer. (978-1-63679-150-0)

The Inconvenient Heiress by Jane Walsh. An unlikely heiress and a spinster evade the Marriage Mart only to discover true love together. (978-1-63679-173-9)

A Champion for Tinker Creek by D.C. Robeline. Lyle James has rescued his dad's auto repair business, but when city hall condemns his neighborhood, Lyle learns only trusting will save his life and help him find love. (978-1-63679-213-2)

Closed-Door Policy by Erin Zak. Going back to college is never easy, but Caroline Stevens is prepared to work hard and change her life for the better. What she's not prepared for is Dr. Atlanta Morris, her gorgeous new professor. (978-1-63679-181-4)

Homeworld by Gun Brooke. Headed by Captain Holly Crowe, the spaceship Velocity's crew journeys toward their alien ancestors' homeworld, and what they find is completely unexpected—and they're not safe. (978-1-63679-177-7)

Outland by Kristin Keppler & Allisa Bahney. Danielle Clark and Katelyn Turner can't seem to stay away from one another even as the war for the wastelands tests their loyalty to each other and to their people. (978-1-63679-154-8)

Secret Sanctuary by Nance Sparks. US Deputy Marshal Alex Trenton specializes in protecting those awaiting trial, but when danger threatens the woman she's falling for, Alex is in for the fight of her life. (978-1-63679-148-7)

Stranded Hearts by Kris Bryant, Amanda Radley, Emily Smith. In these novellas from award winning authors, fate intervenes on behalf of love when characters are unexpectedly stuck together. With too much time and an irresistible attraction, anything could happen. (978-1-63679-182-1)

The Last Lavender Sister by Melissa Brayden. Aster Lavender sells her gourmet doughnuts and keeps a low profile; she never plans on the town's temporary veterinarian swooping in and making her feel like anything but a wallflower. (978-1-63679-130-2)

The Probability of Love by Dena Blake. As Blair and Rachel keep ending up in the same place despite the odds, can a one-night stand turn into forever? Or will the bet Blair never intended to make ruin their happily ever after? (978-1-63679-188-3)

Worth a Fortune by Sam Ledel. After placing a want ad for a personal secretary, a New York heiress is surprised when the woman who got away is the one interested in the position. (978-1-63679-175-3)

A Fox in Shadow by Jane Fletcher. Cassie's mission is to add new territory to the Kavillian empire—murder, betrayal, war, and the clash of cultures ensue. (978-1-63679-142-5)

Embracing the Moon by Jeannie Levig. Just as Gwen and Taylor are exploring the new love they've found, the present and past collide, threatening the future they long to share. (978-1-63555-462-5)

Forever Comes in Threes by D. Jackson Leigh. Efficiency expert Perry Chandler's ordered life is upended when she inherits three busy terriers, and the woman she's referred to for help turns out to be her bitter podcast rival, the very sexy Dr. Ming Lee. (978-1-63679-169-2)

Heckin' Lewd: Trans and Nonbinary Erotica by Mx. Nillin Lore. If you want smutty, fearless, gender diverse erotica written by affirming own-voices folks who get it, then this is the book you've been looking for! (978-1-63679-240-8)

Missed Conception by Joy Argento. Maggie Walsh wants a relationship with Cassidy, the daughter she's only just discovered she has due to an in vitro mix-up. Heat kindles between Maggie and Cassidy's mother in a way neither expects. (978-1-63679-146-3)

Private Equity by Elle Spencer. Cassidy Bennett spends an unexpected evening at a lesbian nightclub with her notoriously reserved and demanding boss, Julia. After seeing a different side of Julia, Cassidy can't seem to shake her desire to know more. (978-1-63679-180-7)

Racing the Dawn by Sandra Barrett. After narrowly escaping a house fire, vampire Jade Murphy is unexpectedly intrigued by gorgeous firefighter Beth Jenssen, and her undead existence might just be perking up a bit. (978-1-63679-271-2)

Reclaiming Love by Amanda Radley. Sarah's tiny white lie means somehow convincing Pippa to pretend to be her girlfriend. Only the more time they spend faking it, the more real it feels. (978-1-63679-144-9)

Sol Cycle by Kimberly Cooper Griffin. An encounter in a park brings Ang and Krista together, but when Ang's attempts to help Krista go spectacularly wrong, their passion for each other might not be enough. (978-1-63679-137-1)

Trial and Error by Carsen Taite. Attorney Franco Rossi and Judge Nina Aguilar's reunion is fraught with courtroom conflict, undeniable chemistry, and danger. (978-1-63555-863-0)

A Long Way to Fall by Elle Spencer. A ski lodge, two strong-willed women, and a family feud that brings them together, but will it also tear them apart? (978-1-63679-005-3)

Barnabas Bopwright Saves the City by J. Marshall Freeman. When he uncovers a terror plot to destroy the city he loves, 15-year-old Barnabas Bopwright realizes it's up to him to save his home and bring deadly secrets into the light before it's too late. (978-1-63679-152-4)

Forever by Kris Bryant. When Savannah Edwards is invited to be the next bachelorette on the dating show When Sparks Fly, she'll show the world that finding true love on television can happen. (978-1-63679-029-9)

Ice on Wheels by Aurora Rey. All's fair in love and roller derby. That's Riley Fauchet's motto, until a new job lands her at the same company—and on the same team—as her rival Brooke Landry, the frosty jammer for the Big Easy Bruisers. (978-1-63679-179-1)

Inherit the Lightning by Bud Gundy. Darcy O'Brien and his sisters learn they are about to inherit an immense fortune, but a family mystery about to unravel after seventy years threatens to destroy everything. (978-1-63679-199-9)

Perfect Rivalry by Radclyffe. Two women set out to win the same career-making goal, but it's love that may turn out to be the final prize. (978-1-63679-216-3)

Something to Talk About by Ronica Black. Can quiet ranch owner Corey Durand give up her peaceful life and allow her feisty new neighbor into her heart? Or will past loss, present suitors, and town gossip ruin a long-awaited chance at love? (978-1-63679-114-2)

With a Minor in Murder by Karis Walsh. In the world of academia, police officer Clare Sawyer and professor Libby Hart team up to solve a murder. (978-1-63679-186-9)

Writer's Block by Ali Vali. Wyatt and Hayley might be made for each other if only they can get through nosy neighbors, the historic society, at-odds future plans, and all the secrets hidden in Wyatt's walls. (978-1-63679-021-3)

Cold Blood by Genevieve McCluer. Maybe together, Kalila and Dorenia have a chance of taking down the vampires who have eluded them all these years. And maybe, in each other, they can find a love worth living for. (978-1-63679-195-1)

Greener Pastures by Aurora Rey. When city girl and CPA Audrey Adams finds herself tending her aunt's farm, will Rowan Marshall—the charming cider maker next door—turn out to be her saving grace or the bane of her existence? (978-1-63679-116-6)

Grounded by Amanda Radley. For a second chance, Olivia and Emily will need to accept their mistakes, learn to communicate properly, and with a little help from five-year-old Henry, fall madly in love all over again. Sequel to Flight SQA016. (978-1-63679-241-5)

Journey's End by Amanda Radley. In this heartwarming conclusion to the Flight series, Olivia and Emily must finally decide what they want, what they need, and how to follow the dreams of their hearts. (978-1-63679-233-0)

Pursued: Lillian's Story by Felice Picano. Fleeing a disastrous marriage to the Lord Exchequer of England, Lillian of Ravenglass reveals an incident-filled, often bizarre, tale of great wealth and power, perfidy, and betrayal. (978-1-63679-197-5)

Secret Agent by Michelle Larkin. CIA agent Peyton North embarks on a global chase to apprehend rogue agent Zoey Blackwood, but her commitment to the mission is tested as the sparks between them ignite and their sizzling attraction approaches a point of no return. (978-1-63555-753-4)

Something Between Us by Krystina Rivers. A decade after her heart was broken under Don't Ask, Don't Tell, Kirby runs into her first love and has to decide if what's still between them is enough to heal her broken heart. (978-1-63679-135-7)

Sugar Girl by Emma L McGeown. Having traded in traditional romance for the perks of Sugar Dating, Ciara Reilly not only enjoys the no-strings-attached arrangement, she's also a hit with her clients. That is until she meets the beautiful entrepreneur Charlie Keller who makes her want to go sugar-free. (978-1-63679-156-2)

The Business of Pleasure by Ronica Black. Editor in chief Valerie Raffield is quickly becoming smitten by Lennox, the graphic artist she's hired to work remotely. But when Lennox doesn't show for their first face-to-face meeting, Valerie's heart and her business may be in jeopardy. (978-1-63679-134-0)

The Hummingbird Sanctuary by Erin Zak. The Hummingbird Sanctuary, Colorado's hottest resort destination: Come for the mountains, stay for the charm, and enjoy the drama as Olive, Eleanor, and Harriet figure out the meaning of true friendship. (978-1-63679-163-0)

The Witch Queen's Mate by Jennifer Karter. Barra and Silvi must overcome their ingrained hatred and prejudice to use Barra's magic and save both their peoples, not just from slavery, but destruction. (978-1-63679-202-6)

With a Twist by Georgia Beers. Starting over isn't easy for Amelia Martini. When the irritatingly cheerful Kirby Dupress comes into her life will Amelia be brave enough to go after the love she really wants? (978-1-63555-987-3)

Lightning Source UK Ltd.
Milton Keynes UK
UKHW011823101022
410250UK00001B/235